WILD ABOUT RAND

Book One:
A WILDING POINT ROMANCE

JOLEEN JAMES

Cover Art by Melissa Russell
Copyediting by Eilis Flynn

WILD ABOUT RAND / JOLEEN JAMES. — 1st ed.
ISBN 978-0-9890504-1-8

Table of Contents

WILD ABOUT RAND

Also by Joleen James

COWBOY, I'M YOURS

LOVING GLORY

UNDER A HARVEST MOON

FALLING FOR NICK

HOSTAGE HEART, A SHORT STORY

HOMETOWN ALASKA MEN SERIES

HOMETOWN STAR

HOMETOWN HERO

HOMETOWN HEARTBREAKER

HOMETOWN CHRISTMAS, A Novella

WILDING POINT ROMANCE SERIES

WILD ABOUT RAND

WILD ABOUT LUCKY   AVAILABLE APRIL 2019

WILD ABOUT CAM   AVAILABLE JUNE 2019

For anyone who has suffered loss.
My heart goes out to you.

Chapter One

"Mom, look out!"

Kristine Wilding hit the brakes. Her heart leapt into her chest as the car screeched to a stop.

"That was close," Carly, her twelve-year-old daughter, cried.

"I'm sorry," Kristine said, her eyes on the red light. She took a breath, releasing it slowly. "My mind's not on driving."

"It's okay," Carly said, giving Kristine a sympathetic look. "I know you're upset about Grandpa."

Upset didn't begin to describe what Kristine was feeling. She didn't want to be here, but there was no one else. She'd tried to find her brother, Lucky. After all, Lucky didn't have a child in school, but he hadn't returned her calls. Who was she kidding? Lucky didn't want to be in Wilding Point any more than she did. In fact, his issues with their father went back farther and were worse than her own.

The light turned green. Kristine accelerated. She couldn't help but trip down memory lane as she drove past the local high school, a place where she hadn't thrived but had merely survived. She turned down the main drag, cutting across the town, then over to the base of the hill where the hospital was located.

She didn't go to Wilding House first, and didn't ask herself why.

Kristine turned into the parking lot of Wilding Point General Hospital. She cruised the lot twice before finally locating a parking spot. She cut the engine, but didn't get out of the car.

Instead, she stared out at the rain, the driving, relentless rain that had been her constant companion on the six-hour drive up from Eugene.

"Are we getting out?" Carly asked.

"In a minute." Kristine hadn't seen her father in six years. Their last meeting hadn't gone well. She'd come to him for help, needing financial support for herself and Carly, but he had told her to grow up. She'd made her own bed getting pregnant out of wedlock, so now she had to figure things out for herself. Going to see him had been a desperate move on her part, but she'd been so alone, so afraid.

She'd been a fool to think her father would help her. Lucas Wilding helped himself and no one else.

Kristine's heart hardened.

"Mom," Carly prompted. "I need to pee."

"Okay." Kristine gave herself a mental shake. She could do this. She was older and stronger now, her father sick and weak.

They exited the car and sprinted for the entrance to the hospital. Once inside, Kristine shook the rain from her hair. Warm air moved over them. The scent of fresh brewed coffee pulled her gaze to a coffee counter. She glanced around. "Let's find the restroom, then grab a warm drink before we find Grandpa."

Carly took off toward the restroom sign, Kristine on her heels.

Afterward, they ordered drinks, black coffee for Kristine, hot cocoa for Carly, then set out for the third-floor ICU where she knew her father was.

As the elevator rose, the knot in Kristine tightened. Her father had always been a man to fear, to be obeyed. She knew from her father's housekeeper, Rowena, that her father's illness had come on suddenly. Rowena had tried to care for him on her own, but

2

Lucas Wilding needed constant care now. Not only was he ill, according to Rowena, he also suffered from dementia—something he'd worked to conceal from them all.

As an attorney specializing in DUI cases, Lucas Wilding had always been sharp as a tack, his legal mind brilliant. Dementia? Kristine still couldn't wrap her mind around the diagnosis.

Off the elevator now, they came upon a waiting area.

"I want you to stay here," she said to Carly. "I'll go inside first, see what's happening."

Carly shrugged before plopping down in a chair, her phone already in hand.

Kristine followed the signs to the ICU. Locked double doors blocked her way and she picked up the courtesy phone.

"May I help you?" a female voice answered.

"I'm Kristine Wilding. I'm here to see my father, Lucas Wilding."

"Come on in." The doors buzzed to let her through.

Kristine hung up the phone then entered. She walked down the sterile hall, her anxiety mushrooming, until she thought she might choke on it. Her father's name was written on the board outside his room. A large neon green sign declared *Quarantine—infectious disease*. A portable hazmat station stood to her left.

She knew from Rowena that in addition to the diverticulitis and colitis that had originally hospitalized her father two months ago, her father had also contracted a highly contagious bacterial infection called *C. diff*, but this looked worse than she'd anticipated.

"Can I help you?" a pretty young nurse asked.

"I'm here to see my father," Kristine said. "Do I need to gown up or something?"

"You do," the nurse said, smiling. "And you can't take that coffee in. Just set it there, at the nurses' station."

Kristine did so, feeling more nervous by the minute.

"I'm just going in myself. Here." The nurse passed Kristine a yellow gown, helping her into the garment. She then handed her gloves. "When you come out, the gloves go in the trash; the gown goes in the hamper. Wash your hands thoroughly; use plenty of soap and water. Hand sanitizer does not kill *C. diff.*"

"How contagious is he?" Kristine asked.

"Very," the nurse said. "When was the last time you saw him?"

"Six years ago."

The nurse smiled sadly. "He's a very sick man."

Kristine nodded as she followed the nurse into the room. The first thing she noticed was the smell, like a baby's dirty diaper times ten.

She held her nose as she rounded the curtain. Was that her father?

She stepped closer. Yes, it was him. His hair was not the steel gray she remembered, but was now a snowy white, uncombed, flattened from being in bed. Pale skin stretched tight over prominent cheekbones, giving his face an angular look. The hospital gown he wore left his collarbone bare, the bone protruding against his thin skin. He was a shell of the man she'd seen six years ago, thin beyond comprehension.

A bevy of IVs stood near the head of the bed. There had to be at least ten of them. Monitors beeped, machines hissed.

Were the machines keeping him alive?

Her heart constricted, the pain sharp and horrific. Where was the rush of love? The sentimental tug on her heart strings? Nowhere. She felt pity for him and nothing else. The smell of feces made her want to retch. More than anything she wanted to turn away, walk out of the room and never look back.

"Mr. Wilding, look who's here," the nurse said brightly.

4

Her father didn't open his eyes, his mouth slack. Was he sleeping?

The nurse beckoned her closer.

"Mr. Wilding," the nurse said again.

Her father opened his eyes. He focused on the nurse. "I'm thirsty."

The nurse held the cup for him so he could sip water.

Kristine turned away, sickened by the sight of her once-robust father reduced to a dying vegetable.

"Who's that?" her father asked.

Kristine moved closer. "It's me, Dad."

"Kristine?" he asked. The word held surprise but no warmth.

No, there would be no joyful reunion between them.

"Yes," she said. "I hear you're not doing so well."

"Get me out of here, Kristine," he pleaded, sounding like a small child. "I want to go home. They're trying to kill me."

She exchanged a worried look with the nurse. "I'll do what I can, Dad. I just got here. I need to speak to the doctor."

"Well, go do it," her father ordered. "They are all against me. I hear them whispering. What are you waiting for, girl?"

Now, there was the man she remembered, the man who always wanted things his way.

"Is your mother with you?" he asked.

"No, Dad. Mom lives in Oregon, remember?"

"Since when?"

Did he truly not remember where his ex-wife lived? "Mom's lived in Oregon over twenty years."

"That's ridiculous," he shouted. "Get me out of here, now. I need to see my wife."

"Let's settle down," the nurse said, the voice of reason. She'd been flitting around Lucas, taking his temperature, monitoring his oxygen. "I think we need to get you cleaned up, Mr. Wilding."

Kristine thought that was an excellent idea. She didn't think she'd ever get the smell of poop out of her nose.

"Why don't you come with me?" the nurse said to Kristine. "I'll find the doctor and you can talk to him about your father."

"Okay." Kristine turned to her father. "I'll be back, Dad."

"Bring me some ice chips," he said, his eyes closed. "So thirsty."

Kristine copied the nurse, disposing of her gown and gloves, then scrubbing her hands with hot soapy water.

When they were in the hall, the nurse said, "I'll page the doctor."

"He looks bad," Kristine said. "How close to the end is he?"

The nurse gave her another sad smile. "I'll let the doctor explain his condition to you."

"All right. Thank you."

Kristine glanced around. This was the ICU. People died here. Obviously her father couldn't control his bowel movements. He was so thin. His once-sharp legal mind muddy and unclear.

Tears pricked her eyes. She needed her brother. She needed Lucky. She couldn't do this alone. She wasn't strong enough. How could she care for a man she'd despised most of her life? Kristine walked away from her father's room, finding a private area to call her brother, but the call again went to voicemail.

"It's me," she said. "I need you, Lucky. Dad looks bad. I don't think he has long to live. I'm waiting to speak with the doctor now. Call me back."

Sick at heart, Kristine went back to her father's room. The door was closed now, leading her to believe the nurses were cleaning him up.

A man came toward her, wearing a white doctor's coat. "Are you Lucas Wilding's daughter?" he asked. He was young, handsome, probably in his late thirties with kind gray eyes.

"Yes. Kristine Wilding."

He nodded. "I'm Dr. Grant. I've been taking care of your father the past week here in the ICU. How much do you know?"

"I know he got sick two months ago. Rowena told me he had diverticulitis and colitis."

"Yes. When he left the hospital the first time he went to a care facility. He was on a rigorous course of antibiotics, which can leave a patient vulnerable to contracting *C. diff*. Unfortunately, we believe he contracted *C. diff* while he was in the skilled nursing facility. In addition, his colon is diseased. In a healthy patient, we would remove the diseased portion, but your father is not a candidate for surgery. He wouldn't survive it."

"Is he going to die?" Was that her voice so emotionless and cold?

"Yes. I understand you have a sibling?"

"I do, a brother."

"He should come. The two of you have some big decisions to make. Your father has a DNR on file. He's suffering. The machines are keeping him alive."

"Are you saying we should let him go?" Kristine asked.

"I'm saying medicine and science aren't working."

"It's time for nature to take its course?" Kristine asked, needing a definite answer from the doctor. She didn't want to be the one to make the decision to let her father die.

"Sometimes all the medicine in the world won't stop the evitable," Dr. Grant said. "I can send the hospital chaplain by to speak to you."

"But you think we should take him off the medications?" Kristine asked, wanting a direct response.

Dr. Grant shook his head. "Sometimes it's the kindest way."

"I don't know if I can," she said.

"Take some time, think about what's best for your father," the doctor told her. "I'm available to answer more questions."

"But I should call my brother again," she reiterated.

He nodded. "And anyone else who would like to say good-bye."

"Okay." Was this really it—the end of the great and powerful Lucas Wilding?

The door opened and two nurses exited her father's room.

"He's all freshened up," one of the nurses said on her way past Kristine.

She didn't want to go back in there. She didn't know that old man in the bed, didn't want to know him. She didn't owe her father anything. Why should she stop her life to care for him? He'd never given a damn about her or Lucky.

And Carly. There was no way she'd let Carly into that room full of disease. She didn't care if her father was dying, she wasn't about to expose her daughter to him. Their relationship bordered on non-existent. Carly barely knew her grandfather, and right now, Kristine was glad.

She pulled her phone out again and called Rowena.

"It's me," she said when Rowena answered. "I'm here, at the hospital. Can you come and pick up Carly?"

"I'll be right there," Rowena said.

And there it was, the rush of love, love for Rowena, the housekeeper who had raised her and Lucky. Rowena, the only mother they'd ever really had, since their own mother, Veronica Wilding, had been an unavailable, emotional train wreck.

"Thank you," Kristine said, her eyes damp with tears.

She headed to the waiting area, to sit with Carly until Rowena came. Once Carly was gone, she'd do her duty and tend to her father.

She didn't know what else to do.

* * *

Hours later, Kristine climbed out of the car, her gaze on her childhood home.

Wilding House.

Six steps and she'd be on the porch, then inside. She inhaled, taking in the salty air rolling off Puget Sound. Wow, she'd missed that smell, the beach, sunbaked seaweed, and mussels. Orange light spilled from the windows, welcoming her. The house sat like a jewel on Wilding Point. A big, beautiful, expensive jewel. Her father's pride and joy. He loved the showpiece of a house more than he'd ever loved his own children.

Somewhere a dog barked. Kristine breathed in the tangy air, trying to clear the scent of death from her nose.

It was after nine. She'd stayed in the ICU until visiting hours were over, although she could have spent the night if she'd wanted to. When people were dying, the ICU didn't limit the amount of time one could spend at the hospital.

Basically, over the course of the day she'd learned her father was dying by shit. He was drowning in it. She'd never seen so much diarrhea. It would be funny if it weren't so sad. Each time it had happened, he'd wanted to know why. He didn't understand and even in his confused state he was embarrassed. He'd cried twice. He was paranoid, and in some ways, he'd become a child, whiny, needy, vulnerable.

This was not her tough as nails father. This Lucas Wilding was a tiny, shriveled, terminally ill man. And right now it was up to her to decide if he should be removed from all machines.

How was she supposed to make a decision like that on her own?

The front door opened. "Kristine," Rowena called. She stood in the open doorway, backlit from the foyer, her hair a little grayer, but otherwise the same, plump, her long hair drawn back into the customary bun.

"Hi, Rowena," Kristine said from the base of the steps. "Can you open the garage door, please? I need to leave these clothes in the laundry room, then take a shower."

"I understand," Rowena said. "He's contagious. I do the same when I come home."

"Yes."

Rowena disappeared and a minute later the garage door opened. Kristine walked through the garage into the laundry room and stripped off her clothes, putting them straight into the washing machine. She didn't bother going upstairs to her private bathroom, but instead made use of the bathroom adjacent to the laundry room, stepping right into the shower.

Kristine scrubbed away the smell of feces and death, embracing the scent of the lavender soap. Only then did she cry, but did she cry for herself and her situation, or for the father who had never loved her or Lucky? For several seconds, she leaned against the shower wall, her tears thick and hot. When she could cry no more, she rinsed away her sadness, telling herself she could handle this. She had to. There was no one else.

When she stepped out of the shower, Rowena was waiting with a thick white towel and a pink guest robe.

The minute she had the robe on, she was in Rowena's arms.

"Oh, my beautiful girl," Rowena said as she stroked Kristine's back. "I've missed you."

"I've missed you, too." She inhaled Rowena, noting the scent of jasmine that was always on the housekeeper's skin. An instant comfort overcame her. She wasn't alone, not with Rowena here.

"Have you eaten?" Rowena pulled back to study her, smoothing the wet hair from Kristine's face.

"No."

"Come on." Rowena linked her arm through Kristine's. "I made your favorite, chicken with fat dumplings."

Kristine smiled. This was home. Rowena was home. "Is Carly okay?"

"She's watching television in her room," Rowena said. "Such a beautiful girl."

"She is," Kristine agreed as they walked into the kitchen. Gone was the kitchen of her childhood, the oak cabinets and black counter tops. "It's been remodeled."

"Yes, two years ago," Rowena said. "I told your father it was fine the way it was, grander than any kitchen I've ever been in, but he wanted it grander."

"Sounds like him." Kristine took a seat at the Carrara marble–topped island. She ran her hand over the smooth surface. "Well, this is beautiful. The white cabinets are gorgeous. Looks beachy in here."

"Yes." Rowena pulled a covered dish from the oven. "I kept the food warm for you."

"Thank you." Again, love tugged Kristine's heart. It had been a long time since anyone had done anything nice or thoughtful for her.

"Eat," Rowena said as she placed the plate of food before her.

Kristine did, savoring the chicken, then the dumplings that melted in her mouth. "This is delicious."

Rowena smiled, taking the seat next to her. "How was he today?"

"Awful." Kristine wiped her mouth on the napkin. "His mind—it's like it's not even him."

"This is true," Rowena agreed. "He's not the same man."

"How long has he had dementia?" Kristine asked.

"I started to notice about five years ago," Rowena said. "Little things, like he couldn't turn his computer on. Bills weren't paid, or they were paid twice. He didn't remember to take his blood pressure medicine, or he took too much, things like that."

"How awful for you," Kristine said, meaning it. "I'm sorry. You should have told me."

"He's a very proud man. He still won't admit he has a problem." Rowena shrugged. "Maybe now he has no idea. He's too far gone."

"I don't know what to say," Kristine said. "I don't know this man."

"This is true." Rowena nodded, her expression thoughtful. "He's different. He doesn't remember every little thing anymore. Maybe you can find it in your heart to know this version of your father."

Did she want to know him, this broken, old man?

Kristine pushed her food away, the knot back in her stomach. "I'm tired."

"Of course you are." Rowena removed the plate. "Come. Your room is ready. Things will look better in the morning."

Would they? Kristine doubted she could even sleep, but she followed Rowena upstairs anyway.

Chapter Two

Kristine awoke to the cry of a gull.

The instant she heard the bird she knew she was home.

She tossed back the covers and went to the window, opening it wide. Oh, the air. She took a deep pull of salt air into her lungs, savoring the fresh, clean scent. The sky was blue, the water of Puget Sound even bluer. She loved this type of sunny day. Living in the Pacific Northwest, they had more than their share of cloudy days that left the Sound an iron gray. But this day was a treat.

Too bad she wouldn't get to enjoy it.

No, she'd be spending her day in the hospital, making hard life decisions regarding a father she didn't know anymore.

Instantly depressed, she closed the window.

She needed another shower. A glance at the clock told her it was after eight. Carly would still be asleep. It was Memorial Day weekend, a five-day weekend for Carly. That meant late nights and sleep-ins.

Kristine showered, then dressed in jeans and a comfy white T-shirt. What did it matter? She'd be wearing a hazmat gown all day anyway. She pulled her hair into a long ponytail before putting on her sneakers. Easy shoes to clean in the washing machine when she came home. She wasn't about to bring any of her father's sickness into this house where loved ones could be exposed.

She left her room. Her father's room was down the hall, but she had no desire to look inside. Thankfully, the door was shut.

Kristine took her time walking down the curved staircase, her shoes making no sound on the polished mahogany steps.

When she hit the foyer she smelled pancakes.

She entered the kitchen with a smile on her face, coming to a stop when she saw a man seated at the island.

Rowena stood at the stove. "Good morning, Kristine."

The man turned around, his eyes on her.

Rand Bell.

She'd had a crush on Rowena's son all through her teen years. He'd been cute then, but he was gorgeous now, a man.

Rand's face had a chiseled look, strong jaw, and his skin already showed a hint of a spring tan. His thick dark hair held a slight wave. He wore jeans and a black T-shirt, leaving his muscular forearms bare. She spied a sizable tattoo on his left forearm, but couldn't make it out without staring. But it was his eyes she remembered most, bedroom eyes the color of dark chocolate.

"You remember Rand?" Rowena asked, the question hopeful.

"Rand," Kristine repeated. "Of course. Hello."

"Welcome home, Kristine," he said, but he didn't smile.

"I hope you don't mind," Rowena said, "Rand rents the guest house. I had to move inside when your father, well, when he needed more daily help."

"I didn't realize," Kristine said.

Rowena smiled. "Pancakes are ready."

Rand slid off his stool. "I better get going."

"Already?" Rowena asked. "No seconds?"

"Nope." Rand patted his flat belly. "I've got a job in Centerville today. Don't want to be late."

"Well, have a good day," Rowena said.

"You, too." Rand nodded to Kristine. "Nice to see you."

"Yes." Rand Bell. Holy cow. She'd had no idea he was still hanging around town. In fact, she'd heard he'd gone to college in California then moved to New York. What was he doing back here?

"Eat." Rowena set a plate of steaming pancakes on the island.

Kristine dug in. "You're going to fatten me up."

"Are you heading to the hospital this morning?" Rowena asked, a cup of coffee in her hands.

"I am." Kristine chewed on her pancakes, then took a swallow of coffee. "I don't know what else to do."

"I think you do," Rowena said. "I think it's time, my darling. He would not want to live like this."

Kristine pressed her lips together. She refused to cry again. "I don't want to be the one to make the decision. How can I? I don't even know him."

"But I do," Rowena said firmly. "Go spend the day with him. Remember who he was, but maybe, enjoy who he is now."

"Enjoy?" Kristine repeated. "I don't see any way to do that."

"Go and see what I mean," Rowena said, her smile gentle. "You will make the right decision. You are a smart, kind, compassionate woman. I have complete faith in you."

Before Kristine could reply, Carly waltzed into the kitchen, halting their conversation. The kid had a serious case of bed head.

"Hey," Kristine said. "Sleep well?"

"A screeching bird woke me," Carly said, the words grumpy.

"The seagull," Rowena said. "He's a pest for sure." She chuckled.

"I'm going to head to the hospital," Kristine told Carly.

Carly slid onto the stool next to her. "Are you staying all day?"

"I might have to," Kristine said. "I'm sorry. Grandpa needs me."

"With Mr. Lucas gone I have a lot of free time," Rowena said. "Why don't we go shopping?"

Carly brightened. "Really?"

"Sure, why not?" Rowena said. "Just the two of us. We'll have so much fun."

Kristine gave Rowena a smile of thanks. "That's a great idea."

"Can I have some money, Mom?" Carly asked.

Money was tight, super tight, but Kristine didn't want to deny Carly this small pleasure. "Sure." Kristine retrieved her purse. She quickly counted her cash before passing Carly forty dollars. "It's all I can spare, sweetie."

"Thanks, Mom," Carly said, all smiles now.

"You go on," Rowena said to Kristine. "Do what you have to do. I have Carly. I'll take good care of her."

"I know you will." Kristine smiled, hugging Rowena. "I'll call you if I have any news."

Rowena nodded. "You're a good girl, Kristine."

A good girl indeed. Kristine left the kitchen, steeling herself for the day ahead.

* * *

Rand dropped the hammer, the tool landing on his foot, bouncing off the steel toe of his boot. "Damn it."

"Mind's not on your work today," Keith Rickman, his boss and friend, pointed out. "That's the second time you've dropped that hammer. What gives?"

"Nothing," Rand said, unwilling to tell his friend about his encounter with Kristine Wilding that morning. He'd been unable to get the blonde out of his head since their breakfast meeting. He remembered her well, even though she'd been four years younger than he was. She'd been a wild, crazy teenager. A risk taker, doing whatever she could to get the attention of her father—a man, who in Rand's opinion, should have never had children.

Lucas Wilding was an unscrupulous, greedy monster, making his money off the misfortune of others.

No wonder his kids had left town and never looked back.

He'd known his mother had been working on Kristine and Lucky, trying to get them both to come home and make peace with their father, but he'd never expected Kristine would show up.

She'd always been too damn beautiful for her own good.

Rumor had it Kristine looked just like her mother, a woman even more broken than her children. Veronica Wilding suffered from manic depression and a host of other mental illnesses. She'd left Kristine and Lucky behind when they'd been small children, left them to a father who'd never recovered from the loss of his wife. A man who didn't like to lose, and prided himself on winning at any cost.

Rand feared Kristine had had it rougher than Lucky. Her pretty face had been a constant reminder of Veronica.

The family was sick and twisted, and Rand didn't want anything to do with Kristine or Lucky. He'd always steered clear of them, and he intended to stay out of their way now. For years, he'd begged his mother to find a job somewhere else, but Rowena was fiercely loyal to the Wildings. It was a loyalty Rand didn't understand. Oh, he knew she loved Kristine and Lucky, feared for them, championed them, but Kristine and Lucky hadn't lived at home in years. Still, his mother wouldn't budge.

He'd often wondered why, but when he'd questioned his mother, her reply was always the same: "How can I leave this beautiful place? I'm happy here."

No, he didn't understand his mother at all.

"This deck isn't going to build itself," Keith said with a grin. "Hey, why don't you come by after work? We could toss back a couple of cold ones and relax."

"Sounds good," Rand replied, his mind back on the deck before him. Lifting his hammer, he drove the nail home.

* * *

Kristine had been sitting with her father for close to four hours when her phone buzzed, Lucky's name flashing on the screen.

"I'll be right back, Dad," she said. "I have to get this."

Her father opened one eye, and even that seemed like too much effort for him. Behind him, the monitors hissed, one of them emitting a relentless beep that was driving her crazy.

"Hey," she said into the phone. "Hold on. I have to get out of my hazmat suit."

"Okay," Lucky said.

Kristine set the phone on the counter. Quickly, she used a Clorox wipe to clean the phone, setting it on a clean paper towel. Once that was done, she removed the gown and gloves, giving her hands a thorough scrub. She had the exit process down to a science now.

She grabbed her phone, praying Lucky was still on the line.

"I'm back," she said on her way to the door. And then she was free, walking as fast as she could toward the double doors that would take her out of the ICU.

"Hey," Lucky returned. "What's going on? Why are you there?"

She shouldered the double doors open, going directly into the family room waiting area. Thankfully, it was empty. "I don't know. Look, can you come home? He's dying. They want me to pull the plug."

"No kidding?" Lucky said, sounding amused.

"No kidding," she repeated, anger rising. "I'm serious, Lucky. I can't do this alone."

"Rowena's there, isn't she?" Lucky said. "She can hold your hand. I don't want to see him."

"This isn't about him. I know how you feel. This is about me. I can't do it. You should see him. I don't even recognize him. He's so sick. He's drowning in his own feces. The smell…" She closed her eyes, willing the unwanted image away. "Please, Lucky. He has dementia. He's different. Still ornery, but there are gaps in his memory. He's only in the present."

There was a pause, and Kristine could almost picture Lucky raking his fingers through his hair.

"I can't," he finally said. "I don't want to see him. The man ruined my life."

Sad thing was, she didn't blame Lucky for feeling the way he did. "I need you, Luck."

He sighed. "I'll think about it. You know I'd be there for you in a minute if you were anywhere but Wilding Point. I love you, sis. It's him I can't deal with."

He wasn't coming. She pressed a hand to her stomach as disappointment filled her, making her weak. She sat on a nearby chair. "Okay," she said. "I understand. Will you at least help me make the decision to stop all the antibiotics and machines? We need to let him go, make him comfortable—use comfort measures only, at least that's what I think the people here are trying to tell me. I guess it's time to let nature take its course. Rowena agrees."

"Do it," Lucky said without hesitation. "But don't do it for him, do it for you."

"No," she shot back. "Not for me, Lucky. This is for him. I know you don't forgive him for what he did to you, but he's suffering."

"I'm here for you over the phone. I promise I'll pick up. You won't be alone, Kris."

She supposed that was the most she'd get out of her brother. "I'll call you back after I talk to the doctor."

"I love you, Kristine," Lucky said. "I'm sorry I can't be there for you."

"I know," Kristine said. "I love you, too. I'll call when I have more info."

"Good luck."

Kristine ended the call. *Good luck.* Good luck with what? Watching their father die? Needing time to collect her thoughts, Kristine made herself a cup of tea in the kitchenette area of the waiting room. It was time to bring Rowena and Carly in to say good-bye. As soon as she finished her tea, she'd call the doctor and make the arrangements to free her father from all the IVs and monitors.

No matter how conflicted her feelings were for the man who had raised her, she couldn't bear the thought of her father spending his last night on earth alone. She'd stay here tonight and give him what comfort she could. If he passed away tomorrow, they could be home in time for Carly to go back to school on Wednesday.

It was a cold thought, but the thought of leaving here was a light at the end of a dark tunnel. She wanted out of Wilding Point.

Some things never changed.

* * *

The monitors were quiet. The IVs gone, the cold metal posts they'd hung on empty and eerie in the dark room, like a row of metal skeletons.

Lucas Wilding had been off all meds for two days, and instead of dying, his vital signs had been steadily improving.

Kristine sat on the makeshift window seat bed, the light from the screen on her phone her only comfort. She'd been researching end of life, and so far her father wasn't showing any of the signs.

Was he really dying?

She didn't know what to believe anymore and no one here, including the doctors, seemed to have any answers. She'd spoken to the infectious disease specialist, who had given her zero hope. Her father's gastro doctor was off today and would be back tomorrow, but Kristine expected the same diagnosis from him. All agreed Lucas Wilding would die, but no one could pinpoint the exact date or time.

She'd expected more from medical science, but the doctors all seemed as clueless as she did.

Kristine set her phone down. Rowena had urged her to come back to the house, sleep there, but for some reason she'd been unable to leave her father. He seemed so helpless. He had no advocate without her.

Rowena was right, he wasn't the same man he used to be. Oh, he was still demanding, constantly thirsty, running her ragged feeding him water and ice chips, but otherwise for the most part he was sweet and confused.

Two words she'd never thought she'd use to describe Lucas Wilding.

This new father perplexed her. He looked at her with love and gratitude, not distaste and hatred.

Her stomach rumbled.

Difficult to eat when you were watching someone die, and worse, wearing a hazmat suit. Food was not allowed in the room anyway.

Her phone pinged as a text message came in.

Rowena's name lit the screen. *Rand is in the waiting area with your dinner. Go eat please.*

Rand? He was the last person she felt like seeing. She was an unwashed, germ-ridden mess. Ugh.

Kristine texted back, *Okay.*

Her father was asleep. She did a check to make sure he was breathing before removing her protective gear and scrubbing with hot water. She ran her fingers through her hair. She wore no makeup and had none with her.

She left the room, waving at the nurse on duty.

"Going home?" the nurse asked, her voice sounding as tired as Kristine felt.

"No, someone brought me dinner. Just taking a break."

"Good, you need to eat," the nurse said with a smile.

Kristine passed through the double doors and into the waiting room.

Rand sat at the round table, a covered dish in front of him. When he saw her, he stood.

"Please," Kristine said, with a wave of her hand. "Sit. Thanks for bringing dinner."

He sat. "Happy to help."

"Still, I don't like to impose." She slid into the chair opposite him.

He looked great, tan, fit, healthy—the opposite of her father. His eyes searched her face. What did he see? A woman in need of a shower, that's what. Kristine frowned, suddenly uncomfortable. She prayed she didn't smell.

"How are you holding up?" Rand slid the dish of food to her.

She gave him a small smile. "I've been better." She unrolled the silverware from the napkin, then uncovered the dish. "Lasagna. Wow, does it smell good."

"It is good." Rand grinned, and it was like the sun came out.

She'd forgotten how handsome he looked when he smiled.

"No one can cook like my mom."

"Agreed." Kristine took a bite of the lasagna, the rich blend of pasta, tomatoes, and cheese a taste explosion on her tongue. "Heaven."

Rand produced a bottle of water. "Here."

"Thanks." Suddenly ravenous, Kristine practically inhaled the food. "Talk to me, Rand. Tell me something that will get my mind off of my father."

He looked thoughtful. "Loved the weather today. It hit sixty-five."

"Not the weather," she said, forking up more lasagna. "Something else. Why are you in Wilding Point?"

"Nothing like a personal question," he returned, his chocolate brown eyes on her. His forehead wrinkled.

"Last I heard you were going to college in California," she said. "Stanford, right? Then you moved to New York."

"Right," he confirmed. "Graduated. Lived in both LA and New York."

"Seriously?" she asked. "Why are you here?"

"Taking a sabbatical," he said with a shrug.

"What do you do here?" she asked.

"A little of this, a little of that. I work for Keith Rickman. We do all types of home repairs and remodels."

"But weren't you always interested in business?" she said. "I seem to remember you were class treasurer."

"I was," he confirmed. "Things changed. I changed. Enough about me. What have you been doing with your life?"

"Raising Carly by myself, her father nothing but a bitter memory."

"I'm sorry," he said softly.

She shrugged. "Me, too. For Carly. She's a sweet girl, but she's turning into a teenager."

He smiled. "It happens."

"Yes." She took a sip of water.

"What do you do in Oregon?" Rand asked.

"Believe it or not, I do intake registration at a hospital."

"Do you make a good living doing that?" Rand asked.

"I make enough." Kristine finished the last of her lasagna. "I'm burning my vacation to be here."

"Don't they have family leave?"

"Working on it." She smiled. "Didn't know I was going to need it, but dying has no timetable. Thanks for bringing me dinner, but more important, thanks for getting me out of his room for a while. It's really isolating in there. I can't eat or drink in his room. I don't want to talk on the phone. I mostly sit on my phone researching his illness and end of life."

Rand gave her a sad smile. "Sounds awful."

"It is." Kristine placed her used silverware in the dish and attached the cover. "Tell Rowena thanks for me. That was wonderful."

"Do you think he'll pass soon?" Rand asked.

Kristine stood. "I don't know. His vitals are better. I keep thinking the doctors made a mistake, but all involved assure me he can't beat this. He will die, but no one knows when."

Rand got to his feet, the dish in his hands. He stood a good four inches taller than her five foot nine. Again, she was struck by his good looks. Those eyes, a girl could drown in them.

She couldn't imagine what he thought of her. Not her finest moment for sure. Even though she'd sworn off men years ago, she was still vain enough to care about what he thought and that bothered her.

Her father was dying, her life was on hold, her daughter needed her. Those were the things she needed to worry about. What difference did it make what Rand thought of her? She didn't plan on sticking around here long enough for his opinion to matter one way or the other.

"Thanks for bringing me dinner," she said, on her way to the door.

"Sure you don't want to step out and take in a big hit of fresh air?" he coaxed, smiling. "Might be just what you need."

Sweet, fresh spring air. "Oh, that sounds tempting."

"Come on, just for a minute." He grinned as he led the way to the elevator.

They rode down three floors and made their way through the lobby and out the automatic doors.

The first thing Kristine noticed was the scent of something sweet—a flower maybe? Then the croak of a frog. The air was warm and soft, making her long to get in her car and head back to the house. Wilding House had three gorgeous decks, all with stunning views of the Sound. She closed her eyes, imagining the view, the lights sparkling on Salmon Island just across the Point.

"Nice night," Rand said.

"Wonderful." She turned to him. "Thanks for suggesting this." She inhaled. "Next time I'm feeling trapped, I'll come out here for air. I feel better already."

"Good."

She met his gaze for a second before looking away. *Careful, Kristine, he's not the guy for you.* If and when she dated again, she wanted a man who made some real money. She was tired of scrimping and saving and juggling bills.

Rand Bell was not that man. Obviously something significant had happened to him to alter the course of his life. Something she didn't want to get involved in.

No, a local handyman was not the guy for her.
Not at all.

Chapter Three

The following morning Kristine watched as they moved her father to the PCU—the Palliative Care Unit. She'd asked if this was good news, but had been told no. Apparently Lucas Wilding wasn't dying fast enough. They needed the bed in the ICU for a patient who had a chance at recovery. A social worker had talked to her about the move and the discharge from the hospital that would soon follow if he didn't pass away quickly.

Discharge? What was she supposed to do with her father? She couldn't care for him on her own, change his diaper—he was a two-person lift. Even if she could care for him, she couldn't bring him back into a house where her daughter was. The social worker suggested a skilled nursing facility. She'd given Kristine brochures on several places near her father's home.

Kristine fought anxiety as she leafed through the brochures. She didn't know what to do. A skilled nursing facility sounded terrible, and while she'd have no qualms about putting the father she'd grown up loathing in a place like that, this Lucas Wilding was scared and sick, his mind muddy and broken. He would not, could not be an advocate for himself. If he lived on, she couldn't stay forever.

The hospital wanted to discharge him as soon as possible. The clock was ticking. She had to make a decision.

"Kristine?"

She glanced up as yet another doctor walked into the room, but there was something familiar about this one.

"Kyle?" she asked.

"Yes." He smiled.

Kyle King. Homecoming king. Captain of the football team. He'd been every girl's dream in high school. Tall, built, with hair the color of brown sugar, and eyes the exact shade of blue as Puget Sound on a summer's day. He'd been Lucky's best friend, two years older than her and totally off limits. They'd never dated, but she'd been as attracted to him as any girl. They'd run in different circles, Kyle with the super popular, the jocks, Kristine with the wild kids.

She came to her feet. "Do you work here? Wait—the gastro doctor, Dr. King. Is that you?"

"Right again." He held out his gloved hand and she shook it. "It's good to see you. I've been in to see your father several times, but never managed to run into you or Lucky."

"I've only been here a few days."

"Is Lucky here?" Kyle asked with interest.

"No," she told him. "Not yet, anyway."

"I see," Kyle said, his attention turning to her father. "How's he doing today?"

She shrugged.

Kyle gave her a sympathetic smile before moving on to her father. "How are you today, Mr. Wilding?"

"Who are you again?" her father asked.

"Dr. King. Kyle. Lucky's friend."

"That's right." Her father closed his eyes. "I want to go home."

"I believe we're working on that," Kyle said. He turned to Kristine. "Have you made a decision about what to do next?"

"No. I don't think I can care for him on my own, even with Rowena's help. The thought terrifies me. I've seen what it takes to change him. I can't do it."

"May I recommend a place?" Kyle asked.

"Please."

"Pinewood. It's the best, and it's hard to get in. I have some pull there. I could make a call."

His kindness touched her. "That would be great."

"Has the social worker talked to you about hospice?"

"Yes."

"Once he's there, get that ball rolling. Hospice will do amazing things for him, and take some of the pressure off of you."

She nodded, so grateful for his help she wanted to cry.

"I'm thirsty," her father said. "So thirsty."

Kristine fed him ice chips. He'd kept her hopping on this chore all night long. If she never saw another ice chip she'd be happy.

"That's good," her father said, sucking on the ice. "You're a good girl, Kristine."

Her eyes widened. What? She'd never received any kind of compliment from her father before. Who was this man in the hospital bed?

"I'm tired," Lucas muttered. "I'm going to die. I want to go home."

"Rest, Dad." She set the cup of ice back on the tray.

"You look beat," Kyle said. "Want to grab a quick cup of coffee?"

"I'd love to."

Kyle smiled.

They got rid of their gowns and gloves and washed up. Kristine followed him to the family waiting area, but when they got there, he said, "Let's go to the cafeteria and sit outside. It's a beautiful day."

"That sounds great." She never got tired of the fresh air.

Kyle bought her a latte and got himself a cup of black coffee. Minutes later, they were sitting in the courtyard.

"Thank you for the coffee, and for getting me outside," she said, her face turned to the sun.

"It's going to be okay," Kyle told her.

She looked at him, saw the compassion in his eyes. "It's tough to know what to do. Everyone tells me he's dying, but there's no timeline. I have a life in Oregon, a job. I have a daughter who should have been in school today."

"A daughter," Kyle said with interest. "How old?"

"Twelve, almost thirteen."

"Twelve?" He smiled.

"I know, I started young," Kristine said. "How about you? Any kids?"

"Nope, no wife either." His hands cradled his coffee cup. "You probably heard I married Beth Barnes. It didn't work out. Since the divorce, I've been busy becoming a doctor, then building a practice."

"Yes, I heard about you and Beth," Kristine said. "I suppose it makes sense you'd turn to each other."

"After Lucky," Kyle said, "well, Beth leaned on me. Things just happened and we fell in love."

"No need to explain," Kristine said. "Lucky and Beth dated a long time ago."

"Still," Kyle said with a shrug. "I wanted to explain."

She smiled before taking a sip of coffee. "It's gorgeous out."

"It is."

"I guess I'll take your suggestion if you're willing to make that call to Pinewood."

"I'm happy to help." Kyle smiled. "Why don't you give me your number and I'll let you know when I've made the call. I'll talk to the social worker, too—help you make the transition."

"I'll owe you big," Kristine said. "Thank you so much."

He passed her his phone and Kristine added her number.

"How's Lucky?" Kyle asked.

"I don't know," she admitted. "Going to prison changed him. He's bitter. He's lousy at staying in touch. He wants nothing to do with Dad or Wilding Point."

"I'm sorry," Kyle said, the words sincere.

"You were such good friends," Kristine said. "You don't keep in touch at all?"

"No," Kyle admitted. "I'm not sure why."

They spent the next few minutes talking about old classmates while they finished their coffees. It felt good to laugh, to have her mind taken off her problems, if only for a few minutes.

When they finished, Kyle escorted her to the elevators, promising to let her know what he found out about Pinewood.

Kristine hadn't been back in her father's room for more than an hour when the social worker popped in to say Pinewood would take her father. They would move him tomorrow.

She had no idea if she was doing the right thing, sending her father to Pinewood, but it was a first step to hospice care, and she needed all the help dealing with end of life she could get.

Since there was nowhere to sleep in her father's new room, she left the hospital around eight-thirty to go home and sleep. She arrived home and managed to get Carly off her phone long enough to watch a movie with her before bed, despite the fact Kristine could barely keep her eyes open.

When she fell into bed around eleven, she tossed and turned, her stomach aching just thinking about her father, his illness, and what it meant for her life. She had to make a decision about

Carly. Should she send Carly home to stay with friends and finish out the school year?

She'd talk to her daughter tomorrow and try to figure things out.

For now, she just wanted to sleep and forget.

* * *

Kristine woke up to the ring of her phone.

She sat up, still groggy with sleep. Locating her phone, she didn't recognize the number. Had something happened to her father?

"Hello?"

"Kristine, it's Kyle."

Relief filled her. Kyle, not the hospital. "Kyle, hello."

"Did I wake you?" he asked. "I'm sorry."

"It's okay. I need to get to the hospital. They are moving Dad to Pinewood today. Thank you so much for your help."

"You're welcome," he said. "I'll try to stop by there later today to check on you and your dad."

"You don't have to do that," she said. "You've done enough already."

"I want to, Kristine," he said softly. "I go back a long way with your family. Let me help."

"Okay, thank you." His kindness touched her. Thank God for his bond with Lucky. Without Kyle's help, she'd be at a total loss. He was helping her, supporting her in a way no one else was. "I'll see you later."

"Count on it," he said. "Bye now."

"Bye." Kristine got up and made a beeline for the shower. She couldn't seem to get clean enough anymore. She dressed in jeans and a spring sweater in a shade of blue that matched her eyes. She fixed her hair and applied makeup for the first time in days.

If she was going to see Kyle, she wanted to look her best, plus cleaning up made her feel better, more like herself.

She went down to breakfast feeling a little more optimistic than she had since returning to Wilding Point.

"There you are," Rowena exclaimed when Kristine entered the kitchen.

"Good morning, Ro," Kristine said. "Carly up?"

"Up and taking a walk on the beach," Rowena said.

"Really?"

"Yes, she's with Rand and Hussy."

"Hussy?" Kristine asked, taking a bite of the cinnamon roll Rowena placed before her. "Yum, this is fantastic."

"Baked fresh this morning." Rowena smiled. "Hussy is Rand's dog, a white German shepherd. Sweet as pie. Carly loves her."

"Carly's always wanted a dog."

"I'll scramble you some eggs for protein." Rowena opened the fridge.

"Thanks. It's going to be a long day."

Carly, Rand, and Hussy entered through the open sliding-glass door. Carly's cheeks held the pink of a cool morning walk.

"Hey, kiddo," Kristine said, giving her daughter a bright smile.

"Hi, Mom." Carly took the stool next to her.

"Good morning," Kristine said to Rand. "And this must be Hussy."

"Morning," Rand said, "and yes."

Hussy sniffed Kristine's leg. "Hey, girl." The dog wagged her tail. "How far did you guys walk?"

"To North Beach," Rand said. "How are things going for you? How's your dad?"

"The same, hanging on," Kristine said. "We're moving him to Pinewood today."

"Pinewood, swanky," Rand said, one eyebrow lifting.

"I guess." Kristine smiled as Rowena set eggs in front of her. "I have to talk to Dad's attorney. I have no idea who has power of attorney, or who is the executor of Dad's estate."

"I can call John for you," Rowena said. "I'll give him your number. I have your father's insurance cards."

"That would be great," Kristine said. "I know Pinewood is going to ask me all kinds of questions. I'll take whatever you have. I know nothing."

"Let me see if I can get John on the phone right now," Rowena said.

"Thank you." Kristine dug into her food.

Rand poured himself a cup of coffee.

"No work for you today?" she asked him, again wondering what his story was.

"Nope, a day off."

"Is the work pretty steady?"

"Usually," he said. "I do okay. I don't need much."

She could never live like that, not knowing where her next paycheck was coming from. She had a daughter to support.

"What are you doing today, Carly?" Kristine asked.

"Rowena and I are going downtown to Pike Place Market."

"I'm jealous," Kristine said on a sigh. "That sounds fun."

"I remember when we went last time. It was so great," Carly said.

"You should go to Beecher's for mac and cheese," Kristine told her, but Carly's attention was on her phone. "Texting with Nan?"

"Yes," Carly confirmed, her eyes on the screen.

Nan and Carly had been best friends since kindergarten. If she had to send Carly back, she'd send her to Nan's. She trusted Nan's parents, Kate and Doug. Kate was Kristine's best friend. They'd been texting the entire time she'd been in Wilding Point.

Kate knew everything about Kristine's strained relationship with her father.

"I should get going," Kristine said. "They are moving Grandpa around noon."

"I'm sorry this is hard, Mom," Carly said after she disconnected from her phone.

She glanced at Carly, surprised by the girl's compassion. "Thanks, honey. I'm sorry, too."

"John's on the line," Rowena said, handing Kristine the house phone.

"Great. Hey, John," Kristine said to her father's attorney on her way out of the kitchen.

Fifteen minutes later, she had her answers. She held the power of attorney for her dad. She was also named as the executor of her father's will. She had access to her father's checking account. John told her where to find everything she needed. Her father had prepared for this moment, had known his memory would be compromised.

According to John, the household bills were set up to pay automatically. Kristine made an appointment to meet with the attorney next week.

She was definitely not going back to Oregon in the near future.

But she had to send Carly back. And she needed to check on her family leave, call her boss.

Death sucked. Dying wasn't for sissies. There was no timeline.

She couldn't leave this new version of her father alone, the version who trusted her enough to leave his estate in her hands, the father who called her a good girl.

As sick and embattled as their relationship was, she was staying in Wilding Point. If her father continued to improve, well, she'd make the decision to go home then. If he declined, she'd stay until the end. Thank goodness summer vacation was approaching. She wanted Carly with her.

Decision made, Kristine set out for the hospital.

It was going to be a long day.

* * *

They were settled at Pinewood, but Kristine didn't have a good feeling about the place.

The room at Pinewood, while very nice, seemed sterile. Not a place she'd want to die. Not a place she'd want for her father. Plus, Pinewood seemed understaffed. She'd rung for the nurse more than once and had to wait several minutes for a response. What would happen to her father if she weren't there to make sure his needs were met?

Her father had hated Pinewood on sight. He wanted to go home, to Wilding House, but Kristine didn't know how she could make that happen. He'd cried as they'd weighed him, then helped him into bed.

He needed full-time, around the clock care. His legs had filled with fluid and no longer seemed to work. She couldn't care for him alone, and it surprised her to discover she was even considering it. No, caring for him at home was not an option.

They'd spent the afternoon watching soap operas, and to her surprise, her father loved *General Hospital*. He knew all the characters, their storylines. Half the time she wasn't sure if he really knew who she was, but she didn't care. This was the father she'd always wanted, needed. A man who wanted to spend time with his daughter.

She spoon fed her father a little yogurt at dinnertime, but he wasn't hungry, hadn't really eaten for days. But he loved his ice chips. She couldn't keep them coming fast enough.

How long could a man exist on ice chips alone?

It was after seven when her phone rang, Kyle's name lighting the screen. A flame of excitement leapt into her belly. Was he really interested in her father's well-being, or was something more happening here?

"Hi, Kyle," she said.

"Hello, Kristine, how did today go?"

"Pretty good," she told him. "He weathered the ambulance ride well, but he wants to go home."

"That's normal," Kyle said. "Have you started paperwork for hospice care?"

"The social worker has been by. Sounds like it will take a few days for hospice to kick in—something to do with the insurance."

"Right," Kyle agreed, "but once hospice care is in place, his quality of care will go up."

"Good, because everyone here seems extremely busy and not really responsive to his needs." Kristine moved her phone to her other ear.

"Can I bring you anything?" Kyle asked. "I was planning to head over."

"That's not really in your job description, doctor," she said, her tone light. "Honestly, there's no need for you to come by."

"I know how grueling end of life can be," Kyle said. "I really do want to help."

"You're sweet, but we're fine. I'll be heading home soon. Sounds like they want me out of here by eight-thirty."

"If you're sure?" he asked.

"I am. You've gone above and beyond. Thank you."

"I have a bit of an ulterior motive," Kyle said. "I know the timing is awful, but I'd love to take you to dinner, or even lunch while you are here."

"You're right, bad timing," she agreed, wishing she could accept the invite. "I can't say yes to either of those right now. My dad needs all my attention."

"I understand," Kyle said, "but I won't give up. I'm here for you personally and professionally. Please call me any time."

His thoughtfulness charmed her. "Thank you, Kyle."

"No thanks necessary," he said. "I'll let you go now, but I'll check in with you tomorrow."

"You don't have to," she said.

"I want to," he replied, his tone firm. "Good night, Kristine."

"Good night."

She tossed her phone in her purse and turned to look at her father. He was asleep, his mouth open.

Was she doing the right thing, deciding to stay with him until the end? Her thoughts turned to Carly. She'd call Kate tomorrow to see if she'd take Carly during the weekdays until her father passed.

Decision made, Kristine felt a little better, more sure of her plan. Rowena was picking her up at eight-thirty and taking her back to her car where she'd left it in the hospital parking lot.

But before she left, she wanted to check in with night nurse, make sure the nurse knew her father needed his ice chips.

Kristine left the room, spoke with the nurse, then sat with her father until eight-thirty. He was still asleep when she tiptoed out of the room, giving a silent prayer he'd sleep all night.

When she entered the lobby at Pinewood, she found Rand waiting for her.

"Hey," she said. "I was expecting Ro."

He smiled. "She was deep into a jigsaw puzzle with Carly. I offered to help."

"Thank you," Kristine said as she followed him out.

Rand's big black pickup truck was one of three vehicles still left in the parking lot.

"Have you eaten?" He opened the door for her, giving her a hand up into the truck.

"No, but I want to shower first," she said. "I take every precaution while I'm with him, but I still worry about being contaminated. In fact, I hate to even get in your truck."

"It's okay," Rand said. "I feel for you. Mom's got dinner ready."

"Ro's the best," Kristine said as they pulled out of the parking lot.

They made the drive in companionable silence. Things were easy with Rand. Again, she wondered why he was back in Wilding Point. Surely he had to want more out of life? She glanced over at him, her gaze going to his tattoo. She could see it clearly now. Pine trees, a lake. A nature scene? She wondered if the place meant something special to him, but she didn't ask.

At the hospital, she directed Rand to where her car was parked. He pulled in behind her, then came around to help her out of the truck. Kristine took his hand, his fingers strong and sure around hers.

"Thank you," she said.

He nodded, waiting while she let herself into her car.

She followed him the short distance home. Suddenly bone tired, she wanted nothing more than to fall into bed. Inside the garage, she stripped off what she could, then finished disrobing in the laundry room before stepping into the shower. She had a routine now. Ro made sure this bathroom was stocked with fluffy white towels and a clean robe for her.

Kristine dried off, slipped the robe on and went in search of Carly.

"Hey, kiddo," she said to her daughter, planting a kiss on the top of her blonde head.

"Hi, Mom," Carly said, looking up from the puzzle she was working with Rowena.

"Let me get your food." Rowena stood. "How was he today?"

"The same. Upset, doesn't really understand where he is, or why he can't come home."

Rowena gave her a sad smile. "Maybe you should bring him home."

"How can we care for him?" Kristine asked. "He's so ill. Just the *C. diff* alone makes the situation unbearable. We'd be bringing contamination into this house."

"We would take precautions," Rowena said. "We could hire help if we need to. He'd have a hospice nurse."

"I don't know," Kristine said. "I don't think I can do it."

Rowena patted Kristine's arm. "Think about it."

Kristine nodded, taking the seat Rowena had vacated. "How about you, Carly? I'm thinking I need to send you home."

"I could stay with Nan," Carly said her expression bright.

"I was thinking the same thing. I'm going to call Kate. I should have a better idea in a few days about Grandpa's condition. Plus, if I did bring him here, I don't want you around the *C. diff*."

"I'm sorry, Mom," Carly said, suddenly sounding super mature.

"Thanks, honey, I'm sorry, too. So sorry for Grandpa. No one should have to die like this, sick, his mind a mess, his own body turning traitor."

Carly nodded.

Rowena returned with a plate of mac and cheese and a beautiful garden salad.

Kristine's stomach growled. "Yum. Thank you, Ro."

"From Beecher's," Rowena said, beaming. "We know how much you love it."

Kristine laughed. "It's true. I do."

The three of them worked the puzzle until bedtime. After she'd tucked Carly in, Kristine went to her room and let herself out onto the third-floor deck.

A million frogs sang. Salt air moved through her body, her mind, her soul. She took a seat in the padded rocker and absorbed Puget Sound, letting the scent of the beach work through her senses. She breathed in and out, letting go of the foul smells she'd been assaulted with for days.

She'd missed Wilding Point. The beaches. The people. The sheer beauty of the Point. She stayed outside until her skin grew cold. Once inside, she opened the window, unwilling to be without fresh, beach air.

She crawled under the covers, thinking about her father, wondering if he were awake, hoping the night staff at Pinewood was compassionate.

Kristine drifted off to sleep, her to-do list heavy on her mind.

Chapter Four

"Help me. Someone help me."

Was that her father? Kristine quickened her step, speeding down the hallway at Pinewood toward her father's room, past patients who sat in wheelchairs, past the nurses' station.

"Help me. Help me."

It *was* her father! At the door to his room, Kristine grabbed her gown and gloves, taking them inside with her.

"Help."

"Dad," she called.

He sat up in the bed. His bib had vomit on it. Kristine's stomach rebelled.

"It's okay," she said. "Hold on." She gowned and gloved up, pressing the call bell for the nurse.

"Yes?" the nurse said through the intercom.

"My father has vomited. He needs to be cleaned up," Kristine said.

"I'll send someone in."

"Thank you." Kristine wiped her father's mouth and removed the bib. A tray of food stood nearby, holding an opened yogurt container and a cup of applesauce. "Did someone feed you, Dad?" Her father couldn't tolerate the food. He vomited after eating. She'd told the staff this, but clearly someone had fed him, ignoring any instructions on his chart. At the very least he should have been watched after being fed.

43

"You have to get me out of here," Lucas said. "They're trying to kill me. They're rough."

"Dad, no one is trying to kill you," she said, feeling like she might vomit herself. "I promise."

"I want to go home, Veronica," he said.

"I'm Kristine, Dad."

The nurse came into the room. "What happened?"

"He was covered in vomit when I got here. I could hear him shouting for help the minute I started down the hall."

Ignoring her, the nurse said, "Mr. Wilding, why didn't you push your call button?"

"He can't," Kristine said. "He has dementia. He doesn't remember what to do. He can't work a call button. Who fed him all that food? He can't keep anything down. It should be on his chart. Small bites, small sips."

"We are required by law to offer the food," the nurse said. "It's his decision to eat it."

"But he can't keep it down," Kristine reiterated. "He has dementia. He can't remember the food makes him sick."

The nurse frowned, then pressed the call button and asked for additional help. Two orderlies came in.

"You can wait outside," the nurse said to Kristine in a curt tone. "We'll get him cleaned up."

Kristine turned away, angry. She stripped off the gown and gloves, washed up and headed for the admin offices down the hall. She went to the social worker and knocked.

"Come in," the social worker said, glancing up from her computer. "What can I do for you?"

"How do I get my father out of here?" Kristine asked.

"Is everything all right?" the woman replied, her eyes kind.

"No. I heard him calling for help the minute I stepped into the hall. He was covered with vomit. The room smelled unbelievably bad. They are forcing him to eat. He can't. I want him home."

"Have a seat," the social worker said, indicating a chair. "You have every right to take him home, but a few things have to happen first. He'll need a nurse assessment. Hospice care. Hospital bed, things of that nature. It can all be done, but it will take a few days to set it up."

"Just tell me who to call." Thirty minutes later, Kristine left the office of the social worker. She went to the waiting room, made an appointment with a nurse certified to do the assessment on her father. Next she called the hospital and told them her story, setting things in motion for home hospice care. Those first steps taken, she called Kate and asked her if Carly could stay there on weekdays while Kristine took care of her father. Kate agreed, promising to pick Carly up at the train station tomorrow. Next, Kristine called her employer and checked on her family leave.

After that was done, her mind clearer now, Kristine headed back to her father.

"Take me home, Kristine," her father said. "Please. They are trying to kill me. They are so rough."

"I will, Dad," she said. "I'm working to get you out of here."

He nodded, his eyes watery and sad.

"Rest now," she said to him. "Rest."

* * *

With Carly gone, Kristine dug into home care for her father with a vengeance. The nurse assessment had gone well. Hospice was in place and four days from the day she'd called, she moved Lucas Wilding home.

A hospital bed had been delivered and placed in a downstairs bedroom. Hospice was set for twice a week. Between Kristine, Rowena, and the hospice nurse, they had Lucas covered.

45

The hospice nurse started tomorrow. Tonight Kristine and Rowena were on their own. She was a little afraid to be so responsible for her father, but something inside told her she could do it. She'd always been interested in medicine. She was strong. Stronger than she thought, both mentally and physically.

"Bring me a bourbon," her father barked when he was settled in his bed.

She smiled. "Okay, Dad." Kristine fed him some ice chips. "Here you go."

"Those are good." He nodded.

"Want to watch a little television?" she asked him.

"No."

"I could read to you."

Her father closed his eyes. Had the ride home been too much? One of the doctors at Pinewood had told her many people in her father's condition didn't survive the ambulance ride home.

"You okay, Dad?" she asked.

He didn't reply. Was he breathing? Yes, she could see his chest rise and fall.

"You go and do something fun," Rowena said, coming into the room all gowned up. "I'll sit with him."

"Really?" Kristine asked.

"Go." Rowena smiled, taking a seat in the leather recliner. "I'm going to knit."

"I think he's sleeping."

"He's worn out." Rowena pulled her knitting from the wicker bag she carried. "Go, shower, take a walk. It's a lovely day."

"A walk does sound good." Kristine headed for the door, putting her gown in the hamper. "Thanks, Ro." She toed off her shoes and stepped into the hallway.

Upstairs, Kristine showered, then dressed in yoga pants, a sweatshirt, and fresh sneakers before heading to the beach. The sun was warm on her face. She walked toward North Beach, enjoying the freedom. For the first time since coming home, she felt present in the moment. Memories of her childhood and teen years spent on this beach came rushing back.

She'd had so much fun here, despite her bad home life.

Growing up on the beach had been wonderful, a magical escape from the unhappiness inside Wilding House.

At North Beach, she sat on a large, sun-bleached log and soaked up the spring sun. She'd had so many plans as a young girl. She'd wanted to be a doctor. What had happened to that dream? She knew the answer. A relationship with a guy her father hated. An unplanned pregnancy. A need to escape her father and Wilding Point. No money for college.

She didn't have a bad life, but it wasn't the life she'd wanted for herself or for Carly.

Thoughtful now, she left the log and began the walk back to the house. Did she have it in her to change her life, start over?

Kristine trekked up the path to the house. She passed by the guest house where Rand lived. His truck was gone. What was his real story, anyway? Did she have the energy to find out? Probably not.

She climbed the stairs to the deck and dropped into an Adirondack chair. Her thoughts turned to Lucky. The time had come to try again to lure him home. Lucky needed closure with their father, she felt sure of it. He needed the closure for himself.

Rand's truck pulled in.

She waved.

He lifted a hand in greeting before starting toward her.

"Hi," she called out.

"Is he here?"

"Yes, your mom is sitting with him," Kristine told him.

"May I?" He pointed to the chair beside her.

"Sure."

"You holding up okay?"

She loved the low baritone of his voice. She even liked the way he looked at her, as if he really cared about her well-being. "I'm okay, it's going to be better having him here. No travel time. More support for me."

"I'm here to help, too," Rand offered.

Her eyebrows lifted in surprise. "Really? What's your relationship with my father like? Were you friends?"

"Friends?" Rand smiled. "Not friends exactly, but we were cordial. I haven't been here long but I noticed right away his memory wasn't working well any longer. He's different now."

"I know."

"I'm glad you're here," Rand said. "He needs you. It's like he's come full circle. You've really stepped up."

"You sound surprised," she said.

"I guess I am." Rand smiled. "I know it can't be easy for you."

"He's the child now," Kristine said, "and I'm his mother."

"Yeah." Rand's eyes were on the Sound. "It will most likely happen for Mom and me, too."

Kristine nodded. "The circle of life."

"I have an idea," Rand said. "Let's have a beach fire tonight."

"As good as that sounds, I should relieve your mom."

"So you sit with him now and we meet at dusk for the fire," Rand said. "Sound like a plan?"

"I don't know." Was spending time with Rand a good idea? She was attracted to him, but she was always attracted to the guy who wasn't a good choice. Rand was gorgeous, but he lacked ambition. He lived in their guest house just steps from his mother. So not the guy for her.

"Check in with Mom and see if she agrees," Rand said. "I'll go and get us some hot dogs and marshmallows and beer."

It was just a beach fire, she told herself. An innocent evening.

"You had me at marshmallows." Kristine laughed. "Okay, I'll see if Ro will sit with him for an hour or two."

"You're on." Rand smiled, and for a minute Kristine got lost in his velvet brown eyes, eyes that promised more than a good time around a campfire.

Rand was dangerous, so not the man for her, but as a friend, she'd take him. He made her feel better, and she liked that.

Maybe a little too much.

* * *

Kristine sat with her father until the scent of wood smoke pulled her to the window. Rand was on the beach, stoking the fire. Was she really doing this? Sitting on the beach with Rand, her teenage crush? Kristine smiled. She needed this, a little down time. A distraction. And Rand Bell was definitely a distraction.

"Rand has the fire going," Rowena said as she came into the room.

"I see." Kristine came away from the window. "Dad, I'm going to take a break. Ro will sit with you."

"I'm so thirsty," he said.

"Here you go," Rowena said, giving him a spoonful of ice chips. "We are going to watch a little television together."

Her father pulled at his hospital gown. He'd been doing that all day, as if he couldn't stand the feel of the cotton against his skin.

"Go on," Rowena said. "We will be fine. I'll call your phone if I need help."

"Thanks, Ro. I won't be long."

"Take all the time you want. I have no plans." Rowena settled into the cushy recliner.

Kristine pulled off her protective gear, then made a stop in her room to do a quick wash. She changed into her favorite jeans and a white T-shirt, adding a light aqua jacket.

As she passed by her father's room on the way out, Rowena called, "I left some cookies for you on the counter."

"Thanks," Kristine said. She snagged the bag of homemade chocolate chip cookies on her way out.

The fire invited her to the beach, the lure of the amber flames irresistible.

Two sand chairs faced the water. A cooler sat between them. Rand added more wood to the fire. The wood spit, hissed, crackled.

"Nice fire," she said.

"I used to be a Boy Scout." He grinned.

"May I?" She pointed to a chair.

"Please, sit."

Kristine took a seat. Rand joined her.

"Hungry?" He popped the lid on the cooler, removed frankfurters, mustard, buns. "Beer?"

"Sure."

He passed her a bottle, leaning over to pop the top.

"Thanks." Kristine took a sip. "I don't remember the last time I had a beer."

"Nectar of the gods." He smiled. "You're long overdue."

She smiled, taking another swig.

Rand produced two thin metal rods, loading a frankfurter onto each one. He passed one to Kristine, and she began to cook her hot dog over the flames. Soon the air filled with the scent of roasting frankfurters. Salt air added to the delicious aroma.

Rand passed her a plate, and they feasted on hot dogs, potato salad, and beer. To Kristine, nothing had tasted this good in a very long time, not even Ro's home cooking could beat this meal. It had to be the fresh air. And maybe the company.

"I'm in heaven," she said. "This is wonderful."

"I'm glad you're enjoying it," Rand said. "I am too."

She smiled. "Let's make s'mores, but without the chocolate."

He laughed. "You're on."

They roasted fat marshmallows, placing the gooey melted sugar between two cookies, washing the dessert down with more beer.

"That was so good," Kristine said, her stomach full and happy.

Rand added more wood to the fire. The sun set behind Salmon Island, turning the sky scarlet. Pink tipped waves lapped gently at the shore.

"I could live in this moment forever," Kristine said.

"I know what you mean. There's something so perfect about a beach fire and a sunset."

"Um hum." Kristine enjoyed the slight buzz she had from the beer. She felt mellow, far removed from her father and his illness. "Tell me something about your life, Rand."

"Not much to tell," he said. "I told you before, I'm a pretty simple guy."

"That's not how I remember you. This you—well, you don't fit. I'm thinking there's a lot more to your story."

"Life throws us curveballs."

"It does," she agreed. "What was your curveball?"

"Burnout?" he said, as if he weren't sure. "Too much, too fast. I lost myself and I didn't like who I'd become. I made mistakes. Take your pick."

He sounded so cynical and bitter.

She nodded. "For me, it was Carly. She was my curveball."

"You've raised her alone from the beginning?"

51

"Pretty much. Her father was a jerk loser with zero ambition."

"Does he help out with her at all?"

Kristine frowned. "Nope, and it's been rough. He's a cliché. A deadbeat dad."

Rand gave her a small smile. "You should go after him. He owes Carly his financial support, if nothing else."

She shook her head. "It's easier to have him out of our lives."

"Even for Carly? She doesn't want to know him?"

"She's never really asked about him," Kristine said. "It's just been the two of us against the world."

Kristine watched the horizon, the ribbon of hot pink in the sky. "I can breathe here."

"Me, too," Rand said. "There's a stillness, a peace that comes with the Point."

She turned to look at him, only to find him watching her. His scrutiny unsettled her while at the same time lighting a spark of desire deep in her gut.

No, not with Rand. He wasn't what she wanted.

He reached out, brushing the hair from her face. His touch sent her pulse racing.

"You're not alone here, Kristine," Rand said.

Her phone beeped, breaking the moment.

"I have to grab this," she said. "Might be your mom." Kristine fished her phone out of her pocket.

"Kyle?" Rand said, his eyes on her phone screen.

She hit the decline button. "Kyle King. He's my dad's doctor."

"Aren't you going to answer it?" Rand asked. "It might be important."

"No. It's personal. He's not in charge of Dad's care right now. Whatever it is, it can wait. I'll call him back tomorrow. Right now, I just want to soak up the atmosphere."

Rand's hand closed over hers and he gave her fingers a squeeze. Kristine's hand tingled where he'd touched her. Rand mixed her up, made her feel things she didn't want to feel.

They sat together, watching the fire die down, the silence between them natural and right. When the phone rang again, it was Rowena, telling her Lucas needed a cleanup.

Kristine helped Rand pick up the remains of their perfect evening. He walked her inside.

"Thank you for tonight," she said when they were in the kitchen.

"No, thank you." He leaned in, kissing her cheek. "Call me if you need me."

And then he was gone.

Her hand pressed to the flutter in her stomach, Kristine headed back to her father, back to reality.

* * *

"Hi, I'm Lauren Baker."

"Kristine," Kristine said, shaking the hospice nurse's hand. "Please, come in."

The woman walked into the foyer of Wilding House. "What a gorgeous home."

"Thank you." Kristine towered over the petite Lauren, who couldn't be more than five foot three. The nurse had thick, honey-brown hair with eyes to match. She was beautiful in an exotic way.

"How's your father today?" Lauren asked.

They'd spoken over the phone twice already. Lauren was here to present the final care plan and set up the schedule.

"The same," Kristine said, "maybe a little worse. He's barely eating anything and hasn't for days. He does drink water and suck on ice chips. We noticed a compression sore on his heel yesterday, and he has another sore on his tailbone I'm worried about."

"Pain level?"

"The sore on his tailbone is bothering him a lot. Sometimes he just cries. We turn him, but he hates it, and begs us to leave him alone."

"Lead the way," Lauren said, her eyes filled with understanding.

Kristine showed the nurse into her father's room. "Dad, this is Lauren, your hospice nurse."

"I'm dying," her father said. "Let me die."

Lauren exchanged a worried look with Kristine. "You're not dying today, Mr. Wilding. Let's take a look and see how we can make you more comfortable."

Kristine stepped to the side as Lauren did her assessment. When she rolled Lucas to his side, he cried out in pain.

"Yes, I'm sure that hurts." After a thorough exam, Lauren said, "Let's go in the other room to talk."

Kristine led the way to the kitchen. They took a seat at the table.

"Let's see your medication log," Lauren said.

Kristine produced the log, which showed her father's medications, when he took them and how much.

Rowena wandered into the kitchen. Kristine made the introductions, and Rowena left them to sit with Lucas.

The hospice nurse talked to Kristine about her father's DNR and his burial wishes. She showed Kristine how to use the hospice kit. Talked to her about morphine and how to administer the drug.

Kristine's heart took hit after hit. A part of her thought that after the assessment Lauren would tell her there'd been a terrible mistake, that her father would recover and didn't need hospice care. The look in Lauren's eyes told Kristine this was real. Lucas Wilding was going to die, and Kristine was the one who had to help him do it.

Lauren also confirmed arrangements for someone to come in once a week and bathe Lucas, and for massage and music therapy. The hospice chaplain would be in touch. So many services, and all covered by insurance.

"You're doing a good job, Kristine," Lauren said. "I'm here to support you. Call if you need anything at all and I'll see you on Friday."

"Thank you so much," Kristine said as she walked Lauren out.

"Take care of yourself," Lauren said. "Self-care is so important."

Kristine nodded. She closed the door, making her way back to her father's room.

"I love you, Veronica," her father said.

Kristine froze in the hallway, eavesdropping.

"I love you, too," Rowena said to Lucas.

"I've always loved you."

"I know," Rowena said, playing along. "Rest now. Be at peace."

"I'm thirsty."

Kristine went into the room. Rowena fed her father some ice.

"I made some lemon cake," Rowena said to Lucas. "When it's cool, I'll bring you some. Would you like that?"

"I would," her father said.

Rowena set the ice down. She smoothed Lucas' hair. "Rest. All will be well."

Her father's eyes closed.

"You're so good with him," Kristine said, appreciating Rowena more than ever.

Rowena nodded. "Everything okay with the hospice nurse?"

"Yes, she thinks we are doing the best we can."

Rowena stood. "I'm going to frost the cake."

"Sounds good." Kristine called Carly and talked to her. Satisfied everything was fine with her daughter, Kristine then returned Kyle's call from last night.

"Kristine," he said on the first ring. "How are you?"

"All right," she said, glad to hear his voice.

"Your father?"

"I think he's declining. The hospice nurse started today. She's great."

"What can I do?" he asked. "Why don't I bring over some Thai food for dinner?"

"You'd do that?" She was touched.

"Absolutely, if it means I get to see you."

"I can't refuse your offer," she said with a smile.

"How many people are in the household?" he asked. "If I bring enough for four, does that work?"

"Yes," she said, thinking Rand usually stopped in for dinner. "I'll let Ro know she doesn't need to cook tonight. It's a treat for all of us."

"Great," Kyle said, sounding happy. "I'll be there around six-thirty."

"See you then."

Kristine glanced at the bedside clock. It was four-thirty. Plenty of time to shower and change.

"Who were you talking to?" her father asked.

"Dr. King," Kristine said.

"Who?"

"Kyle, Lucky's friend. He's going to stop by later." She watched for her father's reaction to hearing Lucky's name.

"That's nice," her father said, his eyes closed.

Did her father even remember Lucky? He didn't seem to. He never asked about his son, and that made her sad.

"Want to watch the news, Dad?" she asked, knowing how much he'd always loved being up-to-date on current events.

"No," he said. "Just hold my hand, Krissy."

Tears pricked at her eyes. Kristine held his hand. His thin fingers closed around her gloved ones.

"I love you, my darling," her father said.

She had no idea if her father even knew who she was, but for now, Kristine would take this act of love to heart, whether it was real or not. For this moment, she wanted to pretend she had a loving father. She needed this, needed his approval and love.

Chapter Five

The doorbell rang at six-thirty sharp, and Kristine knew without looking it would be Kyle, right on time, with dinner.

A dinner she so badly needed and for more reasons than just being hungry.

The afternoon with her father had been brutal. He'd cried for an hour non-stop before becoming paranoid. She had no idea if the morphine was making him act like that or if it was his dementia. When Rowena had come in to relieve her, the worst of the episode had passed. He'd calmed at the sound of Rowena's voice, and had even eaten two bites of lemon cake.

Kristine met Kyle at the door. She'd showered and changed into a pink sundress, her feet in pink flip-flops. She'd even applied makeup.

When Kyle saw her, she noted the appreciation in his eyes. He liked what her saw. Her heart danced.

He held up a bag. "Hungry?"

"Starving." She held the door wide and he came inside.

"How's Dad?" he asked, his caring tone touching her heart.

"Rough day," she admitted. "Rowena is with him now. She's able to calm him down when I can't." She pointed to the food. "Smells great. My stomach is rumbling."

He grinned. "Then let's eat."

In the kitchen, Kristine unloaded the bag of food. So many yummy dishes, including her favorite, sweet chili chicken.

Rowena joined them first, followed by Rand, who entered the kitchen via the sliding glass doors.

"I think you know everyone," Kristine said to Kyle.

"Yes," Kyle said. "I've met Rowena, of course, at the hospital, and I remember Rand from high school."

"How's it going, Kyle?" Rand asked easily as he slid into his chair at the kitchen table.

"It's going nicely," Kyle said, his eyes on her.

Kristine's cheeks heated. She couldn't remember the last time any man had paid attention to her the way Kyle was.

"Are you living in Wilding Point again?" Kyle asked Rand.

"For the time being," Rand said, not giving much away.

"Are you living here, at Wilding House?" Kyle asked.

"In the guest house," Rand said, helping himself to a hefty portion of swimming angel. "I didn't know doctors made house calls anymore."

"I'll admit I have an ulterior motive." Kyle smiled at Kristine. "I'm here for the good company."

Rand raised his eyebrows in a way that told Kristine he didn't approve of Kyle. Well, too bad! Kyle was exactly the kind of man she needed in her life, both ambitious and attentive to her.

"Thank you so much for the food, Kyle," Kristine said.

"Yes, thank you," Rowena echoed. "It's so nice to have a night off from cooking, especially when I'm spending so much time helping Mr. Wilding during the day."

"Glad I could help." Kyle turned to Kristine. "Are you able to leave once in a while? I'd love to take you out to dinner, or a movie."

"Right now, I'm needed here," Kristine said with regret. "It takes two of us to change Dad, to turn him."

"Of course," Kyle said, clearly disappointed.

"But if you plan ahead," Rowena said, "I could have Rand help me for an evening."

"That would be wonderful." Kyle beamed.

Kristine met Rand's eyes.

"Sure, happy to help," Rand said.

Was he happy or not? Kristine couldn't tell. Rand seemed mad, almost jealous. Of what? Kyle? His reaction didn't make any sense at all. She and Rand were friends, nothing more.

"What do you say, Kristine," Kyle said. "Saturday night, you and me, dinner and a movie?"

"I don't know," she hedged. "I'm not sure I could leave my dad. It seems wrong to have fun when he is so ill."

"Say yes," Rowena said in a firm tone. "If you need to cancel, you can cancel, but you know he's usually asleep around seven."

True, her dad did tend to sleep around that time, but was usually up moaning in pain around midnight. She could be back before then in case she was needed.

"Okay, Kyle," Kristine said. "Saturday night sounds great."

"Fantastic," Kyle said.

The rest of the meal passed with light conversation. Kristine cleared the dishes, and Rowena went to sit with Lucas. Rand excused himself, leaving Kristine and Kyle alone.

"Glass of wine on the deck?" she asked Kyle.

"You read my mind."

Kristine opened the wine refrigerator. "Do you know anything about wine? Want to choose?"

"Absolutely." Kyle looked through the bottles, producing a bottle from the Châteaunef-du-Pape region of France. "This one, from Château la Nerthe. I went to the vineyard when I was in the south of France. It was breathtaking, the wine first rate."

"Is it expensive?" Kristine asked.

"This one is. Is it all right to drink it? Your father won't mind?"

"I don't think my father will miss it." Her father would never drink wine again. A veil of sadness fell over her, leaving her with a deep melancholy.

Kyle obviously sensed her shift in mood, because he said, "If you'd rather not."

"No, I want to open it. I'd like to think he'd want me to."

Kyle nodded, uncorking the wine.

Kristine produced two wine glasses.

Kyle made a great show of sniffing the wine, twirling it in the glass, tasting in, rolling the wine around in his mouth. Kristine had seen her father open plenty of expensive wine, but never had she been treated to a show like the one Kyle put on. When he finally pronounced the wine fit to drink, she had to bite back a full-out belly laugh.

Kyle poured her a glass. To humor him, she swirled the wine in her glass, inhaling the bouquet, then took a sip.

"You're too quick," Kyle said. "You should savor the wine, push it through your teeth, let it open up."

Holy cow, if this is what it took to drink expensive wine, she'd stick with wine coolers.

"Let's go outside," she suggested.

They settled on the thickly padded lounge chairs, their eyes on the setting sun. Another beautiful day. Kristine sipped her wine, hoping Kyle wouldn't comment on the way she drank it.

"It's quite beautiful here," he said.

"You grew up in Meadow Park. Most of those homes have a view of the Sound—did yours?"

"Guilty." He took a sip of wine, and thankfully, he swallowed it.

"Where do you live now?" she asked.

"In Meadow Park," he told her. "I bought my parents' house when they sold it."

"That's nice." A soft breeze gently ruffled her dress, her hair, the breeze caressing her skin. She inhaled the intoxicating air and let the wine relax her.

A tanker cruised past, its pace snail slow.

She glanced at Kyle who studied his wine glass.

"What are you thinking about?" she asked him.

"Funny how things work out. Just thinking it's strange I'm here with you. I mean, I was married to Beth. Now I'm not." He took another sip of wine.

"I remember Beth well," Kristine said. "Cheerleader. Super pretty and popular. Homecoming and prom queen. Lucky was really into her for a while."

"Yes," Kyle agreed, sounding bitter.

"What happened? Why did you divorce?"

"I didn't want any children," Kyle said. "She did. It became a problem."

"Oh."

"She has a child now."

Kristine could feel his distaste for children as if it were a tangible thing in the air. "You know I have a daughter, right?"

"She's older?" Kyle asked, his attention on her now.

"Twelve."

He grimaced. "That's right."

"I was eighteen when she was born."

"What were you thinking?" he asked with a smirk.

His attitude upped her irritation. "I got caught up in the moment."

"I'm not sure that would ever happen to me," Kyle said matter-of-factly. "I like control. You don't have control with children. They are unpredictable."

She grinned. "True, but as a parent, you learn to roll with anything your child does. You'd be fine, Kyle. Sometimes it's nice to lose control."

"Not for me." He topped of their wine glasses. "I am a control freak. I'll admit it."

Kyle's personality was so different from Lucky's. She found it hard to believe they'd been friends, Kyle with his control issues and Lucky with his wild streak. If Lucky had possessed even one quarter of Kyle's self-control, maybe his life would have taken a different path. Maybe he'd be here now, helping her with their father.

Kristine sipped her wine. Hussy cut across the yard, coming up the deck steps. The dog stopped in front of Kristine.

"Hey, girl." Kristine petted the dog. "Aren't you a sweetheart?" She glanced at Kyle. "Not a dog person?"

He shook his head. "I'm afraid not. Again, animals are challenging to control."

"What do you like, Kyle?" she asked, curious. "What makes you happy?"

"Fine wine, beautiful women, you."

He said the words softly, his tone meant to stir the flame within her, but she was having trouble picturing herself with him and that bothered her.

The guest house door opened and Rand stepped outside. He gave a soft whistle and Hussy took off like a rocket. Kristine watched as Rand got down on one knee to pet the dog. A few minutes later, Rand and Hussy set out for the beach.

Suddenly, she longed to go with them.

No, Rand was not the man she wanted, not at all. She was always drawn to the handsome recluse. The man who didn't really want a job. The man who was damaged. One of those men who wanted a tiny house so he could live a life with no responsibilities. She did not want a man like that. She wanted a man with ambition, a man with a house in Meadow Park. She had a daughter to think about.

"Kristine," Rowena called.

"Out here."

Rowena stepped out onto the deck. "He's asking for you. He's agitated. I think he's in pain."

Kristine rose. "I'm coming. I'm sorry, Kyle, I need to go."

"Of course," Kyle said with obvious regret. "Do you need my help?"

"It's sweet of you to offer, but no." She picked up the bottle of wine, passing it to him. "Cork it and take it home and enjoy. I insist. It's the least I can do since you brought us dinner."

"Thank you," he said, inclining his head in a way that told her the offer pleased him. "I will."

They went into the kitchen, where Kyle corked the wine. Lucas' cries reached them.

"I need to go," she said to Kyle. "Thank you for a wonderful evening."

"My pleasure," he said, wine bottle in hand. "I'll pick you up at six Saturday night."

"I'll be ready." She gave him one last smile before going to her father.

The lovely evening was over. Back to the reality that was her life.

* * *

Rand walked the beach, his eyes on the setting sun. Hussy ran ahead, chasing shore birds. The rosy sun turned the Sound pink. The same pink as the color of the dress Kristine had been wearing tonight.

Damn.

Why couldn't he get her out of his mind? She obviously had her eye on Dr. Love. He didn't get it. Kyle King had to be one of the most arrogant guys he'd ever met. Pompous. Even Beth Barnes had finally seen through him and divorced his ass.

Good looks didn't buy you happiness.

Money didn't buy happiness.

No one knew that better than he did.

He paused, his focus on the water now, on the way the waves lapped softly at the rocky shoreline.

What the hell was he doing here, living in the Wildings' guest house? He didn't belong there and he knew it. Time was running out. He had a decision to make, but he wasn't ready to make it. He was stuck, on so many levels.

Why couldn't he move on with his life? He'd wanted so many things, gotten so many things. Was he ready to throw it all away?

He had no answers. "Come on, Hussy, let's head back."

The dog turned and looked at him expectantly. Rand gave a nod toward the house. Hussy understood, running to catch up.

The second-story deck was empty when he reached Wilding House. His gut tightened. Where were Kristine and Dr. Love? Had she taken the doctor to bed?

The thought turned his stomach.

Unable to help himself, Rand walked around to the front of the house. There were no extra cars. The doctor was gone. So soon? Kristine and Kyle had looked cozy just minutes before. Alarmed something might be wrong with Lucas, Rand let himself in the back door. The kitchen was empty. And then he heard it, a pitiful whimpering. His mother's soothing voice. Kristine telling Lucas they were working as fast as they could.

Rand didn't hesitate. He followed the sound of their voices.

"Let me help," he said, when he found Kristine trying to prop her father up while his mother worked to clean the man.

"No, don't come in," Kristine said. "You know he's contagious."

His mother and Kristine were fully gowned, gloved, and wore masks.

Rand took those same items from the cart in the hall and suited up. A minute later, he nudged Kristine aside, easily holding the frail Lucas Wilding in place so both women could clean and diaper him.

He didn't focus on the smell in the room—he couldn't. How did his mother and Kristine do this by themselves? No child should ever have to diaper their parent, yet Kristine had stepped up, even though her relationship with her father was less than warm and stellar. Watching her now, Rand formed a new, solid respect for her.

She was stronger than he'd thought.

"Let him down easy," his mother instructed. "He has bed sores. Then we need to turn him on his right side. We prop him up with pillows."

Lucas cried out when Rand moved him. Kristine quickly pushed the pillows into place, then stepped back.

"All done, Dad," she said with relief. "You did great. I know it hurts. The morphine should kick in now. Rest. I'll put on your classical music."

While Kristine talked, his mother bagged up the soiled clothes and laundry, removing them from the room.

Kristine stripped off her gloves, re-gloved, then opened the window wider, letting the fresh beach air into the room.

"Thanks for the help," she said. "He's heavier than he looks."

"You should have let me know sooner," Rand said. "I don't mind helping."

"I don't like exposing you or your mother to the *C. diff*," Kristine said. She stroked her father's hair. "Better, Dad?"

He didn't reply. Kristine used a tissue to wipe the tears from his cheeks.

Rand couldn't take it. Is this what dying was like? The loss of dignity? Your son or daughter taking care of you when you were at your worst? Could he do this for his mother?

Of course he could, but he also knew it would break his heart and most likely, hers.

"We're fine now," Kristine said to him. "Rand, you should get out of here. Put your gown there." She pointed to the hamper. "Gloves and mask in the garbage, then go scrub."

"Sure," he said, sensing she wanted to be alone with her father.

His mother came back into the room.

"He's doing better?" Rowena walked to Lucas, her eyes on the sleeping man.

"I think so," Kristine said. "The morphine is working."

"You gave him the medicine for the agitation?" Rowena asked.

"Yes."

Rowena sat in the chair near the bed. "Then you go and finish your wine."

Kristine gave her a small smile. "I sent the bottle of wine home with Kyle."

Rand stripped the gloves and gown off. "How about a beer? I think we could both use one. Meet you on the deck in ten?"

"I don't think so," Kristine said, shaking her head. "It's been a long day."

"Go," Rowena urged. "He's fine. I'll call if I need you. I enjoy my time with him."

"See you in ten," Rand said, leaving before Kristine could say no again.

He sprinted over to his place, snagged a couple of cold ones, and went back to Wilding House.

Kristine was waiting for him on the deck on a lounge chair.

Without saying a word, he offered her a beer, taking the seat next to her.

She took a long pull, then rolled her head to the side to look at him. "Thank you, not just for the beer, but for helping with Dad."

"Like I said, no thanks necessary."

Hussy came up the steps and flopped down at Kristine's feet.

"She likes you," Rand said.

"I like her, too." Kristine's hair blew in the gentle breeze, making him long to touch it.

The sun slipped into the horizon, favoring them with a gorgeous pink glow. Rand glanced at her dress, even more rosy in this light.

Kristine Wilding didn't belong with Dr. Love, no way. Kyle was way too uptight for her. Kristine was wild, untamed.

Not liking where his mind was going, Rand took another sip of beer.

He needed to get his own shit together before he worried about adding someone to his life.

They sat there in silence, sipping their beers. The night went from pink, to purple, to black. Beside him Kristine snored softly. Rand went inside and retrieved a blanket, covering her. He settled back in his chair, keeping watch on the woman who had made him remember what it felt like to feel again, to remember the life he'd once had. A life that had at one time filled all of his senses to bursting.

The life he could have again, if he made that choice.

Chapter Six

Her father's cries woke Kristine around six a.m.

He called for her by name, his voice pulling her out of bed and downstairs to his bedroom.

"Dad, I'm here," she said, turning on the bedside lamp.

Rowena came in after her. She belted her robe. "What's wrong?"

Her father's mouth worked, but no sound came out.

"Let me check him," Rowena said. "He's been making less urine, but I'm sure he's wet."

"Thirsty, Dad?" Kristine picked up his cup. "Ice."

He nodded.

"I'll be right back." Kristine padded to the kitchen, grabbing a clean cup, filling it with crushed ice off the fridge door.

A knock sounded at the slider.

Rand stood on the other side of the glass. He'd been so kind to her last night, helpful, even covering her with a blanket while she'd slept. Her cheeks heated. She wasn't used to feeling so vulnerable.

She unlocked the door.

"I saw the light," he said. "Do you need help with him?"

She smiled. "Your mom is checking him, but I'm sure he needs changing."

She started for the bedroom, Rand on her heels.

Rowena was already gowned and gloved. Kristine and Rand followed suit and the three of them changed her father quickly while he sobbed silently in pain. When they were finished, Kristine gave her father his meds. Rowena tucked him in.

"How about some banana pudding today?" Rowena coaxed. "I know it's your favorite."

"Sounds good," her father said in a gravelly voice.

"Good." Rowena smiled.

"You're so pretty," he said to Rowena.

"You're an old flirt," Rowena teased on her way out of the room.

Lucas Wilding a flirt? Kristine had never witnessed any flirting between her father and another woman. She exchanged an amused look with Rand.

"Not sure what that was about," she said, smiling.

"Me, either. Creeped me out."

Kristine laughed. She fed her father some ice.

"Good," Lucas said. "More."

"Thank you again for the help," Kristine said to Rand. "It's easier when you are here, for sure."

"Happy to help when I'm around." Rand pulled off his gown and gloves. "I've got to get ready for work."

"What's on the agenda for today?" she asked.

"Starting a deck for a house on Wilding Road."

"Should be a nice day for it. Supposed to have clear skies."

"Yeah." Rand paused in the doorway. "Hope he does well today. Take care."

And then he was gone. Kristine released a breath. Rand Bell, while not the guy for her, was certainly a guy. Sweet, handsome, the entire package minus his lack of ambition and obvious emotional damage.

Kristine took care of her father while Rowena made breakfast. She chatted with Carly via phone while the teenager got ready for school. Her heart ached for her daughter. She prayed she was doing the right thing leaving her at Nan's. Rowena appeared in the doorway.

"How's he doing?" she asked.

"Sleeping," Kristine replied. "He seems to sleep more now, don't you think?"

Rowena nodded sadly. "Come have breakfast with me."

"Okay." Kristine removed her protective gear, ran upstairs, showered and dressed before meeting Rowena in the kitchen.

Rand sat at the table, scarfing French toast, eggs, and bacon.

Kristine took the seat opposite him. Rowena placed a plate of food in front of her.

Rand took a swallow of coffee. He didn't speak, but the way he looked at her, as if he were trying to figure her out, unnerved Kristine a little.

She forked up a bite of French toast.

"I better get going." Rand pushed back in his chair and stood. He carried his plate to the sink. "Call me if you need me. I'm just up the road."

"Thank you, sweetie," Rowena said, "but we'll manage. We have the hospice nurse today and I think music therapy. Isn't that right, Kristine?"

Kristine nodded, her mouth full.

Rand smiled. "Bye, girls."

Kristine waved.

"I'm going to start on that banana pudding," Rowena said, her tone cheery.

"Do you really think he'll eat it?" Kristine asked. "He's barely eaten anything for days."

"I'm not going to stop trying." Rowena gave her a tired smile. "He's always been good to Rand and me, giving me a paycheck and a place to live. Taking care of him during his final days is the least I can do."

"Thank you, Ro," Kristine said from the bottom of her heart. "I couldn't care for him at home without you."

Rowena squeezed Kristine's shoulder as she passed by.

Kristine finished her breakfast, helped Rowena do the dishes, then made a check on her father. Her eyes went to his chest, to the rise and fall. He'd grown so thin. Skin hung from his arms. His sunken chest and belly reminded her of a painting she'd seen of Christ on the cross. Skin on bones, nothing more.

She pressed her lips together to keep from crying.

What was wrong with her? She'd spent most of her life despising her father. Now she was crying for him?

For the millionth time she wished Lucky were here. Only he could understand the plethora of emotions waging war inside her.

She needed air, needed to get out of this room.

"Ro," she called on her way to the glass doors. "I'm going for a short walk."

"Take your time," Rowena called back. "I've got him."

"Thank you." Kristine bolted down the deck stairs, taking the path to the beach. Rocks and mussel shells crunched under her feet as she walked. Seaweed littered the beach, making the air more fragrant than usual. She loved being on the beach. Needed this air.

She inhaled deeply.

Breathe. Breathe.

The air, like a tonic, eased her anxiety. She came back to earth, ready to face the day and whatever it brought.

Calmer now, Kristine walked home and went inside. She heard Rowena humming. Smelled banana pudding.

For some insane reason, Kristine smiled.

* * *

The hospice nurse arrived around noon.

"How are you holding up?" Lauren asked Kristine.

"I've been better," Kristine admitted. "I worry about him constantly. Am I doing the right thing giving him morphine? Am I killing him?"

"Kristine," Lauren said, taking her hand. "He's dying. He's in pain. You are doing the right thing. You are making him comfortable."

Kristine nodded, wanting desperately to believe her.

"I'm going to take a look at his sores," Lauren said. "Will you help me turn him?"

Kristine did as Lauren asked. Her father sobbed the entire time. When they made him comfortable once more, Lauren said, "You can give him more morphine. Once an hour if he needs it."

"How close do you think he is?" Kristine asked.

"Close," Lauren said. "Do you have siblings? Anyone who would want to say good-bye?"

"I have a brother. I've asked him to come."

"Sometimes loved ones hang on, waiting for closure, waiting to say good-bye."

"There's no love lost between my father and Lucky," Kristine said. "In fact, my father hasn't asked for him once."

"Still," Lauren reasoned. "You might mention those things to your brother. Plus, you could use the support."

"True." For a young woman, Lauren was unusually wise. Kristine envied her wisdom and her profession. Where had she gone so wrong, straying from medicine and settling for a data entry job at a hospital?

She knew where. Money. Education was expensive.

Lauren looked through Lucas' supplies and medications, ordering more of what was needed. She went over the comfort kit with Kristine again, making sure she understood what was included and when to administer each drug.

All too soon Lauren's visit was over. Kristine hated to see her go. Having the nurse around was super comforting. As Lauren was leaving, a van pulled in. Kristine waited in the open doorway to Wilding House.

"Are you Kristine?" a pretty forty-something brunette asked as she exited the van.

"Yes."

"I'm Sarah," she said, smiling. "We spoke on the phone. Music therapy. I'm a harpist."

"Of course." Kristine smiled. "Come in, please. Do you need help unloading?"

A man exited the van.

Sarah shook her head. "You said you had steps, so I brought my husband, Mac, to help."

"Thank you," Kristine said to Mac.

"No problem," he said easily.

Minutes later Sarah was set up just outside of Lucas' room. She began playing the most beautiful music on her harp.

Kristine sat with her dad, and they both had a view of Sarah, although Lucas kept his eyes closed.

"Angel's music," Kristine said.

"Yes," her father agreed. "Angels."

Kristine lost herself to the beautiful music. She had no idea if the music calmed her father, but it made her feel good. Rowena came into the room, taking a seat in the other easy chair. She exchanged a soft smile with Kristine.

When the music stopped, Kristine said, "That was absolutely wonderful. Thank you so much."

"Beautiful," Rowena agreed.

"I hope he enjoyed it," Sarah said, her eyes on Lucas.

"I know he did," Kristine said with certainty.

"Should I come again next week?" Sarah asked.

"Yes, please."

Mac already had the harp packed up.

Kristine walked the couple out. "Thank you again, Sarah."

Sarah smiled before following her husband out of the house.

Kristine went back into her father's room.

"What a treat that was." Rowena leaned over Lucas, stroking his hair.

He nodded, but seemed tired.

"How about some banana pudding?" Ro said to Lucas.

"I might try a little," Lucas said in a faint voice.

Kristine had no idea how Rowena got her father to eat. The woman was amazing.

While Rowena fed her father, Kristine let herself out onto the deck. She scrolled through her contacts list and called Lucky.

The phone rang three times before he said, "Hi."

"Hi," she said and suddenly she wanted to cry. "I—"

She couldn't breathe, couldn't continue. Emotion choked her throat.

"Are you there? Kris?"

"I need you," she managed to get out. "It's awful, Lucky. He's wasting away. He's like a child." She gulped for air. "The hospice nurse told me he might be hanging on, waiting for you. He's suffering. Please."

Silence stretched between them.

"Okay," he finally said. "It's going to take me a few days, but I'll come."

Kristine wiped her tears with the back of her hand. "Thank you."

"I'll see you soon."

The line went dead.

Kristine buried her face in her hands, sobbing, letting loose everything she'd been feeling.

And then arms were around her.

She blinked through her tears. Rand.

He sat beside her, holding her as she cried.

His hand found her hair and he stroked her head gently, then her back.

No words were exchanged. Slowly her tears dried up. She sucked in a big breath and pulled away from him.

"I'm sorry," she said.

"Is he—?"

"He's alive. It's just, well, it's been a day. I just got off the phone with Lucky. Hearing his voice set me off. I didn't realize I was so upset."

Rand gave her a tender smile. "You were overdue for a good cry."

She nodded. "I suppose. Thanks for the shoulder, or whole T-shirt." She noted the wet spots on his chest.

"No problem." He stood, holding his hand out to her.

She took it, his strong fingers closing over hers. He pulled her up. For a split second she looked into his delicious chocolate eyes before glancing away from everything she was starting to feel for him.

"Come on," he said, covering her awkward moment. "I'm starving. Let's raid the kitchen."

"You'll spoil your dinner." Kristine followed him inside.

"Not likely. I never ate lunch, worked straight through."

Kristine pulled out the fixings for sandwiches, her own stomach growling.

Together they assembled thick turkey sandwiches.

Kristine took a big bite of her sandwich just as the front doorbell rang. "Probably another hospice delivery," she said, her mouth full. She grabbed her napkin and went to the door.

"Kyle," she managed while trying to swallow. She wiped her mouth.

"Hi." He smiled. "Thought I'd stop by and check on you. Is this a good time?"

"Just having a sandwich," she said. "Can I make you one? Rowena roasted the turkey herself."

"Love one," he said, following her to the kitchen.

Rand sat at the table, half his sandwich gone, a bag of open barbecue potato chips in front of him.

"Rand," Kyle said, the word sounding distasteful.

"Kyle." Rand gave him a nod. "What brings you around?"

"Just checking on Kristine."

"Have a seat, Kyle," Kristine said, in an attempt to diffuse the obvious tension between the two men.

Kyle did so.

"I invited Kyle in for a sandwich," Kristine said, as she worked to put the sandwich together.

Rand picked up his other half, eating, ignoring Kyle.

Kristine set Kyle's sandwich on the table. "There you go."

"Thank you." Kyle smiled before digging in.

Kristine was finishing her own sandwich when Rowena came into the kitchen, the bowl of banana pudding in hand.

"He didn't eat much?" Kristine asked.

"Just one bite." She smiled sadly.

Kristine rose, taking the pudding from her. "Sit, I'll make you a sandwich."

Rowena waved her hand. "I'm not hungry."

"You sure?" Kristine asked. "You've been at it as long as I have today."

"Yes."

"You look tired, Mom," Rand said. "Why don't you lie down for a while?"

"Me nap?" Rowena scoffed. "I don't nap. I'm fine. How was work today?"

"Great." Rand stood and put his plate in the dishwasher. "I'm going to take Hussy for a walk."

Kyle finished his sandwich. Thankfully he'd been silent during the exchange between Rand and Rowena.

Rand gave Kristine a long look before leaving.

Kristine brought her attention to Kyle.

"How was your day?" she asked.

"Good." He took a sip of bottled water. "Feel like getting out of here for a while?"

"I can't. My father is a two-person job," Kristine said.

"Rand's around," Kyle said.

"It isn't Rand's job to care for my father."

"I suppose not," Kyle said. "Okay, how about a walk? We can stay close."

"I don't know."

"Go, Kristine," Rowena urged. "I'll text you if I need help."

Kristine gave the housekeeper a smile. "Okay, but I'll stay close by."

Kyle rose. Kristine went with him out into the sunshine. A light wind stirred her hair. Kyle took her hand as they reached the beach.

She spotted Rand and Hussy.

Kyle tugged her in the opposite direction.

"Will you stay on in Wilding Point after he passes?" Kyle asked.

"I don't think so," Kristine said. "My life is in Oregon. My daughter has friends there, school."

"I'm sure you stand to inherit money, and there's the house. You could start over anywhere," Kyle pointed out. "You could stay here."

"I haven't really thought about that," Kristine said. "I didn't even think to ask the attorney about the money. It doesn't seem important right now. And for all I know, my father has squandered everything away. He's had dementia for some time, according to Rowena."

"Someone else has been in charge of paying the bills, right?" Kyle asked.

"Yes, he has an accountant."

"Your life may be about to change," Kyle said.

Kristine stopped walking. "I don't know. It seems wrong to even think about inheriting when my father is still alive."

"Put the thought in your head, Kristine. I'd love it if you stayed on in Wilding Point. I know this is a sad time, but eventually you will crawl out of the darkness and begin to live your life again. Just put Wilding Point on your radar." His fingers squeezed hers.

Did she want to stay in Wilding Point after her father passed? She didn't know and the decision wasn't hers to make alone. Carly would have a vote, if and when she did inherit any of her father's estate.

For now, it was something to think about.

Chapter Seven

Rand sat on the patio outside of the guest house, his eyes on the deck, on Kristine and Kyle. Hidden in the evening shadows, Kristine's laughter drifted across the yard to annoy him.

What did she see in Kyle King?

Rand would never understand women. Was a man's paycheck the be-all, end-all? Money wasn't everything. Money caused problems, added pressure to life. He knew that better than anyone.

Yes, a simple lifestyle was better. He liked what he did now, liked working with his hands, liked the lack of big responsibility that had come with his former job. He wasn't responsible for anyone's retirement fund anymore. He wasn't paying an outrageous rent on an apartment he never had time to enjoy.

He didn't want those things anymore, or did he? Hell, he was living in the Wildings' guest house. No wonder Kristine didn't look at him like she looked at Kyle King.

Once a rich girl, always a rich girl.

Kristine Wilding had grown up with a silver spoon in her mouth. Yeah, her father might have yanked it away, but her love for expensive things had been bred into her. She liked the lifestyle Kyle could offer, no question about it.

Rand sighed. Melancholy settled around him and he let himself remember how he'd wound up here. Grif Jones. Sadness and guilt moved through Rand with a swiftness that stole his breath.

Grif, his college roommate and best friend. They'd both been recruited by Stern and Rogers Investment Services right out of college. They'd risen up through the ranks quickly, elbowing their way into private client services, where the big money was. They'd lived the high life, wearing expensive clothes, driving expensive cars, dating expensive women.

But somewhere along the way, Grif had gotten in too deep financially. Rand had suspected something was wrong, but he'd been too caught up in his own fast-paced life to really pay attention.

When Grif had asked him for a sizable loan, he'd been shocked. He'd told his friend he needed to think about lending that much money. Grif had said he understood.

But he hadn't.

Rand closed his eyes. He'd been the one to figure out where Grif had gone. The one to find him.

He took a deep breath, steadying breath, his eyes on his tattoo—the constant reminder of his friend, a constant reminder of the life he'd once had.

Deep down, Rand knew he was to blame. Hell, he accepted the blame, wallowed in it to the point he'd left everything behind to come home to Wilding Point.

He should have lent Grif the money, no questions asked. Why hadn't Grif given him time to think things through? He'd had no idea Grif had been in debt up to his eyeballs. No idea he had lost everything, including his girlfriend, Cory.

No idea Grif had been so depressed.

Anger beat in Rand's chest, anger directed at Grif, a dead man. He knew it didn't make any sense, but the anger stayed with him. He had no idea how to let the destructive emotion go.

And at the root of his anger was money.

Money destroyed people. It had destroyed him. It had killed Grif.

It had destroyed Kristine and the relationship she had with her father, with Lucky.

Too much money was bad for the soul, he truly believed that now. It was why he was back here, in Wilding Point. He didn't need money to be happy. He'd give everything he had if he could have his friend back.

Kristine and Kyle stood, breaking Rand's train of thought. He shifted in his chair. Was Dr. Love finally leaving? It was after ten.

Kyle leaned in, kissing Kristine.

Rand's gut tightened. His fists clenched. Kyle King rubbed him the wrong way on so many levels.

Kyle opened the door for Kristine and they disappeared inside.

Rand kept his eyes on the house. Out front a car started, the sound eventually dying away.

Dr. Love was finally gone.

Rand released his breath.

Kristine came back out onto the deck, carrying a blanket.

Rand stood and was walking to her before he even had a chance to think about what he was doing.

"Hi," she said as he joined her.

"May I?" he asked, indicating the chair Dr. Love had just vacated.

"Sure." She worked to spread the blanket over her legs.

"How's your dad?" he asked.

"Sleeping," she said. "Thanks for asking. Ro is sleeping, too. I have this." She held up the receiver that was linked to the nursery monitor in Lucas' bedroom. "I just can't get enough of the air out here. I'd sleep out here if I could."

He studied her. Her hair was a bright beacon in the darkness, her features concealed in shadows. She'd grown into a beautiful woman, albeit a slightly damaged one thanks to her father.

That fact alone made her more interesting, added layers to her personality.

"Pretty evening," she said softly. "So many stars."

"Yes." He trained his eyes on the sky. "It's my favorite time of day, when I can stargaze."

"Um hmm."

"When do you think Lucky will get here?" he asked.

"In a few days," she said. "I pray he's not too late. Dad slept a lot today. Everything I've read says that's an indicator that the end is near. I keep praying for mercy. No one should have to die like he is. I don't care if he wasn't a nice man a lot of the time."

"You know the saying—what goes around, comes around," Rand reminded her. "Some people would feel joy at the awful way he's dying."

"Not me," she said. "And I'm not sure why. I think it's because he's so different from the man I left behind. He's sweeter, appreciative, and horrified he has these unspeakable health issues. No matter our pasts, I'm oddly thankful I've had this time with him, where it wasn't about him getting his way, or about money. This time has just been about being together, and me supporting him."

Rand didn't comment.

"Would he have done the same for me?" she asked. "Or for Lucky? I'd like to hope so, but probably not. And that's sad."

"Yes."

"You're so lucky to have Ro for a mother."

"I am," he agreed. "She's the best. A woman with a heart of gold and a pure spirit."

Kristine laughed softly. "I agree."

"Help," Lucas called through the walkie-talkie.

"He's up," Kristine said, tossing the blanket back.

"Need a hand?" he asked, not willing to let her go yet.

"That would be great. Otherwise, I'll have to wake your mom and I don't want to do that. She's exhausted."

Together they changed Lucas, working effortlessly as a team now. When they were done, Kristine settled in the bedside easy chair, where she admitted she slept most nights.

Rand covered her with her blanket. "Can I get you anything?"

"No," she said, her eyes on him. "Thank you for helping. Please go home and get some sleep. I'm fine with him."

Rand nodded. "Sweet dreams, Kristine Wilding."

"You, too." She smiled.

And for Rand, it was enough.

* * *

"Why didn't you wake me?" Rowena asked the following morning. She stood in the doorway of Lucas' room, her hands on her hips.

Kristine, having just awakened minutes before, blinked the sleep from her eyes. She'd actually gotten four hours of sleep in a row. Worried about her father, she focused on him. Yes, he still breathed. More than anything she wanted him to live long enough for Lucky to get closure.

"I'll make you some tea," Rowena said.

"That would be great." Kristine stood, adding the blanket and her protective gear to the hamper. "I'm going to shower."

"I'll listen for him," Rowena said as Kristine passed. "I feel like a new woman after a full night's sleep."

"I'm glad." Kristine started up the stairs. In her bathroom, she stripped and showered, enjoying the hot spray. She dressed in jeans and a yellow T-shirt, her feet in slip-on sneakers.

In the kitchen, she accepted a cup of tea from Ro.

"How did you manage last night?" Rowena asked.

"Rand helped me," Kristine said, taking a sip of tea.

"He did?" Rowena stirred what Kristine hoped was waffle batter.

"Yes, after Kyle left, Rand came over and kept me company. Dad woke up and he offered to help."

Rowena smiled. "He's a good boy."

"He's a man, Ro." Kristine grinned.

"I guess he is." She chuckled. "He's had a rough time. I'm glad he has you to talk to."

"What happened to him?" Kristine asked. "He was always so driven, so interested in business. I thought he had his life mapped out."

"You'll have to ask him," Rowena said. "It's not my story to tell."

More curious than ever, Kristine cast her gaze out the window to the guest house. What was Rand's story? Did she even want to find out?

Rowena produced the waffle iron and ten minutes later, Kristine enjoyed her breakfast. When she was done, she placed a quick call to Carly to check in, like she did each morning. They made plans for her to come up on the train Friday evening.

Kristine couldn't wait to see her daughter. Seemed like they'd been apart forever. Next, she did a check on her dad. Still sleeping, and that upped her worry. Something was different. He wasn't producing as much urine, and he hadn't had a bowel movement in twenty-four hours. So not normal with *C. diff.*

Concerned, she placed a call to Lauren, who assured her everything seemed fine. If things didn't break loose soon, Lauren would intervene, but for now Kristine could relax.

She had to admit it was nice not to have that type of cleanup.

Yet, her worry for her father increased. Around noon he woke up long enough to get changed. He cried the entire time, his bed sores getting the best of him. Kristine gave him morphine, unable to stand his anguished crying.

Rowena settled in next to the bed, urging Kristine to get out of the house.

Kristine took a walk, thinking about what Kyle said about a possible inheritance. What would she do if there was money? Without a doubt she knew the answer. She would go back to school, finish what she'd started and become a nurse.

The possibility of a career she wanted bloomed in her like a summer rose, giving her a hope she hadn't felt in a long time. She refused to let the guilt over her father's impending death squash her hope for a brighter future for herself and Carly. Money would also buy Carly an education, something Kristine now had no easy way to give her daughter.

When Kristine returned to the house the hospice massage therapist was in with her father. Lucas slept through the massage. Afterward, Kristine stayed with Lucas. She sat by the open window in the bedroom, breathing the restorative air rolling off of Puget Sound while reading on her phone about end of life. She'd become obsessed with the topic, unable to stop researching, looking for something, anything that would let her know where her father was on his journey to the other side.

"Kristine?" her father said, her name so faint she barely heard it.

"I'm here, Dad." She moved closer to him, so he could really see her.

"There's something wrong with my eyes," he said. "I can't see you. A shadow."

She'd read about people who lost vision when they were close to death. "I'm here."

"Why is this happening to me?" he asked, silent tears rolling from his eyes.

"I don't know," she replied, her heart breaking. He really didn't understand any of this. "I've called Lucky. He's coming home."

"Lucky?" her dad asked, as if he had no idea who she was talking about.

"Your son, Lucas Junior," she reminded him. "He's coming to see you, Dad."

"That's nice," her father said.

This man was so not the Lucas Wilding she'd grown up with. "Yes."

"I'm thirsty."

Kristine fed him some ice chips.

"That's good," he said. "More."

She spooned more ice into his mouth. "Can I get you anything else? Are you hungry?"

"No." He pulled at the hospital-style gown he wore. "I can't stand this. Take it off."

"You'll get cold, Dad," she said.

He began tearing at the gown, pulling it off his shoulders, leaving his chest bare.

She wanted to weep at the bones she could see through the thin skin. She tried to cover him. He pulled the gown off. Kristine gave up, instead attempting to cover him with the blanket.

"I want to get up."

"No, Dad," she said. "You're fine."

He hadn't been out of bed or able to move his legs in days.

"You're keeping me prisoner," he accused. "I know what you're doing."

"I'm not," she said.

"Untie me."

"Dad, you're not tied down." She lifted the blanket so he could see she spoke the truth.

"You never loved me," he cried. "You don't love me."

"I do, Dad," she said, his words tearing at her. "I love you."

"No." Her dad shook his head. "You don't, Veronica."

"Dad, I'm Kristine," she reminded him. "Mom isn't here."

"She left me," he said, crying now.

"She was sick, Dad," she said. "She's still sick. She can't help it."

"Kristine?" he asked, his eyes on her.

"Yes, Dad, it's me." Tears ran from her eyes. She wiped them away.

"I love you, Krissy," he said, before closing his eyes. "I love you."

"I love you, too, Dad," she said, her heart beaten and bruised. "I love you, too."

* * *

Kristine was waiting on the platform when the train pulled in Friday night.

Never had she been this excited to see Carly. She'd missed her daughter something fierce.

The train braked to a stop, the screech of metal against metal announcing their arrival.

Kristine watched eagerly as the first passengers disembarked. It seemed to take forever before she saw Carly's blonde hair. Kristine made her way to her daughter, and then Carly was in her arms.

"Hi, honey." She kissed the top of Carly's head.

"Hi, Mom," Carly said brightly.

"Oh, I missed you."

"Me, too. Kate's great, but she's not you." Carly smiled up at her. "How's Grandpa?"

"Failing," Kristine said, wanting to be honest with her. "Ro and Rand are with him now."

"Rand?" Carly asked, the word holding more than a hint of disbelief.

"He's been a godsend," Kristine told her as they headed to the parking lot. "I don't know what we would have done without him. He helps us turn Grandpa. Grandpa is total deadweight now."

"Sad," Carly said as they got in the car.

Kristine pulled out of the parking lot.

"How long do you think Grandpa has?" Carly asked. "I miss you."

"I know. Me, too," Kristine said. "And I do have a job that I'm sure misses me, but I really have no idea. The hospice nurse thinks he's close. I know it sounds awful to speculate on how long he has left, but he's so miserable. He's in pain all the time. He has no quality of life."

"That sucks," Carly said, frowning.

"Yeah, it does."

They passed the rest of the drive time talking about school, then Carly filled her in on her friends—a subject she could go on and on about for days.

By the time she pulled into the driveway, Kristine felt more like her old self. Doing something as simple and normal as having a conversation with her daughter had brought her back to her own reality. She was glad Carly had come for the weekend.

Rowena was waiting with a hot meal for all of them, including Rand, and they gathered around the kitchen table to eat.

Rowena served up burgers with homemade hand-cut fries—Carly's favorite.

"Having Carly back agrees with you," Rand said, right as Kristine took a bite of hamburger.

She nodded.

He smiled, and Kristine's heart sang. He made her feel good, and she liked that.

Her thoughts went to Kyle. He might not be the right guy for her either, but he was miles closer to her ideal.

Was she a snob? Was she more her father's daughter than she thought? Even if she did inherit money from her father's estate, the type of guy she wanted would be the same.

No, it would never work between her and Rand, no matter how sexy and good looking he was. She just couldn't go there.

And that made Kristine sad.

* * *

The following morning Kristine set out for a walk.

Her father had suffered a rough night, the pain keeping him awake and crying. Kristine had finally called hospice in the middle of the night to discuss upping his morphine. Once she got the okay, she did just that, and he'd fallen into a drug-induced sleep.

Never had she thought about what it would be like to watch someone suffer. Death should be peaceful, but after watching her father, she realized death came in all kinds of packages, most of them not pretty.

She struck out down the beach, enjoying the fresh air. The hour was early, not quite seven. Carly was still asleep. Kristine walked for about forty minutes before she turned around and started back. The sun was higher in the sky now, the water a cool blue. She was about ten minutes from home when Hussy came into view, followed by Rand.

Her heart sped up.

Why did he have to be the one? She could no longer deny her attraction to him. Her physical attraction, she reminded herself. The dog reached her first and Kristine squatted to give her some love.

Hussy ate up the attention.

"She sure likes you," Rand said as he reached them.

"The feeling is mutual," Kristine said as she came to her feet. "Working today?"

"Yep, need to be on the job by nine."

"Working sounds good." She smiled.

"You worried about your job?" he asked as he fell into step beside her.

"A little," she admitted. "I know they can't hold this time off against me, but it's weird not going to work."

"I suppose," he said, "but you are doing the right thing."

"I couldn't do it without you," she told him.

"I'm glad you don't have to."

She glanced at him. He studied her. She saw so much in his eyes, tenderness, acceptance. He knew so much about her family, yet he was there, helping out, no questions asked.

"What do you say we do a beach fire tonight for Carly?" he asked. "It's going to be a gorgeous evening."

"I don't know," she said. "I'd love to, but I'll have to ask Rowena to sit with him."

"Trust me," he said. "She doesn't mind."

"You say that like you know something." Kristine stopped. "Is something going on between them?"

He shrugged, but she could see the truth on his face.

"Are you kidding me?" she asked.

"She's never admitted it, but I see things."

Kristine shook her head. "I've seen things too, like the way he responds to her, how tender she is with him, but I just assumed she is such a good person and it's in her nature to handle him like that."

"Maybe."

"No," she said, "I think you're right." Kristine laughed. "Well, maybe some of her goodness has rubbed off on him. He always seemed so unhappy, so bitter and caustic."

"Not with her, at least not in the past few years."

"Wow." Kristine struggled to process what Rand was saying. "Wow."

He laughed. "I know."

They reached the house.

"I'll see you tonight?" Rand asked as they parted ways at the guest house.

"Okay, sounds good—if I can get Rowena to sit with him. Hot dogs and s'mores?"

"That's a given," he said with a wave.

Kristine flew through her day. In the early afternoon, her phone rang.

"Kyle," she said.

"Kristine, hello," he returned. "Are we still on for tonight?"

"Oh, no," she said. "I totally forgot. I can't. I have Carly."

"I could come there," he offered, his tone hopeful.

"I promised her a beach fire," Kristine said. "She's just here for the weekend. She leaves tomorrow. It's mother–daughter time." The lie was bitter on her tongue, but she couldn't invite him. It was weird between Kyle and Rand.

"I see," he said the words tight. "I'm sorry. I was looking forward to the evening."

"I'm the one who's sorry," she said. "The timing is just so bad. My dad is close. I need to stay home."

"Why don't you call me when you are free," he suggested. "I like you, Kristine. I'd like to pursue this."

"I like you, too, Kyle," she said. "Thank you for understanding. I'll let you know when things are better."

"Okay." He paused. "Good-bye, Kristine."

"Bye." She put her phone back in her pocket. She'd just lied to Kyle. Maybe she didn't like him as much as she thought.

Ugh. Why did life have to be so difficult? Why couldn't she make the smart choice, the safe guy, the guy who had goals like hers?

Kyle was a doctor, for Pete's sake. Perfect for her in every way.

Her thoughts turned to Rand. He was everything she wanted to avoid and everything she wanted—all wrapped up in one gorgeous package. She was playing on dangerous ground with him, yet that didn't stop her from agreeing to the fire.

A safe evening, with her daughter present.

What could happen?

* * *

Wood smoke mixed with the sultry breeze.

Kristine inhaled, loving the two scents. She unfolded her beach chair and placed it next to Carly's. Rand continued to work on the fire, adding more wood.

The sun hovered on the horizon like a giant peach, casting a golden glow on everything.

It felt so good to be here, on the beach and out of the house that was beginning to smell more and more like death each day. Earlier, she'd called Lucky to check on his progress. He'd told her he was wrapping things up as quickly as he could and he'd be there soon.

"A penny for your thoughts," Rand said, his eyes on her.

She smiled. "Just thinking about Lucky. Hoping he arrives in time."

"He will, Mom," Carly said with certainty. "Grandpa is waiting for him."

Earlier, she'd had Carly gown up and say good-bye to her grandfather. They'd never been close, but Carly had wanted to say good-bye one last time. Everyone needed closure.

Rand settled into his chair. Hussy wandered over and plopped down at Carly's feet. A single star shone in the sky and Kristine made a wish for a peaceful death for her father.

"We'll let the fire burn for a bit before we roast anything," Rand said. "Need those good coals."

Carly fiddled with her phone, then music came on. Teenage music.

Kristine shrugged. "Tell us something fun, Carly."

"I don't know," Carly said. "Wait, you know that girl, Melissa?"

"The one with the wild hair?" Kristine asked.

"Yes. She tried to dye it purple, but it came out this super ugly shade of gray. You should see it, Mom. She looks like an old woman."

Rand's mouth curved in a half smile.

She wondered what he thought of her daughter. He seemed to like Carly. They got along fine. She also wondered why he wasn't married, didn't have a girlfriend. He was so good looking.

Carly entertained them with teen gossip, keeping the conversation light, far away from death, and Kristine needed that, needed her daughter to keep her sane. She dreaded putting her back on the train tomorrow.

"It's great here, Mom," Carly said. "You were lucky to grow up on the beach."

"I know," Kristine agreed. "I didn't always feel lucky to grow up in Wilding House, but it certainly had nothing to do with the house or the setting."

Rand nodded and she could see the compassion in his eyes.

Rand finally pronounced the coals ready, and they roasted hot dogs, followed by sticky, sweet s'mores, this time made with peanut butter cups. They were all going into sugar shock for sure.

The sun set and the night took on a velvety softness. One of Carly's friends called and she chattered away.

Rand moved his chair closer to Kristine's.

"She's got a lot of energy," he said with a grin.

"I know. I didn't realize until now how much I need that energy in daily life. She keeps me going. She keeps me young."

"She's a great kid," he said. "You're lucky."

"Ever want any kids of your own?" she asked, prying just a little.

"No, always too centered on my career," he said, sounding sad. "Never had my priorities in the right order."

"No girlfriend or wife?"

"No and no, but plenty of one-night stands."

"Okay," she said, letting the word trail off. "Probably more than I wanted to know."

"I'm a guy, Kris."

"I know."

"You?"

"You know about Carly's dad. I'm lucky to be rid of him, but like I told you before, I'm sorry for her. She deserved a better father. It's his loss."

"For sure. And after him?"

"No one, really," she said. "I was too busy raising a baby, working, and for a time, going to school."

"You're incredible." He said the words softly.

Her pulse revved. "No, I'm nothing special. Just a mom."

"From where I sit, you had your priorities right. Your daughter comes first. It's what every kid wants."

"I guess it is. I know I secretly wished for that when I was a kid."

Carly ended her phone call.

"Everything okay?" Kristine asked her.

Carly smiled. "It was Nan. She went skating tonight. Everyone was there. Jack Reece tried to hold her hand."

"Seriously?" Kristine asked. "You girls are twelve. Too young to be holding hands."

"Mom," Carly said, the word long and drawn out. "Sometimes you are so lame."

Kristine smiled.

"I'm going up," Carly said. "I told Nan I'd call her back in ten minutes. She has more stuff to tell me."

"Okay," Kristine said. "I should get back and relieve Rowena."

Rand stood. "I'll put the fire out."

"I'll pack up," Kristine said. "Take your chair, Carly."

The teenager took both chairs, trudging up the path to the house. Kristine waited for Rand to put the fire out, then the two of them started up the path. He carried her cooler and followed her up onto the deck and into the house, where he placed it on the kitchen counter.

"Thanks," she said. "We had a great time tonight. Thanks for building the fire. Carly loved it."

"No thanks necessary," he said. "I enjoyed it, too."

She turned, finding he'd come up behind her. He was so close. And the way he was looking at her. Her mouth went dry.

"Rand—"

"Good night, Kristine." He grinned, leading her to believe he was on to her discomfort.

Kristine stared after him with regret, for a full minute, before snapping back to reality and going to check on her father.

Chapter Eight

Sunday night and she was alone again.

Kristine sighed. She missed Carly already and she'd only been gone a couple of hours. Lucas had been sleeping all day, rousing long enough for a few ice chips. In her heart Kristine knew the end was near.

She sat at her father's bedside. For something to do, she'd begun reading the newspaper to him. He'd always enjoyed the paper, and reading helped pass the time. She started with the sports page tonight, giving him the stats on the baseball games that week.

Her father remained unresponsive.

Kristine set the paper aside. She hated this. The waiting. The worrying. Lucas Wilding was shutting down. He hadn't had a bowel movement in days. His urine output was pitiful. He'd grown so thin. He slept all the time.

"It's okay to go, Dad," she said, rubbing his arm. "It's okay."

Nothing.

"I want you to be at peace. Please go, Dad. Please."

She broke off, ashamed of herself for telling him to go. Who did that?

"Hey," Rand said from the doorway. "You okay?"

"No." She stood, ripping off her protective wear.

"How's he doing?" Rand asked.

"The same." She went into the bathroom and washed up, then left the room, Rand on her heels. "I need some air."

"I know where you can get some," he said easily.

"Ha ha." She breezed through the kitchen.

Rowena glanced up from something she stirred on the stove.

"Watch him, Mom," Rand said. "Kristine needs air."

"I won't be long, Rowena."

"Take your time," Rowena said unable to keep the worry from her tone. "I'll watch over him."

And then she was free. Kristine ran down the deck steps, down the path to the beach. When she reached the waterline she stopped and inhaled.

"Better?" Rand asked, when she turned to face him.

"You shouldn't have followed me." She didn't need him so close all the time. His nearness was unnerving. He made her doubt everything, and she hated that about him right now.

"You looked like you needed a friend," he said.

"Quit being so nice to me." She turned away.

He caught her arm. "Why? I think you need someone to be nice to you."

"But not you," she said.

"Why not me?" He looked into her eyes.

Something inside her gave way. "I just don't need any complications in my life."

"I'm a complication? What about Kyle?"

"He's a complication, too," Kristine said, knowing she sounded like a loon. "I need to focus on my father. He's all I can handle right now."

"Okay," Rand said. "Would you rather be alone?"

"Yes. No. I don't know." She shook her head. "I'm sorry. I'm a mess."

"Watching someone die will do that to a person."

"You say that like you have firsthand knowledge."

He shrugged. "Not really."

His hand was warm on her arm, and she was instantly aware of him as a man. Her body tingled with sexual excitement. She tugged her arm free.

"You're trying awfully hard not to like me," Rand said, the words soft. "Quit fighting so hard. I'm nice. I really am."

She smiled. "Okay, if you want to be my friend, be my friend. But that's it."

"Well, friend," he said, "why don't I bring over a comedy tonight and we can watch a movie. Take your mind off of things for a couple of hours."

She had to admit a little mindless entertainment sounded great. "I'm game. I'll make the popcorn. Tell me you like butter and parmesan cheese on it."

He smiled. "Love it."

"Seven?" she asked.

"Works for me."

They walked back to Wilding House, parting ways at the guest house. Once inside Wilding House, she headed to her father's room to check on him.

A muffled crying came from the room.

Had he passed?

Panicked, Kristine raced into the room. Rowena was holding Lucas's hand, tears running freely down her face.

"Rowena?"

The older woman quickly wiped her eyes with a tissue. "He's alive. I'm sorry."

"Don't be sorry," Kristine said. "You love him, don't you?"

Rowena nodded. "He's not the same man you knew. He changed as he grew older. Had regrets. He made room in his heart for love."

Kristine wanted to believe Rowena, but she remembered her father as a man with zero warmth in his heart.

"He loves you and Lucky," Rowena said. "Never doubt that."

"And he loves you?" Kristine asked.

"We were lovers, yes," Rowena told her, no shame in the words.

"I suspected." Kristine smiled. "I'm glad he had you, Ro. You are everything good. I'm sure you rubbed off on him."

"I'm losing him," Rowena said, the tears back in her eyes.

This time Kristine comforted Rowena, hugging her as she cried for Lucas Wilding.

* * *

Rand showed up, movie in hand, at seven.

Kristine stood at the stove, making popcorn.

"Hi," she said. "I pop in olive oil. I hope that's okay."

"Absolutely." Seeing her made him happy and he hadn't felt happy in a long time. He'd been moving through his life like a shadow, doing all the right motions, but feeling nothing. She wanted to be friends, and that was fine, but deep down he wanted more from her.

The popcorn popped, the sound growing louder and louder. Kristine shook the pan. When the popping slowed, she removed the lid and overturned the pan into a large metal bowl.

She took melted butter from the microwave and used a spoon to mix the butter with the popcorn. When she finished, she added a liberal portion of grated parmesan cheese.

"Finished." She smiled.

Rand scooped up a handful, sampling the popcorn. "Delicious."

"I know." She carried the bowl toward the media room. "Can you grab us a couple of drinks from the fridge? There's beer, or soda, or water."

"Water works," he said.

"For me, too."

In the media room, she took the movie from him. It was an old Tom Cruise movie, the perfect blend of comedy and romance.

"Good choice," she said as she loaded the DVD.

They settled into side by side recliners, the bowl of popcorn between them.

Rand's fingers brushed against hers ever so often as they ate the popcorn. He lost himself to the movie and the good company. When the movie ended he knew he didn't want to go home yet.

"That was great," Kristine said. "I should probably go and relieve Ro."

"Thanks for hanging out with me, friend," he said.

She smiled. "Thanks for cheering me up."

"That's what friends are for," they both said in unison, before laughing.

Kristine stood and gathered up the empty popcorn bowl and water bottles.

He walked her to the kitchen.

She set the bowl in the sink.

"Kristine," Rowena called from the hallway, her tone urgent.

"I'm in here," Kristine said, passing him.

Rand followed.

"I hear the rattle," his mother said, the words worried, frantic.

Rand wasn't sure what his mother was talking about.

They were in the bedroom now. Lucas' breathing had an odd rattle, as if phlegm were caught in his throat.

"I'm calling Lauren," Kristine said, pulling her phone from her pocket.

"What can I do, Mom?" Rand asked.

"Gown up and come here," Rowena said. "I want to turn him on his side."

Rand did as she asked, helping her turn Lucas.

Kristine stood nearby, talking to the hospice nurse. "Thank you," she said, before rejoining them. "Lauren said putting him on his side might help. I think we need to be with him all the time now. I don't want him to die alone. He's getting close."

"I agree," Rowena said.

"I wish Lucky was here," Kristine said. "I don't know if Dad will be coherent enough again. It breaks my heart they might never make peace with each other." Tears filled her eyes.

Rand forgot he was just supposed to be her friend. He went to Kristine and pulled her into his arms, holding her while she cried. Her arms came around him.

The scent of her shampoo teased his nose. Her soft body felt as good as he'd imagined. He wanted to protect her, make the hurt go away, but he knew from experience grief had its own timeline.

He kissed the top of her head.

His mother watched them, her eyes sad.

He was about to have two grieving women on his hands.

Time to get his own life together. Kristine and his mother needed him to be strong, to be their rock, and Rand wouldn't have it any other way.

* * *

Kristine woke up with a crick in her neck. She moved her head to the side as the room came into focus. She'd passed the night on the easy chair in her father's room. She didn't have to look at her father to see if he lived—the rattle in his breath told her he was still with them.

She stood and stretched, giving a silent prayer Lucky would arrive today. Kristine checked her father. He was still dry and as comfortable as she could make him given the circumstances, so she headed for the shower.

Thirty minutes later she felt like a new woman. She found Rowena with Lucas.

"Breakfast is on the stove," Rowena said. "Go eat."

"Thanks."

In the kitchen, Kristine dished up a bowl of oatmeal, adding raspberries and a bit of honey before taking the food outside to the deck. The air was cool, but not cold. She sat at the table and ate her breakfast.

She really did love it here. Wilding House had a charm, a magic. She'd missed looking at the raw beauty of the beach every day.

Her phone rang. Kyle.

"Good morning," she said into the phone.

"Good morning," Kyle said. "How is Lucas?"

"He has the death rattle." She set her spoon down.

"I'm sorry," Kyle offered. "Can I help in any way?"

"No, Ro and I are taking turns sitting with him. I don't want him to be alone."

"No sign of Lucky?" Kyle asked.

"Not yet."

"Do you really think he's coming?" Kyle asked.

"He said he was." She sighed.

"I'd like to come by and sit with you tonight, help you pass the time," Kyle said. "Would that be all right?"

"You don't need to do that," Kristine said. "Dying is so personal. I'm not sure my father would want outsiders in the room when he's so close to passing."

"I understand, of course."

"I do appreciate the offer," Kristine said in an attempt to soothe him.

"I'll check in with you later," Kyle said. "Please know I'm thinking about you."

"Thank you. Bye." She ended the call, her eyes going to the guest house. Rand's truck was gone. She tried to ignore the disappointment in her chest, but failed. Rand was the one she wanted to see, the one who seemed to understand what she and Ro were going through.

Kristine picked up her dishes and placed them in the dishwasher. Lauren had arrived and she was busy doing a check on Lucas.

"How is he?" Kristine asked.

"He's close," Lauren said, her eyes sad. "I'm here to help in any way I can. Like I told you before, there's no real timeline. He could go on like this for days, or pass suddenly."

Kristine nodded.

"You are doing everything you can, Kristine," Lauren said. "Dying is natural."

"I have so many doubts," Kristine said. "Am I doing the right thing giving him the morphine? I've been reading end of life blogs. Some people believe morphine is responsible for death. I don't know what to believe."

"He's suffering," Lauren reminded her. "He's in so much pain now. You know him. Would he want to suffer, or would he want the relief morphine brings?"

Rowena took Kristine's hand. "He wouldn't want to suffer."

Kristine knew in her heart they were right, but being the one making the decisions was hard.

After the nurse left, Kristine and Rowena sat with Lucas. They took short breaks for food and walking and stretching. When Rand showed up at six, Kristine was shocked the day had passed so quickly.

"How's it going?" Rand asked.

Rowena shook her head sadly.

"How about I order some pizza?" Rand offered, his eyes on Kristine. "You two need to eat."

"I don't think I can eat." Rowena pressed a hand to her stomach.

"When you smell pizza, you'll change your mind," Rand predicted before disappearing.

Kristine stood. Her father's rattle had been the same for hours now, consistent and troubling, but not so bad he was choking.

She pulled off her protective gear. "I'm going to help Rand get dinner. Call if there's any change."

"You know I will," Rowena said.

Kristine washed up and left the room, heading for the kitchen. Rand was on the deck on his phone, no doubt ordering pizza.

She didn't question why she wanted to be with Rand. Instead, Kristine stepped outside.

Rand turned to look at her as he ended the call. "Pizza will be here in twenty-five minutes."

"I had to get out of there."

"Oh, baby." Rand gathered her in the strong circle of his arms. He didn't speak, he just held her. Kristine didn't cry, she absorbed him, his scent, the feel of his solid shoulder under her cheek, the way his touch felt large, bigger than life.

He was alive.

Rand wasn't struggling for breath.

She needed this, someone far removed from sickness and death.

Rand stroked her back.

Kristine pulled away slightly, enough to look into his dark eyes.

"Don't look at me like that, Kristine," he said. "I can't stand to see you so sad. If you don't look away, I'm going to kiss you."

Kristine didn't look away.

Rand took her face in his hands and kissed her.

Kristine opened her mouth to him, and he deepened the kiss, taking her mind off of everything but him. The kiss went on and on, making her drunk with passion, with need.

Something nudged her leg, once, twice.

They broke the kiss. Hussy.

What had just happened? Kristine dragged her hand across her mouth, as if the action would erase the kiss.

"I'm sorry," she said, embarrassed and confused. "God, I threw myself at you. I—" She broke off at a loss for words.

"You're entitled to a little mindless kissing," Rand said softly. "I get it. I've been where you are. You needed a distraction, and I was here."

He was so much more than a distraction, but she couldn't tell him that. Her emotions weren't her own at this moment. They belonged to a crazy woman.

She nodded. "You're right. I wanted to feel something good."

"In that case," he grinned. "I'm glad I could help."

Kristine ran a hand over her hair. "I don't know what I'm doing anymore."

"Come on," he said, taking her hand. "Let's get ready for dinner. It was one wild, hot kiss, even if it wasn't for the right reasons. Next time, we'll get it right."

Kristine opened her mouth to tell him there wouldn't be a next time, but he was already gone, whistling as he walked away from her.

Chapter Nine

Another day slipped by with no great change in Lucas Wilding.

Another day of waiting for the absent Lucky to show.

Kristine rarely left her father's room now, certain he'd be taken from them at any moment. Her own life had come to a screeching halt, other than her daily phone calls to Carly.

School was winding down. Only a couple of days left, then Carly would take the train back to Wilding Point. At least they'd be together here.

Kristine shifted in the recliner. She was going to get recliner butt. Ugh. It was almost seven. She had another endless night ahead of her. The thought depressed her.

Her father's mouth was open, shaped into a perfect oval. He'd been that way for days. She constantly cleaned his mouth and lips, using the soft sponges Lauren had provided.

Her phone chimed. A text from Kyle.

How's it going? he asked.

The same.

I'm sorry. Do you want company?

No, I'm good. It's too sad here.

If you change your mind, please call any time.

Thanks.

Kristine set her phone on the bedside table.

Her father's gurgle changed to a full-out, wet sound. He began coughing, sounding like he was drowning in the phlegm.

Alarmed, Kristine shot to her feet. "Dad."

He continued to choke.

"Rowena," she shouted, while at the same time grabbing her phone and calling Lauren.

"It's Kristine, my dad is choking. What should I do? I don't know what to do."

"Calm down," Lauren said, in a soothing tone.

Rowena ran into the room. "What's happening?"

"In the comfort kit," Lauren said. "Open it, remember, there's something you can give him that will help."

Kristine followed Lauren's instructions, putting the drug into her father's mouth while Rowena held the phone.

Her father continued to drown in his mucus.

Rowena touched Kristine's shoulder. "He's going."

"No," Kristine said, her eyes filling with tears. "Lucky's not here yet."

Lucas began to quiet.

"It's working," Kristine said, wiping her eyes on her sleeve.

"Maybe," Rowena said, "but he wants to go. He's being called. We have to let him go. He can't suffer like this anymore."

Kristine knew in her heart Rowena was right, but she wasn't ready. "I can't."

"It's all right, my love," Rowena said, stroking Lucas' hair. "Go now. Be at peace. Go." Tears streamed down Rowena's cheeks.

Kristine held her father's hand. She had to put her father first, no matter how much her heart ached. "I love you, Dad. Go, please go."

Her father shuddered, then drew two very shallow breaths before going still. Rowena laid her head on his chest, crying openly now.

Kristine cried too, tears of sadness mixed with relief. It was over.

Lucas Wilding was gone.

She didn't need a doctor to tell her, she knew. His spirit had gone on to a better place.

She rubbed Rowena's back and the woman sat up, embracing Kristine.

"He's at peace now," Rowena said, patting Kristine's back.

Kristine nodded. A movement at the door caught her eye.

"Lucky." She jumped from the bed and into her brother's arms. Tears poured out of her, onto her brother's shirt. "He's gone."

Lucky held her. He didn't say anything, but she could feel the slight tremor in his arms.

"What's going on?" Rand's voice called as he came down the hall. "Lucky," he said with surprise.

"He's gone, Rand," Rowena said to her son.

"Oh, Mom, I'm sorry." Rand held his mother as she cried.

Kristine stepped away from her big brother. Lucky's dark hair was longer than she remembered and he wore a close-cropped beard. He looked lean, tan, his blue eyes sad and tortured.

"I'm sorry," Lucky said with a shake of his head.

"He just passed," Kristine told him.

"I saw."

"You did?" she asked hopefully.

"Yeah." He glanced away.

"Do you want to say good-bye?" she asked him.

"No, I'm good. We pretty much said all we had to say to each other when he sent me to prison." A haunted shadow filled Lucky's eyes.

Kristine ached for her brother and all he'd been through. "He was different at the end. Softer, more like a child than the father you remember."

Lucky shrugged.

Rowena separated herself from Rand, and moved on to Lucky.

"My beautiful boy," she said to Lucky, hugging him tight. "Welcome home."

Lucky hugged Rowena back, his love for her written on his face along with a hefty helping of anguish. "Hi, Ro."

Kristine's heart broke. Lucas Wilding had damaged his son. She couldn't begin to understand Lucky's feelings for their father. Right now, she was thankful Lucky was here.

With Lucky in Ro's capable hands, Kristine called Lauren. She needed the nurse here, needed someone to confirm the death, help with getting him ready, someone to follow up with the funeral home they'd picked out.

"He's gone," Kristine said into the phone when Lauren answered.

"I'm sorry," Lauren replied. "Would you like me to come?"

"Yes, please."

"On my way."

Kristine closed her eyes. Her body had gone numb. She felt trapped in a dream. She was doing all the right things, but she had no idea how she was doing them.

Rowena turned up the classical music Lucas liked. "I'll clean him up, get him ready. Kristine, will you help, or should I wait for Lauren?"

Lucky said, "I'm outta here. I'll be on the deck."

Disappointed her brother didn't want more closure, but understanding why he didn't, Kristine watched Lucky go.

"Do you need my help?" Rand offered.

"Yes," Rowena said. "I'll be back with water."

Rowena left the room. Kristine opened the window wide. She could hear a million frogs. She inhaled, needing the scent of the beach.

"You doing okay?" Rand asked.

"I guess. It's surreal. I can't believe he's really gone."

Rand pulled her into his arms. "I'm sorry," he whispered against her hair.

"Thank you." She held him tight, her hands twisted in his soft T-shirt. He made her feel so alive. Hopeful. She never wanted to let him go.

Rowena returned with the water and they broke apart, but not before Kristine saw a longing in Rand's eyes that matched her own.

Together the three of them worked to clean Lucas Wilding for the last time.

They'd just finished dressing her father in the black power suit that had been his uniform for years when Lauren arrived.

"You did all this?" the nurse asked. "You people are amazing."

"Can you make sure he's really gone?" Kristine said. "I know he is, but I need to be sure."

Lauren examined Lucas. "He's gone. Time of death?"

"Seven-ten," Rowena said. "I made sure to note the time."

"Okay," Lauren said. "The funeral home is on the way, but they said it could take a couple of hours."

Kristine nodded.

Lucky hesitated in the doorway.

"Lucky," Kristine said, dragging him into the room. "Meet Lauren Baker, our hospice nurse and resident angel."

"Ah, the infamous Lucky," Lauren said, extending her hand.

Lucky shook her hand, his expression grim. "That's me."

"I'm glad you made it." Lauren smiled. "I'm glad you're here for Kristine."

Lucky nodded.

"Well," Lauren said brightly, "I think you are all set here. If I can do anything else, please let me know."

"All this equipment?" Rowena asked.

"I'll make arrangements to have it picked up," Lauren said. "The meds too."

"Thank you," Kristine said, more grateful to Lauren than she could voice. "I'll walk you out."

"No need," Lauren said with a wave of her hand. "You all stay with your loved one." She headed for the door. "Nice to meet you, Lucky."

"Likewise," Lucky said.

Lauren smiled at Lucky on her way past.

And then they were alone. Rowena insisted on cleaning the room around Lucas, making everything spick and span, ridding the room of anything toxic.

Kristine sat with her father, rubbing his arm. "I'm so glad you are at peace, Dad, so glad I had this time with you."

She felt a touch on her arm. Lucky squeezed her shoulder, his eyes on their father.

The bond was there between them, the bond of a brother and sister. Love for Lucky filled her. Together they'd get through this, it was what they did, what they'd always done.

* * *

The undertakers—two of them—showed up around eleven p.m.

Young men, probably in their mid-twenties, obviously brothers, they both stood around six foot seven. Dressed in formal black suits, one with long wavy hair to his shoulders, the other with short curly hair, they seemed like something out of a black comedy or horror movie.

They introduced themselves, shaking the hands of each family member while delivering a perfect condolence line.

Kristine exchanged a look with Lucky, and she knew he could read her thoughts. Were the undertakers for real? Or was this some kind of shtick they'd dreamed up to make their jobs more bearable?

Rowena explained that Lucas had been contagious, may still be. She warned the boys about the open sores on his back. The young men nodded, unfazed, and asked if they all wanted to watch while they moved Lucas to the gurney they'd brought in.

Lucky bolted immediately. Rand followed him. Kristine and Rowena held hands as Lucas Wilding was moved from the bed to the gurney. They followed as the boys took him down the hall, then carried him down the front stairs to the hearse.

Watching her father disappear into the creepy hearse brought tears to Kristine's eyes. Rowena's grip on her hand tightened.

"Bye, Dad," Kristine whispered as the car pulled away.

"Go in peace, my love," Rowena said.

When the car disappeared from view, Kristine and Rowena embraced.

"It's over," Kristine said. "I can't believe he's gone."

"I know," Rowena agreed. "The house won't be the same without him. I won't be the same without him."

Arm and arm they went inside.

"Let's close the door on his room for tonight," Kristine said. "I need a shower."

"I agree." Rowena nodded. "I'll stop by the kitchen and let Rand and Lucky know we'll join them in a few minutes."

"Sounds good."

Kristine climbed the stairs, so tired. Her emotions felt pulverized, yet she wasn't ready to go to bed yet. She wanted to talk to Lucky. Wanted to be near Rand.

Fifteen minutes later, showered and dressed in comfy pajamas and a thick white robe, she padded to the kitchen.

Rowena was already there, putting on a pot of coffee.

Rand and Lucky sat at the table, engrossed in conversation.

"Hey," Rand said when he noticed her. "You okay?"

"I think so." She took a seat at the table.

"Thanks for taking care of him," Lucky said his voice a hoarse rasp. "I couldn't. And for that, I'm sorry."

"I know." She reached for his hand, squeezing it. "It's all water under the bridge now."

"What comes next?" Lucky asked. "Is there a funeral planned?"

"He didn't want one," Rowena said. "He told me he wants his ashes buried under the pink dogwood tree near the gazebo. There's a view of the lighthouse from there. Lucas loved that lighthouse."

"So he's being cremated," Lucky said.

"Yes," Kristine said. "I have paperwork to do, but I imagine it will take a few days. I'm going to have to shift gears and go home to Oregon to pick up Carly. I'll bring her back here and we can plan a family memorial. Will that work?"

"Sure," Lucky said. "I can stick around."

She had no idea what her brother had been up to, or even where he'd been living. Did he have a life, a girlfriend, a mortgage? These were all questions she longed to ask him, but she didn't want to do that in front of Rand and Ro. There'd be time for twenty questions later.

"Will you leave tomorrow?" Rand asked her.

"No, I need a day to just be. I'll go the following day and be there for Carly when school gets out."

Rowena set a cup of coffee in front of her.

"I don't know if I can do coffee, Ro," Kristine said.

"It's decaf and I put a shot of Bailey's in it," Rowena said with a sad smile. "It will help you relax and sleep."

Kristine nodded, before taking a sip. "There's a lot to do. The house needs to be gone through. Lucky, if there's anything you want, take it."

"I don't want anything," Lucky said, his mouth tightening.

Kristine sighed. "There's a will. I'll call the attorney and let him know Dad has passed. I know I'm the executor, but that's all I know. There's a copy here somewhere, but I haven't come across it."

Lucky sipped his coffee, his expression thoughtful.

Kristine glanced up to find Rand's eyes on her. The way he looked at her, as if he were trying to judge if she was all right, melted her heart.

"I'm beat," Lucky said, pushing back in his chair. "I'm going to head up to bed. Okay if I take my old room?"

"Of course," Kristine said.

"I made it up fresh for you the second you said you were coming," Rowena told him. "I'll walk you up."

"Good night," Lucky said as he followed Rowena from the room.

"I'm exhausted, too," Kristine said. "I don't think I've ever felt this tired."

"It's been quite a ride." Rand stood, stretching. His T-shirt rode up, giving her a view of his flat stomach.

Kristine glanced away, standing. "Thank you for everything you did for my father."

"This is the beginning of the rest of your life, Kristine," Rand said.

"I guess it is."

He opened the sliding door. "Want to look at the stars before bed?"

Suddenly, she did. Outside, she looked up. Stars twinkled everywhere. There was a whole, big world out there. A world where people were alive, living their lives.

She had a lot to think about. Did she want to go back to her job, her lonely life in Oregon? There was a chance her father had left her some money. Money opened the door to possibilities. She did have to consider Carly's feelings. Could she get her daughter to stay in Wilding Point, where they had Rowena and Rand? And maybe Lucky, now that he didn't have to hide from their father anymore?

Kristine didn't know, and right now her head was too tired to figure out a life plan that made sense.

"Thanks for the stars," she said, smiling at Rand.

"For you, any time."

"Good night." She touched Rand's arm as she passed, wanting him to know how much his help with her father meant to her. He snagged her fingers giving them a tight squeeze.

"Sleep well, Kristine."

He let go of her, and Kristine left him. Once in bed, Kristine couldn't shut her mind off. Her life was now one big question mark.

It had been years since she'd been hopeful about her future. Years. Maybe she was putting the cart before the horse, maybe there was no money, but it didn't matter. Wilding Point had changed her, made her want things she hadn't wanted in a long time—a better job, and most of all, family ties.

No matter what the will said, Kristine's life was about to take a dramatic turn, for better or worse.

Chapter Ten

Kristine pulled into the parking lot of her apartment complex and shut off the engine.

"Is this it?" Lucky asked, his eyes on the ugly building before them.

He'd come with her to collect Carly, and while he hadn't said much on the drive down, she'd appreciated his company.

"Yep, home sweet home—not," she said with a grin. "The rent is decent. I'm a poor single mom, Lucky."

"I'm sorry, Kris," Lucky said. "You should have stayed in school."

"School is expensive." She got out of the car and Lucky followed her in.

The apartment had a musty smell. She opened the sliding glass door to let the fresh air in.

Lucky wandered over to her bookshelf, looking at the photos of Carly displayed there. "She's a little beauty," he said.

"I know." Kristine went to her room. "I need to pack for both of us. I'm officially out on bereavement for the coming week, but when bereavement is over I'm either going to have to return to work or have a different plan."

"Do you really think he left you money?" Lucky asked. "He was a spiteful man. I know he didn't leave me anything. He hated me."

"He didn't hate you," Kristine said, so sad for Lucky. "For some reason, we didn't live up to his expectations."

"Because he was an asshole." Lucky frowned. "He made sure we didn't love him."

"I loved him," Kristine said, "at the end. I forgave him."

Lucky pressed his lips together. "I'm happy for you. I don't think I'll ever be able to forgive him."

"Then I'm sorry for you," she said. "Hate eats at your heart. To be happy, you have to forgive. Trust me, it's true. Forgive him for yourself, for the peace you will find."

Lucky didn't reply and she knew the subject of forgiveness was closed.

Kristine glanced at the clock on the microwave. "Yikes, I need to pick up Carly."

Her daughter had taken the news of Lucas' death well. She'd elected to go to school and have her last day. She'd been understanding about returning to Wilding Point, giving Kristine hope that Carly might fall in love with the beach lifestyle this summer.

"Want to come with me to pick her up?" she asked.

"Sure."

They were waiting for Carly when she exited the school.

"Hi, Mom," Carly said, hugging Kristine. "Uncle Lucky, hi."

"Hi, squirt." Lucky grinned, hugging Carly. "You've really grown up."

"I know." Carly smiled. "I'm sorry about Grandpa."

"He's at peace now," Kristine said.

"Kristine."

Kristine turned. Her friend Kate approached, Nan trailing behind her.

"Hi, Kate," Kristine said, hugging her friend.

"I'm so sorry," Kate said, her brow creased with worry. "What can I do?"

"You've done enough," Kristine said. "Thank you for taking care of Carly."

Kate passed her Carly's bag of clothes. "My pleasure. You know she's always welcome at our place."

Kristine squeezed Nan's hand. "You're a good friend."

Nan smiled. "I'm sorry, too, Kristine."

"Thanks, honey."

"Who's this?" Kate asked, her eyes on Lucky.

"Oh, I'm sorry," Kristine said, "this is my brother, Lucky."

"Nice to meet you, Lucky," Kate said, shaking his hand. "This is Nan."

Nan raised her hand in greeting.

"Is there going to be a funeral?" Kate asked.

"Just a private family service next weekend," Kristine told her. "Dad's wishes."

"Okay," Kate said. "Well, I won't hold you up. I know you want to get back on the road."

"Thank you again, Kate," Kristine said. "You're the best."

"Take care, Kristine." Kate gave her a wave before moving on.

Kristine, Carly, and Lucky got in the car. Back at the apartment, the girls packed up more clothes and toiletries. Lucky helped them load the car, and then they were on the road back to Wilding Point, back to the place of beach fires and endless summers.

Kristine smiled, her eyes on the road.

"What?" Lucky asked.

"Nothing," she said, but the smile didn't leave her face, because in her heart she knew she was going home.

* * *

125

The attorney called on Wednesday, asking to meet with Kristine and Lucky as soon as it was convenient for them. Kristine made an appointment for Friday. The memorial for Lucas was on Saturday. Come Sunday, she'd need to make a decision regarding her job.

Everything was happening so fast.

Kristine and Carly spent their days at the beach, soaking up the sun, reading, relaxing. Although the time was tinged with a certain sadness, she didn't want their time together to end.

Thursday evening, as they were heading back to the house after yet another lazy afternoon she was surprised to find Kyle coming down the path toward them.

He raised a hand in greeting. "Hey, there."

"Hi, Kyle." They met and embraced.

"I'm sorry about Lucas," he said, his arms around her. "I wanted to come sooner, but without an invitation I hesitated."

Kristine pulled back. "I'm sorry. Carly and I have been taking it easy." She smiled at her daughter.

"Hello, Carly," Kyle said, smiling.

"Carly, this is Dr. Kyle King. He was one of Grandpa's doctors and he's my friend."

"Hi." Carly gave a nod toward the house. "I'll see you inside. I want to call Nan."

"Okay, honey." Kristine watched her daughter go. "Lucky's back, but he's in town."

"He's here," Kyle said with surprise. "At last."

"Yes." She smiled.

"Well, it will be good to see him," Kyle said. "Do you have dinner plans?"

"Not really," Kristine admitted. "Rowena cooks for us every night. Would you like to join us?"

"I'd like to steal you away," Kyle said, smiling. "I'd love to take you to dinner. Italian?"

"Italian does sound good," she said, still unsure. "I don't know."

"You have to eat, Kristine," Kyle coaxed. "I'm sure it would do you good to get away from Wilding House for a bit."

The setting sun cast a glow on everything, even Kyle. He looked even more handsome in the golden light. Did she like him enough to date him? Was this even a date?

"Say yes," he urged.

"Let me talk to Carly," Kristine said. "See if she's okay with me going out."

"Deal." Kyle's smile widened.

She left Kyle in the kitchen and went to find Carly, who was on the phone.

"Can I talk to you a sec?" Kristine asked.

"Hold on, Nan," Carly said. "Mom wants to ask me something." Carly gave Kristine her attention.

"Kyle asked me out for dinner. Is that okay with you?"

"Sure," Carly said. "You need to go out, Mom. I'm okay here with Rowena and Uncle Lucky."

Kristine smiled. "Thanks, honey. I won't be late. Just dinner, then back."

Carly nodded, the phone already pressed to her ear.

Kristine cleaned up quickly, slipping into a blue floral sundress and strappy sandals.

She found Kyle in the kitchen with Rowena.

"I hear you have dinner plans," Rowena said, from her place at the sink.

"Yes," Kristine confirmed. "If you don't mind keeping an eye on Carly."

"You know I will," Rowena said with a smile. "It will do you good to go out. Have fun."

"You look beautiful, Kristine," Kyle said, and she could see the appreciation in his eyes.

"Thank you," she said, warmed by the compliment. She turned to Ro. "Just dinner. I'll be home right after."

Rowena beamed. "Don't you worry about Carly. I'll take good care of her."

"I know you will, Rowena." She looked at Kyle. "Shall we?"

"Absolutely."

He offered her his arm, and she took it. They made the short drive to the restaurant. It seemed Kyle was a regular. The waitress made a great fuss over him, bringing Kyle his favorite bottle of cabernet sauvignon.

Menus appeared, food was ordered.

"So how are you holding up?" Kyle asked.

"I'm doing all right," Kristine said. "I have a lot of decisions to make fast."

"Decisions?" he prompted.

"I'd like to stay in Wilding Point for the summer, but for that to happen certain things need to fall into place."

"I see." He sat back in his chair, his expression thoughtful. "Well, I would love it if you stayed on."

"You would?"

"I like you, Kristine, you have to know how much." His eyes glowed. "I think I've always had a secret crush on you, but you were younger, and the timing wasn't right then. It is now."

"I like you, too," she returned, a warmth settling in her chest. For a second, she thought of Rand, but she banished the thought, didn't want to think about him now. Rand Bell mixed her up. Didn't she owe it to herself to give Kyle a chance?

Their appetizers arrived, then their entrees. Wine flowed. They talked, they laughed. When Kristine finished the meal she felt like a new woman, sated and happier than she'd been in a long time.

They left the restaurant, taking a walk around town. So much had changed. Kyle pointed out new places to eat, to shop. He showed her around the newly renovated town square, so cute with its old-fashioned light poles and park benches.

"I should probably head home," Kristine said with regret. "This has been a wonderful break from the sadness."

"I'm glad," Kyle said, giving her hand a squeeze.

Kristine stared out the car window at the water as they made the drive home. Houses along the water were lit, the golden glow in their windows beautiful. They drove through the gates to Wilding House and down the driveway, stopping in front of the house.

Kyle came around the car and helped her out.

"Thank you again for the wonderful evening," Kristine said.

"I'll call you tomorrow," Kyle said, "if I can wait that long."

Kristine stared into his eyes, unsure of what she was feeling. Excitement? Hope? She'd had too much wine for sure.

He leaned in. Her breath caught as his lips brushed against hers.

"What the hell is going on here?"

Lucky's voice came out of the shadows, his tone deadly.

"Lucky," she said, her eyes going to her brother.

He walked down the front steps. "Are you kidding me?"

She didn't understand why he was angry. Was he mad at her, or Kyle?

Lucky stopped in front of Kyle. "Stay away from my sister."

"What are you doing?" Kristine said to her brother. "Stop it."

"Leave," Lucky growled, his eyes locked on her date.

"Lucky," Kyle began. "Kristine told me you were back. Welcome home."

"Welcome home?" Lucky said, the words incredulous. "Are you really glad to see me, Kyle? It sure as hell didn't feel that way fifteen years ago."

"Kristine," Kyle said, his eyes on her now. "I'm sorry."

"For what?" she asked, shocked by Lucky's anger. "Someone tell me what's going on?"

"Ask your boyfriend," Lucky said before stalking away.

"Kyle?" she asked, giving the doctor her full attention.

"We didn't part on good terms," Kyle offered. "I'm sorry. I thought you knew. It was a long time ago."

"Knew what?" she asked. "Lucky never said anything."

Kyle glanced away from her then back. "A misunderstanding between Lucky and me. I'm sorry you got caught in the middle of it. I never expected Lucky to still be angry."

"Why is he angry?"

"We had a falling-out over Beth," Kyle told her. "I guess he hasn't forgiven me for marrying his ex-girlfriend."

Kristine glanced toward the house. Lucky waited for her on the porch, his arms crossed over his chest. To say he looked formidable was an understatement.

"That was a long time ago," she said. "That doesn't sound like Lucky."

"I guess he holds a grudge, or maybe he still carries a torch for Beth?"

"You should go," she said to Kyle. "I'm sorry Lucky ruined the end of our evening, but again, I had a wonderful time."

"So did I," Kyle said. "I'd kiss you again if I didn't think he'd come down here and kick my ass."

She smiled. "Go."

"Good night, Kristine."

She waved.

Kyle drove off. Kristine started up the porch steps. Lucky was gone. She walked straight to the kitchen then out the back door, finding Lucky on the deck.

"What the heck is going on?" she asked. "If this is about Beth Barnes, it has nothing to do with me."

"Is that what he told you?" Lucky asked, his words less harsh and more tired now. "Beth has nothing to do with this."

"Then what?"

"Stay away from him, Kristine," Lucky said. "The guy doesn't have a loyal bone in his body."

He left her, taking the path to the beach.

Shaking her head, Kristine sat down on the lounge chair, more confused than ever.

*   *   *

Rand sat up straighter in his chair.

First Lucky had come out onto the deck, now Kristine. He didn't have to strain to hear what they were saying.

Lucky bounded down the stairs, sailing right past Rand. He didn't even glance his way, didn't see Rand sitting in plain sight on his porch.

Uncomfortable eavesdropping, Rand considered going inside, but their conversation was over now. Kristine remained on the deck. Was she upset? He couldn't tell from here.

Rand tried to remember what he knew about Lucky's arrest. He'd been high and drunk, hitting a car head on, killing the driver, an elderly woman. The police had found ecstasy in the car. Lucky had tested positive for the drug and his blood alcohol level had been sky high. The case had gone to trial, with Lucky getting four years in prison.

But the worst part was his own father had refused to lift a finger to help Lucky. Lucas Wilding had been a crackerjack DUI attorney. He'd made his living representing people exactly like Lucky. He'd built Wilding House with money made from DUI crimes. Not only had Lucas refused to represent his son, he'd left Lucky in the hands of a lazy public defender.

Lucky had maintained all the way through the court process the drugs weren't his, said he'd never taken ecstasy, not once. He didn't remember driving the car. He'd sworn he'd been passed out in the backseat. They'd been no witnesses to back up his story, or any story. No one had seen his car leave the party.

Everyone believed Lucky had simply been too wasted to remember what had really happened.

After his release from prison he'd left Wilding Point, and as far as Rand knew this was his first time back in town.

"Rand?" Kristine called.

Busted. He stood, heading toward her.

"Have you been sitting there the whole time?" she asked as he came up the steps.

"Guilty," he said. "I didn't know what to do. I felt like a deer caught in the headlights."

"I'm glad you heard what Lucky said. Was he totally irrational or was it just me? I only had dinner with Kyle, as friends, nothing more."

"I don't know," Rand said, still trying to digest the news she'd had dinner with Kyle King. "Lucky seems pretty upset about something Kyle did."

"I don't know what to think." Kristine frowned.

"You aren't going to find any answers tonight." He glanced up at the stars.

"I suppose not." She sighed.

"Go to bed," he said. "Things will look better in the morning."

She gave him a tired smile. "Good night."

"Sweet dreams, Kristine."

She waved before going inside, closing the door behind her.

Chapter Eleven

"How much?" Kristine asked, certain she'd heard the attorney wrong.

She sat next to Lucky, across the desk from her father's longtime attorney, John Emmery.

"Five point six million," the attorney confirmed. "That doesn't count Wilding House, the five rental properties he owned, the cars, or the office building on Main Street."

"Holy shit," Lucky said. He exchanged a surprised look with Kristine.

"What does that mean for us?" Kristine asked.

"All children will inherit the cash equally, with a few exceptions I will outline for you. Wilding House has been left to both of you equally. However, should you wish to live in one of the other properties your father owned, it's also a choice either of you can make. Assets can be sold, or divided up equally on paper. You'll have to go through probate, but I'll help you through the process. I have very explicit instructions from your father. There are no stipulations on how the money must be spent, but there are a couple of things you should know."

"Such as?" Lucky asked.

Lucky had been avoiding her since his outburst regarding Kyle. Kristine didn't know what to think about any of it. Instead, she focused on the attorney, glad Lucky was at least taking an interest in their inheritance.

"One hundred thousand has been set aside for Carly's education," the attorney said.

"Oh my," Kristine exclaimed. Never had she dreamed there'd be this much money.

"Lucas also left money to Rowena, five hundred thousand dollars."

"I'm glad," Kristine said, happy for Ro.

"There's more," John continued. "This will come as a shock." He leveled his direct gaze on them. "Your father had another son."

"What?" Kristine and Lucky said at the same time.

"He was born between the two of you. He is your half-brother."

"Dad cheated on Mom?" Kristine said in horror. "Did she know?"

"I believe so, yes," John said. "Your father has set aside money to find this son. I will be hiring a private detective."

"So you're saying the bulk of the estate will be split three ways?" Kristine asked.

"Yes, you're correct." John sifted through the papers on his desk. "With the exception of Wilding House. The house has been left to you and Lucky jointly, as I said earlier."

"Does this son know that Lucas was his father?" Lucky asked.

"I don't believe so," the attorney said. "Your father had an arrangement with the boy's mother. In exchange for child support, she would not tell the boy anything about Lucas."

"Surprise," Lucky said dryly. "The way I see it, this kid was the lucky one."

"Lucky," Kristine said, her own heart taking a hit. "Come on."

"I mean it, Kris. He grew up in a normal household."

"We don't know how he grew up," Kristine said. "He's going to be as shocked as we are."

"I doubt it," Lucky said. "This is so like the old man. Even dead, he's delivering one last nasty surprise."

"God, you're cynical," she said. "Can't you try and see things another way? We have a brother. Frankly, we can use all the family we can get. Let's hope we like him."

"Commendable attitude, Kristine," John said, peering at her over the top of his glasses.

"What's his name?" Kristine asked.

"Cameron Butler," the attorney told them.

"Cam Butler?" Kristine said. "I went to school with a Cam Butler. He was a grade ahead of me."

"Holy shit," Lucky said again, his mouth twisting in disgust.

"Do you remember him, Lucky?" she asked.

"No, I was older. He wouldn't have been on my radar."

"He was different, artsy," Kristine said, remembering the high-school Cam. "Had a girlfriend. She had a tattoo of a hummingbird on her shoulder."

"How do you even remember?" Lucky asked.

"She was in my gym class. He'd walk her there, make out with her. I've seen her change clothes. I remember the tattoo. She was goth, black hair, edgy. No one had a tattoo in those days. I remember her. I remember him. I can't remember her name, or her face, just that tattoo."

John removed his glasses and set them on the desk. "You're correct, Kristine. The boy did go to school with you."

"He was here, right under our noses," she said. "What kind of man does that to his son, to his other children?"

"You know what kind," Lucky said quietly. "He was a manipulative son of a bitch."

Kristine's memories of the father she grew up with came crashing back. In an instant, her days with the new and improved

Lucas Wilding melted away. Sadness hung heavy in her heart. She wanted to be sick. Wanted to crawl in a hole and never come out.

Lucas had betrayed them one final time, managing to ruin all her latest memories with him. Lucky was right.

Lucky must have sensed her shut down because he reached for her hand. "It's going to be okay. We will get through this."

She pressed her lips tightly together to keep from crying.

"Do you need some time?" John asked. "I know I've given you a lot to think about."

"No," Kristine said. "Let's just get this over with."

"Very well." He passed them some paperwork. "There are other valuables listed here. There's a complete list of assets. Take your time, look things over."

Kristine's stomach turned. "This is too much. All of it. I'm not sure how I feel about Dad's money. Right now I'm considering running away and not looking back."

"Ditto." Lucky shook his head.

"No matter what feelings you had for your father," John said, "I hope you'll enjoy his money. Money can open doors for you, give you security and the freedom to pursue your dreams."

Kristine closed her eyes, giving a silent prayer for strength.

"You two have come into a great deal of money," John said. "You will need financial advisors. Nothing needs to be decided now. Kristine, as executor, you can take all the time you want. Go home, get through the memorial service, take some time to breathe."

She nodded. Another surreal experience. "What else do you know about our half-brother?"

"He is the son of a nanny who worked for your parents after Lucky was born. Her name was Susan Butler. She passed away seven or eight years ago. I don't have the exact date here. Cancer. After her death, Cameron disappeared."

"You have no idea where he is?" Kristine said.

"I believe he's out of the country," the attorney said. "But as I said before, I will be putting a detective on the case."

She looked at Lucky. "What are we going to do?"

Lucky shook his head. "I don't know."

"I suggest the two of you give all of this some time to sink in," the attorney said. "Wilding House will continue to run as it always has, your father has seen to that."

"I need some air," Lucky said, rising.

"So do I." Kristine stood. "Thank you, John. We'll be in touch. And please let us know when you find Cameron."

"Of course." The attorney walked them out. "Call if you need anything at all."

"We will," Kristine said.

They stepped out into the sunshine.

"I'll say it again," Lucky said. "Holy shit. I never imagined there would be so much money, or that we'd have another sibling."

"Me either," she said. "And I was worried about making rent."

They were at the car now.

"I love you, Kris," Lucky said.

"I love you, too." She hugged him.

"It's five o'clock somewhere," Lucky said. "Are you game?"

"Absolutely."

* * *

Rand had just ordered a draft beer when Kristine and Lucky walked into the Wilding Point Bar and Grill.

"Hey," he called out, waving them over.

Kristine smiled, making her way to him. "Hi."

"Can I buy you two a beer?" Rand asked. He was seated at the bar. His co-worker, Keith, had gone off to use the john. He offered Kristine Keith's vacant barstool.

"Sure." Kristine slid onto the seat.

Lucky took the stool on the other side of Rand. "You bet. It's been a hell of a day."

"For us, too," Rand said. "Knocked off early when we ran out of materials. Mix-up on some order. What went wrong with your day?"

Kristine smiled. "Let's just have a drink."

"Okay," Rand said, taking the hint to change the subject. "Two more drafts, Joe."

"Sure thing," the bartender said.

Keith returned. "Hey." He grinned. "Company. Now we don't have to drink alone, Rand."

Their beers arrived and both Kristine and Lucky took a long drink. Something was definitely wrong with the Wilding siblings.

"Hey, do you remember a kid named Cameron Butler?" Kristine asked.

Rand shook his head. "No, why?"

"Apparently, he's our half-brother," Kristine said with a shake of her head.

"Whoa," Keith chimed in. "That's heavy. You didn't know?"

"Nope." Lucky took another long drink. "Lucas Wilding was full of secrets."

"Is this good news or bad news?" Rand asked, suddenly understanding their need for afternoon alcohol.

"I'm not sure," Kristine admitted. "I guess time will tell."

"Hey, can I get a shot of tequila?" Lucky asked the bartender.

"Sure thing." The bartender poured the shot and slid the glass to Lucky.

"Want one?" Lucky asked Kristine, right before he shot the tequila.

"No, thanks." She sipped her beer. "One of us has to drive home."

"What's on the agenda for tonight?" Rand asked. "Any interest in barbecuing?"

"I'm in," Lucky said, "if there are steaks involved. Hell, we can afford them."

"I'll supply the steaks," Rand said. "You two look like you can use some cheering up."

Kristine gave him a tight smile. "I just want this week to be over. I need Dad buried. I need closure so I can move forward."

"Any idea what you're going to do?" Rand asked.

"I know I want to go back to school," she said, "and thanks to Dad I'll have the means to do that."

"Will you stay here, or go back to Oregon?" He wanted her to stay and that surprised him.

"That's the million-dollar question," Kristine said. "And a joint decision I'm going to make with Carly." She looked at Lucky. "What will you do after the funeral? Will you leave Wilding Point?"

"I don't know." He sipped his beer. "There's really nothing to go back to. I had a job, but I can work anywhere. I really don't know."

"What were you doing before you came here?" Rand asked. "You haven't said much."

"I moved around, a lot. Worked construction, mostly," Lucky said.

"So you were a drifter?" Keith asked with a grin.

"I guess I was," Lucky said, "until recently. I attempted to get my life together. I've been going to school. I just graduated."

"What?" Kristine said, obviously surprised. "You never mentioned anything to me. What were you studying?"

Lucky smiled. "I completed culinary school."

"Like you're a chef?" Keith asked.

"I studied to become a chef, yes," Lucky said. "However, getting work with a felony on your record is tough."

Kristine set her beer down. "Lucky, you don't need to work for anyone now. You could buy your own place, run your own kitchen."

He shook his head. "I don't know enough about the business end. I just want to cook, create."

"Hire someone," both Rand and Kristine said at the same time.

Kristine's eyes lit with excitement. "Hire someone with the business savvy to run the day-to-day side of the restaurant. You could find a place to buy or rent one that's already open, or start from scratch. It's exciting, Lucky. You can be your own boss."

Lucky's brows furrowed. "I don't know. I'll think about it."

Kristine smiled, the shadows gone from her eyes. "Cook for us tonight. I'd love to see you in action."

"Yeah," Rand chimed in. "I agree. Give me a list. I'll go by the store then meet you at home."

Kristine rummaged around in her purse, producing a pad of paper and a pen. She pushed the items down the bar to Lucky. "Here."

"Steaks?" Lucky said. "Okay. Why not?" He began to write.

For the first time since Lucky had come home, Rand saw a spark of excitement in the guy's eyes. Kristine had the same look. She was jazzed Lucky had an interest in something exciting. If he knew anything about Kristine, he knew she took on everyone's problems, holding the stress tight in her chest. She needed to relax and think about herself now.

Maybe Lucas Wilding had just given her the permission to make her own dreams come true.

"Am I invited to this dinner?" Keith asked, his brows raised in question.

"Of course," Kristine said easily. "The more the merrier. We are going to have a wonderful party tonight."

Lucky passed the shopping list to Rand. "If we're going to do this, let's head home. A meal like this takes time."

"Okay." Kristine stood, pulling out her wallet.

"I've got your tab," Keith said. "It's the least I can do in exchange for a great meal."

"Thanks, Keith," Kristine said, smiling.

"Yeah, thanks, man," Lucky echoed.

Rand stood. "Okay, I'm on my way to the store, see you at the house."

He watched Kristine and Lucky go. They'd come into the bar beaten down and upset, and had left upbeat and smiling.

Rand grinned all the way to the store.

Chapter Twelve

Kristine set the outdoor table, using pretty blue plates that had once belonged to her mother.

The late afternoon was warm, the sun baking the deck, but Kristine didn't mind. The table had an umbrella, providing them shade from the setting sun.

She'd set six places, placing wine glasses at the head of five plates. No wine for Carly. She'd cut some early roses, putting the flowers in a Mason jar. On each side of the bouquet, she had thick, white candles.

To her, the table looked magical, and judging from the smells coming from the kitchen, the food would be top notch.

Lucky had kept the menu a secret from the group, shooing them all outside.

Rand, Keith, Rowena, and Carly sat nearby in the padded deck chairs.

"The table looks so pretty, Kristine," Rowena said.

The housekeeper had wanted to help set the table, but Kristine had declined the offer. Rowena rarely relaxed. Kristine wanted to give Ro a special evening. She'd earned it, after the way she'd cared for Lucas.

"I still can't believe Lucas left me money," Rowena said, her hand on her heart.

"He loved you, Mom," Rand reminded her. "He wanted you to be comfortable."

"We haven't talked about what will happen now," Rowena said. "I guess my job here is done. I should probably move out, get a place of my own."

Kristine turned. "Not necessarily."

Rowena gave her quizzical look. "How so?"

"Let's all just sit tight for a few weeks and see how things shake out," Kristine said. "Our lives are changing. We need time to adjust."

Carly gave her a weird look. Kristine had explained about the money and what it would mean for their family. Carly had been happy for them, eager to do whatever Kristine wanted, even stay in Wilding Point for the summer.

Rowena nodded. "I suppose I could use some time to adjust."

"So you really knew nothing about our mysterious half-sibling, Cam?" Kristine asked Rowena.

Rowena shook her head. "No, hearing about him has been a huge surprise. Your father never mentioned him to me."

"I put in another call to Mom," Kristine said, "but so far she hasn't called back. I wanted to pick her brain, gather all the info I can about Cam. I hated telling her about Dad in a message, but she never picks up."

"You had to let her know," Rand said, his eyes on her.

"I guess." Kristine looked out at the water, so blue against the sky. The sun was still a couple of hours away from setting. She loved this time of evening. The stillness, the beauty.

Lucky appeared in the doorway. "Everyone gather around the table. I'm ready to serve the appetizer." He pointed to Carly. "Hey, squirt, how about you help me serve?"

"Okay." Carly jumped up, smiling. Carly loved Lucky, a fact that pleased Kristine to no end.

Each of them found a place at the table. Rand took the seat to Kristine's right. Keith sat across from Rand, Carly next to him, leaving one end of the table for Rowena, the other for Lucky.

Carly and Lucky exited the house, carrying bowls. They placed a bowl on each plate. Carly ran back inside, returning with more bowls.

"Mussels?" Rand asked, glancing at the dish.

"Mussels," Lucky confirmed. "But not just any mussels. These are infused with a Roquefort sauce." He took his seat at the head of the table. "Watch."

He picked up a mussel, using his fork to dislodge the shellfish. He then dipped the mussel into the bowl, dragging it through the sauce before popping it into his mouth.

They all followed Lucky's lead.

"Oh my," Kristine said, "these are delicious."

"I second that," Rand said.

They spent the next minutes eating, washing down the mussels with a chilled white wine from Lucas' collection.

The next course appeared, a salad dressed with a spicy lemon dressing. Herb-crusted steaks were grilled and served with fingerling potatoes and tender grilled asparagus.

"You're a master," Rand said to Lucky. "This is probably the best meal I've ever eaten."

Lucky grinned. "I only had time for a simple dessert. I hope everyone likes chocolate mousse."

"Are you kidding?" Kristine asked, licking her lips in anticipation.

"I'll invest in your restaurant," Keith said. "I mean it, man. This food is fantastic."

Lucky took a sip of wine. "Eating with friends makes the meal great."

"Hear, hear," Rowena said, lifting her glass. "To Lucky and his grand adventure."

"Cheers," Rand said.

"Cheers," they all echoed, clinking their glasses together.

They enjoyed their dessert as the sun set. Candles sparkled on the table. The air was still and warm. The sky grew pink.

Kristine mellowed, relaxed, melted. This was what she'd wanted all along, family, friends. This was life.

Carly excused herself after dessert, wanting to go inside and play video games. Kristine gave her the go-ahead. She'd been a trouper hanging out with the adults all evening.

Keith headed for home after thanking Lucky profusely for the meal, and again offering to buy into any business Lucky might start.

Rowena rose to clear, but Kristine made her sit back down. "I'll do it. You relax."

"I'll help you," Rand said.

And Kristine let him. They cleared the dishes.

In the kitchen, she loaded the dishwasher and Rand brought the pans to her. It was a team effort. They didn't speak; they didn't need to. It was as if they'd done this before, working as a team. It was easy between them.

When the last counter had been wiped down, Rand handed her the wet towel.

"Done," he said.

"Yes." She surveyed the tidy kitchen, satisfied they'd done a good job.

"One more glass of wine?" he asked.

Being with him was dangerous, but she said, "Love one."

They rejoined Rowena and Lucky.

"Tomorrow will be busy," Kristine said. "Emotional."

"Yes," Rowena agreed. "But we all need this closure the burial will bring. This time to grieve together."

Lucky didn't comment. He toyed with his wine glass. Kristine wondered how he felt about burying their father. Did Lucky regret not having closure with Lucas?

"I think I'll head inside," Rowena said. "I'm tired. All this fresh air will help me sleep like a baby. That and my extremely full stomach." She smiled. "Thank you for the wonderful meal, Lucky."

"My pleasure," Lucky said, his gaze on Rowena soft and filled with love.

Rowena squeezed his shoulder as she passed.

"I'm going to head in, too," Lucky said. "Thanks for cleaning up, but I feel my bed calling me." He rose.

"Good night," Kristine said, praying Lucky would find peace his own way.

"Night," Rand echoed.

Lucky went inside, leaving them alone in the candlelight.

"How are you really doing?" Rand asked her, his attention on her now.

She knew she should end the evening, keep her distance from Rand, but she didn't want to, not yet. "I'm okay," she said. "My life is up in the air. I have decisions to make."

"Will you go back to Oregon?" he asked.

"I don't want to, but that will depend on Carly," Kristine said. "I don't plan on going back to my job. I need to call my boss and break the news."

"So you will stay for the summer." A hopeful note lit his words.

Kristine's heartbeat picked up. "For sure. There's so much stuff to go through. I expect I'll find more than one ghost in Dad's office."

Rand leaned back in his chair. He'd taken the seat beside her, so he too could look out at the water.

"I'm glad you're staying," he said. "You belong here. Wilding House has its princess back."

"I don't know," she said. "I'm not much of a princess, but my roots are here. My family is here. I just have to convince Carly."

"See, sounds like you've made up your mind."

"I guess I have." She smiled at him.

Rand returned her smile. It would be so easy to get lost in his eyes, so easy to kiss him, touch him. Maybe it was time to find out what his real story was.

She might belong in Wilding Point, but she didn't believe Rand belonged here. Like her, he was running from his past. Eventually, he'd figure things out and go back to the life he once loved.

It seemed so clear to her now.

He was kidding himself if he thought this town was big enough for him. Funny, she no longer saw him as a man with no ambition. In fact, he was so far from that man, she couldn't believe she'd ever pegged him as such. Rand Bell was as driven as she remembered, but he'd been through something life changing. Yet she had no doubt he'd find his way back to the life he'd left behind.

Which was precisely why she could never fall for him.

They wanted different things.

"Kristine," he said, her name filled with need.

"I should go in." She stood, putting the brakes on her feelings for him. "Big day tomorrow." She blew out the candle nearest to her.

"Yeah, you're right." Rand took care of the flame closest to him. "I'll see you tomorrow."

She nodded before leaving him there, alone on the deck.

* * *

Kristine had just crawled under the covers when her phone rang.

Kyle.

Should she answer? What had really gone on between Kyle and Lucky? Didn't she owe it to Kyle to give him a chance to air his side of the story?

"Hello," she said, keeping her voice low.

"Kristine," he said with obvious relief. "I wasn't sure you'd take my call. How are you?"

"Okay," she said. "Adjusting to life without Dad."

"I'm so sorry."

"The memorial service is tomorrow," she said. "Family only. That's how Dad wanted it."

"I understand," he said. "I know I wouldn't be welcome."

She shifted onto her side. "What happened between you and Lucky? Why is he so angry?"

"Jealousy?" Kyle said. "Who knows?"

"He says it's not about Beth," Kristine said.

"Really?" Kyle asked, sounding unconvinced. "Then what?"

"Maybe you should ask him?" she suggested.

Kyle sighed.

She switched the phone to her other ear, snuggling more deeply under the covers. "I like you, Kyle, I do. And it looks like I'll be here through the summer for sure. If we are going to be friends, you and Lucky need to clear the air."

"I understand," he said, sounding resigned. "I can be the bigger man."

"I think it's more about airing the truth, whatever the truth is," Kristine said. "Lucky's been through a tragic, horrible ordeal. He was a kid. He made a mistake. He went to prison for four years. I don't know what happened between the two of you, but you need to clear things up with him."

"Okay," he agreed, sounding tired. "Is there anything I can do for you?"

"Just make peace with Lucky," she said. "I like you, Kyle. I don't want to lose your friendship."

"You're a good sister, Kristine," he said.

"I try to be. Family is everything."

"Yes," he said, "I suppose it is."

"It's late, I was about to go to bed."

"Of course," he said, taking the hint. "I'll be thinking of you and your family tomorrow. Please convey my condolences."

"Thank you. I will. Good night, Kyle."

"Good night, Kristine."

She placed her phone on the nightstand. Was Kyle telling the truth? Did he really have no idea why Lucky was angry with him? Tired, Kristine didn't want to think about Kyle anymore.

She turned out the light, closing her eyes. Rand filled her mind. Kind, handsome, sexy Rand. The kind of man a girl had a summer romance with. She couldn't stop thinking about him. He'd gotten under her skin. He invaded her thoughts all the time. Her heart beat faster when Rand was around.

She didn't expect him to stay in Wilding Point, but could they have a summer romance?

Summer romances weren't real. They were a product of sunshine, long days, and hot, steamy nights.

Rand was definitely summer romance–worthy.

But could her heart take the hit when he walked away, went back to the life he'd left behind?

She didn't know. She did know she desperately needed a diversion, and Rand Bell fit the bill to the T.

If Rand was game for a summer romance, she was in.

Chapter Thirteen

They gathered for the memorial near the gazebo, around the pink dogwood, standing in a semi-circle.

The day had dawned clear and hot. Too hot to be wearing black. Kristine felt a trickle of sweat run down her back.

"Bye, Dad," she said, setting the urn deep into the hole Lucky had dug earlier. "I hope you are at peace."

Rowena cried, blotting at her eyes with a tissue.

Kristine took the shovel and scooped up some dirt, tossing it on the urn. Lucky went next, followed by Carly, Rand, and finally Rowena. Lucky completed the burial, packing the last of the dirt on what was left of Lucas Wilding.

A hot breeze blew Kristine's hair across her face and she pushed the strands away.

"He's where he wanted to be," Rowena said. "Part of Wilding House forever."

Kristine nodded. She had no tears—those had already been spent. A melancholy filled her heart. Rand stood near, and his hand found her back, rubbing it. She wondered if he could feel the sweat.

They'd ordered a headstone, but it wouldn't arrive for four more weeks. For now, Lucky placed some flat stones on the grave.

Kristine picked up the box of flowers she'd had delivered, orchids, roses, and stargazer lilies. They all chose flowers, placing them on the rocks.

An offshore breeze stirred the dogwood, sending the leaves shivering. Kristine looked up, half expecting her father to be hiding high in the branches of the old tree.

"It's done," Rowena said. "He's officially laid to rest."

Kristine put her arm around Rowena. "He lives on in your heart, Ro."

Rowena gave her a small smile. "I guess he does."

A car came down the drive.

"That's odd," Kristine said. "We didn't buzz anyone in. Wait, is that Mom?"

The group watched as the car rolled to a stop. The door opened and Veronica Wilding stepped out. Tall, her blonde hair faded now, there was no mistaking Kristine and Lucky's mother.

"Mom." Kristine left the group, surprised and happy to see her mother.

"Hi, honey," Veronica Wilding said, as she embraced her daughter.

"Mom, I can't believe you came," Kristine said.

"I came for you kids," Veronica replied. "Hello, Lucas."

Lucky stepped forward. "Mom."

Veronica embraced her son, holding him tightly. "I've missed you. You look good."

"I've missed you, too, Mom."

Their mother, while she had mental health issues, loved them very much. She'd done the best she could for her children, fighting for them when she was up, leaving them behind when she was down. Over the years, they'd had a sporadic relationship. Veronica had tried harder with Carly, and while the two weren't close, they loved each other.

When Veronica finally let go of Lucky, she zeroed in on her granddaughter.

"Hi, Grandma." Carly hugged her.

"Hi, baby." Veronica embraced Carly tightly. When they parted, she turned to Rowena. "Hello, Rowena, Rand."

"Veronica," Rowena said, smiling. "I'm glad you came."

Veronica and Rowena had a deep mutual respect for one another. Veronica knew Ro had raised her children when she couldn't. Rowena understood Veronica's mental health issues. Together, the two women had done the best they could for Lucky and Kristine.

"Let's all go up on the deck," Rowena suggested. "I helped Lucky put together a delicious lunch for all of us."

They feasted on oysters roasted in the half-shell, barbecued pork sliders, delicate white cheddar cheese pastry puffs, and a spring pea salad that was to die for. They washed everything down with ice-cold champagne.

They didn't share stories about Lucas because there weren't many good memories to share. Instead, they celebrated being together again as a family.

The afternoon wore on. The sun rose higher in the sky.

Carly asked if she could take Hussy for a walk on the beach. Rand said yes. Carly called the dog, who followed her readily.

"How are you doing, Krissy," her mother asked.

"Fine," she replied. "Watching him die was brutal."

Her mother nodded. "I'm sorry you had to go through that."

"I'm not," Kristine said. "It's the best I've ever gotten along with him. I know his personality was altered by dementia and sickness, but it felt good to be needed by him."

"I can imagine," Veronica said wistfully. "He wasn't one to need anybody."

"He thought I was you much of the time," Kristine said. "He'd call me Veronica."

"Goodness, I hope that wasn't too upsetting." Her mother looked at her with sad eyes.

"Not really. I got used to it."

"How about you, Lucas," her mother said, focusing on her son. "Were you able to make peace with him?"

"I made peace with him the minute he cut all ties with me," Lucky said, his mouth tight. "I came home for Kristine."

Veronica smiled sadly. "He was always so tough on you. I'm sorry, Lucas."

"Not your problem, Mom," Lucky said. "And could you call me Lucky?"

"I'm sorry," Veronica said again, her brows drawing together.

"Stop staying you're sorry," Lucky said in a teasing tone. "It's okay, I just prefer Lucky."

"I know." Veronica stared out at the water. "My poor babies. Lucas and I both put you through so much."

Kristine blew out a breath. "We are grownups now. We are fine, right, Lucky?"

He grimaced. "If you say so."

"Mom, did you know about Dad having another son?" Kristine asked.

Her mother frowned. "I did."

"Will you tell us what you remember?" Kristine asked. "Dad has left him an equal share of the estate."

"Well, I'm glad to hear he's doing right by the boy," Veronica said. "It's bad enough the boy had to grow up fatherless."

"The attorney told us Dad had an affair with Lucky's nanny," Kristine prompted.

"He did. I was devastated."

"Ouch," Kristine said. "How awful for you."

Veronica shrugged. "It was a long time ago. Have you met him?"

"No one knows where he is," Kristine said. "There's a detective looking for him."

Veronica nodded. "I can tell you this much. His mother was a good woman. I'm sure she raised him right. After all, I trusted her enough to help me with Lucky. She loved you, Lucky."

Lucky brought his attention back to Veronica.

"Do you remember her at all?" Veronica asked him.

"No," he said. "I don't."

"You were too young, I suppose," Veronica said.

"How long can you stay, Mom?" Kristine asked.

"I have to head back tonight. I work tomorrow." Veronica smiled. "I'm glad I came."

"I'm glad, too," Kristine said, reaching for her mother's hand.

Veronica squeezed her fingers. With her free hand she reached for Lucky. He took Veronica's hand.

"I love you both so much," Veronica said, her eyes bright with unshed tears.

"Love you, too," Kristine replied, her heart full.

Lucky glanced away, but said, "Love you, Mom."

Lucas Wilding had brought them all together again. If he'd done nothing else, he'd done that.

* * *

Kristine couldn't sleep.

She let herself out onto the deck. The scent of the beach calmed her. Inside Wilding House, everyone was asleep, the house silent.

The guest house was dark, leading her to believe Rand was asleep, too.

Probably a good thing.

Today had been emotional, but in a good way. They'd laid Lucas Wilding to rest.

They'd bonded as a family.

In a lot of ways, it had been a really good, healing day.

Still restless, Kristine headed for the beach. There was a full moon and she negotiated the path to the water easily. She knew the path by heart anyway, knew every bush, every rock, knew right where the path ended and the beach started.

Kristine walked straight to the water's edge and breathed.

Nothing smelled better than this beach, salty and clean.

Tomorrow a new chapter would begin for her. A new phase of life where she'd make better choices, fulfill dreams, make a better life for her daughter.

In her heart, she knew their future was here in Wilding Point. She just had to convince Carly.

"Kristine."

Rand. The sound of his voice poured over her like sun warmed wine; desire filled her.

She turned. "You're up late."

"Hussy must have heard you. She woke me. When I let her out I saw you."

Kristine spied Hussy a few feet away.

"Good ears," she said.

"Yep."

Rand reached her. "Everything okay?"

"Just thinking," she said. "Can't shut off my brain tonight."

"I have lots of nights like that," Rand said.

She longed to ask him if he planned on staying in Wilding Point forever, but in her heart she already knew the answer.

He brushed the hair from her cheek.

The touch of his hand on her skin sent a shiver of longing up her spine.

"Have you ever felt like doing something crazy?" she asked.

"Such as?"

She glanced out the water. The moon cast a bright beam on the surface. "I have the strongest urge to get in the water, to swim in the beam of moonlight. Sort of like a cleansing. Out with the old life, in with the new."

He grinned. "I'm game if you are."

Kristine took his outstretched hand. Together they waded into the shallow water. Fully dressed in shorts and T-shirts, sandals on, they trudged on, until the Sound pulled at their knees.

"Ready," Kristine said. "Dunk."

They both executed shallow dives, coming up in the center of the moonbeam.

"It's so cold," Kristine said, laughing.

"I'll say. I'm pretty sure there's shrinkage, if you know what I mean."

She smiled.

They stood now, in the hip-deep water, face to face.

"I'll race you back to the house," she said.

Rand took off before she had the words all the way out. She chased him up the path to the guest house. Once there, he caught her hand.

"Come on in," he said. "I have towels."

"Okay."

He pulled her inside and shut the door.

The guest house looked the same as she remembered it, cozy, worn furniture, faded tile floors. Rand disappeared into the bathroom, bringing them each a towel.

Kristine wrapped the towel around her. "I'm freezing."

"There's a robe hanging on the back of the bathroom door. You're welcome to get out of those wet clothes and use it."

She nodded, going into the bathroom and closing the door. She stripped off her wet clothes, quickly pulling the robe on. Using the towel, she dried her hair, but was still chilled. She spied a hairdryer hanging from the towel bar.

She poked her head out the bathroom door. "Mind if I use your hairdryer?"

"Be my guest."

His voice came from the bedroom and she guessed he was changing into dry clothes, too.

Kristine blew her hair dry. She left the bathroom warm, but with a clean feeling that came from swimming in cold water.

Rand was in the kitchen, dressed in pajama pants and a T-shirt.

"Tea?" he asked when he saw her.

"Love some." She smiled.

The kettle whistled. He made the tea, passing her a mug.

Kristine blew on the tea before taking a sip. "This is great. Just want I needed."

He glanced at her. "Me, too."

They wandered to the living area, sitting on the sofa, sipping their tea.

"Thanks for everything you've done for my family," she said to him.

He took another drink of tea. "What can I do for you, Kristine?"

"What do you mean?" she asked. "You already do so much. You've been there for me, Rand, maybe more so than anyone else."

Their eyes met. Held. The air between them became sultry, an invitation. Kristine's long-dormant sexuality roared to life. Her pulse revved, her heart sped up.

Rand leaned in, kissing her. A soft kiss, gentle, perfect. They parted and he took her tea from her, placing it on the coffee table next to his own.

She had no doubts as to what he wanted because she wanted it too.

Kristine drew in a shaky breath. She willed him to kiss her again.

Rand looked deep into her eyes, and then he was kissing her. She tasted him, her tongue touching his. The kiss deepened, and his need thrilled her. Never had she been kissed like this, consumed, Rand's desire for her a palpable thing.

The robe parted and his hands found her breasts, cupping them, his thumbs finding her nipples.

Kristine moaned. If this was a dream, she never wanted to wake up.

The robe dropped off her shoulders to pool around her waist. She helped Rand pull his T-shirt off and they came together, skin to skin, naked from the waist up.

A hunger built in her, a hunger for him. She couldn't get enough. She ran her hands over his shoulders. His hands found her waist, and he pulled her on top of him, so she faced him, straddled him, the robe still twisted around her hips.

He kissed his way down her neck, to her breasts.

"Oh, yes," she moaned as he sucked her nipple.

He had one hand on each of her butt cheeks and he moved her against him, his pajama pants between their most sensitive parts.

She wanted him, wanted him inside her. She didn't care about anything but the way Rand made her feel, wild, hot, crazy for him.

"Hold on." He left her aching for him as he went into the bedroom, returning a few seconds later, a condom in hand. He smiled devilishly. "Now where were we?"

Kristine returned his smile. "Have a seat and I'll remind you."

He sat, freeing his sex before he pulled her back onto his lap. He jerked her robe away, leaving her naked.

"Ride me, Kristine," he said, his bedroom eyes filled with heat. "I want to watch you. Use me."

He lifted her, and Kristine took him inside. Her back arched as she made room for him. He slid in so easily, she was that ready.

"Man, that's good." He moaned, his hands still on her butt.

He tugged at her, and she caught the rhythm he wanted. Moving up, down, around, faster, until she couldn't catch her breath.

One of his hands slipped between them, inside her, coaxing her to the edge, and then she was gone, arching into an orgasm so powerful it left her gasping.

His cry of pleasure met her ears, and he stilled, gripping her butt, holding her tight against him.

So tight.

Sweat beaded his brow.

No one was cold now.

Her hands were on his shoulders, and she leaned back to better see him. His eyes were closed, as if he couldn't bear to let go of the sensations riding him. She loved the pleasure she saw on his face, loved that she'd put the intense emotions there.

"You okay?" she teased.

His eyes glowed like two hot embers.

"You're kidding, right?" He gave her a wicked smile before sitting up a little taller and kissing her. "Stay with me tonight."

"I can't," she said with regret. "I have a daughter, remember?"

She climbed off him, locating the robe and slipping it on.

When she looked at him again, his pants were back where they were supposed to be. His chest, however, was still bare, the pecs and rock-hard abs doing a number on her. For a second her gaze touched on his tattoo, so sexy she longed to press her mouth to the black ink, but she held back, not sure he'd be receptive to the move.

Instead she settled back down next to him, and Rand drew her into the circle of his arm. He kissed the top of her head.

"You've given me a gift," he said.

"A gift?"

"Remember when you told me you needed to feel alive again?" he asked.

"Yes."

"Baby, I feel alive all over." He grinned.

She smiled. "Me, too."

His arms tightened around her.

"Want to be my summer romance?" Kristine asked, half joking.

"Summer romance?"

"I know you don't belong here, and most likely will leave, but I want a summer romance, and I want it with you. No strings attached. No thoughts for tomorrow. Just time together. I want more of this."

"Makes me sound a little like a piece of meat," he said, but he didn't sound offended, just amused.

"No," she said, staring into his eyes. "Not at all. Just giving you an out. A no-strings summer girlfriend. Heck, I don't even know if I'll be here when summer ends."

"Are you suggesting mutual booty calls as needed?" He smiled.

"I guess I am, and maybe more, someone to take walks with, watch movies, all the things we've been doing anyway, but without the illusion that this is permanent. We both need time to regroup. I know I don't know your whole story, and maybe I don't need to, but if your story is anything like mine, well, what just happened between us is a great stress reliever. It's a summer fling."

"You're an odd one," Rand said, studying her. "Okay, I accept."

She smiled. "And by the way, there was no shrinkage."

He laughed, right before he kissed her again.

Chapter Fourteen

Kristine woke up refreshed, ready to start the next chapter in her life. She stayed in bed an extra five minutes, thinking about her stolen evening with Rand.

She smiled.

He'd been perfect, as good in bed as she'd dreamed he'd be.

And if that made her crass, well so be it. She was a modern woman with wants and needs.

She got up when she heard the front doorbell. Wrapped in her own robe, she went downstairs, finding Lucky had already opened the door.

The sound of Lauren's voice cheered Kristine.

"Lauren," she said, coming to stand beside Lucky. "Come in."

The hospice nurse stepped inside. She carried a beautiful hanging basket of flowers.

"I brought you this," Lauren said. "I hope it adds some cheer to your summer."

"Thank you so much," Kristine said, the gesture of kindness filling her heart. "It's gorgeous."

Lucky took the basket from Lauren. He didn't say anything. Kristine would have been surprised if he had.

He walked toward the back of the house with the flowers.

"Don't mind him," Kristine said. "He's a man of few words."

"He's fine," Lauren said, her eyes lingering on Lucky. "How was the memorial service?"

"Good." Kristine motioned toward the kitchen. "Can I offer you some coffee? I was just heading to the kitchen."

"I'd love some," Lauren said. "But I can only stay a few minutes. I need to be in Centerville in forty-five."

Rowena stood at the sliding glass doors.

"Lauren," Rowena said, when she saw the nurse. "Did you bring the flowers?"

"I did."

"How thoughtful." Rowena touched her heart. "Coffee?"

"Please," Kristine said.

Lauren moved to the door, watching Lucky.

"He didn't say a word," Rowena offered, "just hung up the basket and started for the beach."

Kristine shrugged as Ro passed her a mug of coffee. "That's Lucky. Lots of demons."

Lauren turned to face them. "I am sorry for your loss. I wish I could have done more."

"You did so much." Kristine pointed to a chair. "Let's sit."

Ro passed Lauren a cup of coffee and the three women seated themselves at the table.

"Can I ask you something?" Kristine said to Lauren.

"Of course." Lauren took a sip of coffee.

"Do you enjoy being a hospice nurse?"

Lauren smiled. "I love it, and I'll tell you why. Not only am I helping people leave this world, making them as comfortable as I can, I love working with the families. There's so much love in the room. I feel honored to be a part of someone's passing."

Kristine nodded. "I've always wanted to be a nurse, or a doctor. Thanks to my dad, I can make my dream come true now."

"How wonderful, Kristine," Lauren said.

"I'm considering hospice nursing," Kristine told her. "I think I want to do for other families what you did for us. I couldn't have taken care of Dad without you."

"She's right," Rowena chimed in. "It's truly wonderful what you do."

"Thank you." Lauren gave them a soft smile. "I was happy to help." She set her cup on the table. "I should run. I just wanted to check on you, make sure you were both okay."

"We will be," Rowena said. "We have each other."

Kristine nodded. "I'll see you out."

When Lauren was gone, Kristine went upstairs and dressed. She had a full day planned. First up, a conversation with her boss. Next, a phone call to her landlord to give notice. She couldn't see paying for an apartment she wouldn't be in all summer. If they did go back to Oregon, Kristine wanted to find a little house. If not, they'd stay here, in Wilding House.

Most important today, she needed to have a conversation with Carly about their future. It was this conversation she dreaded the most.

Kristine quickly took care of her calls to her boss and landlord. A few minutes ago, she'd heard Carly come downstairs and join Rowena in the kitchen.

She wanted this, wanted to live here with Rowena. How good would it feel to have another adult around, an adult who had her back, an adult who would step up and be there for Carly if Kristine could not?

And while Rowena had come into her own money, she'd told Kristine she wanted to stay on at Wilding House. The house was home for Rowena.

"Hey, sleepyhead," Kristine said to Carly when she entered the kitchen.

"Hi, Mom," Carly sipped a cup of hot cocoa, a bowl of oatmeal in front of her.

"How about a walk this morning?" Kristine asked. "We could walk to One Way Beach."

"Okay," Carly said easily.

They left the house half an hour later, walking along the shoreline. There was a low tide today, giving them a lot of beach.

Two houses down, Kristine spotted some kids Carly's age. Kristine wondered if the Coopers still lived there, or if they had sold.

The kids also caught Carly's attention.

Kristine waved at the kids. The girl waved back.

"You know we are inheriting some money," Kristine said, breaking the ice on the conversation she'd dreaded as they continued to walk.

"I know." Carly lifted her face to the morning sun.

"We also have Wilding House to think about," Kristine said.

"You mean, like we could stay here?" Carly asked.

"Yes," Kristine admitted.

"Do you want to?" Carly asked, stopping.

"I think so," Kristine said, "but it's a decision we should make together."

Carly looked out at the water. "I'd miss my friends."

"I know, honey, but growing up here, on the beach, it's a once in a lifetime experience."

Carly met her gaze. "Can I think about it?"

"Of course," Kristine said. "I quit my job today."

Carly's eyes went wide. "You did?"

"I don't need to work right now."

"There's that much money?" Carly asked.

She understood her daughter's concern. Money had always been tight for them. Carly had been on a free lunch program at school. They'd had to find creative ways to stretch their budget.

"What are you going to do, Mom?" Carly asked.

"I'm going back to school," Kristine said. "Get my nursing degree. Then I'm going to get a better-paying job."

Carly nodded. "A good plan."

"Let's take the summer and decide what we want to do," Kristine said. "I'd like to stay here and go to school. We'd have Rowena to help out. She could be there for you when I'm at school. She loves us, honey, but bottom line—I want you to be happy."

Carly nodded. "I wasn't all that happy in Oregon."

"You weren't?" Kristine asked, surprised.

"I mean, I love Nan, but school—" Carly pulled a face.

"Nan can visit," Kristine said. "In fact, invite her whenever you want. It would be fun for you to have someone to explore the beach with."

"Okay," Carly said.

"Our lives are going to be different now," Kristine told her. "We don't have to worry about money."

"Can we get a dog?" Carly asked. "You said dogs are expensive. Can we afford one now?"

Kristine laughed. "I suppose we can afford a dog, but before we make a big decision, let's see where we end up. A dog needs a house."

"A beach?" Carly smiled. "If we stay here, a dog would love it. Hussy does."

"Yes, Hussy does," Kristine agreed.

They spent the rest of the walk talking music—a subject Carly loved.

Back at the house, they parted ways, with Carly going to call Nan to invite her friend up for a visit.

Kristine settled in a deck chair.

She'd done it.

She'd quit her job, given notice at her apartment, and had the talk with Carly.

Her eyes settled on Rand's place. She knew he was at work, yet she longed to see him, wanted to be with him.

She had no idea how she'd get away tonight, but she knew she would.

She definitely wanted more of Rand. Much more.

* * *

Rand's mind had been on Kristine all day.

Because they'd gotten behind on the job Friday, they'd worked until after eight tonight. Anxious to get home, he'd made a stop for fast food, pulling into the guest house at eight-thirty.

Would Kristine be waiting for him?

Inside, he ate his meal, his eyes on Wilding House. The lights were just coming on inside, giving the house the welcoming glow he loved.

The light was on in Carly's bedroom, but Kristine's room remained dark.

He'd turned his own lights on, hoping Kristine would see them and come over.

His hunger for food sated, he climbed into the shower, the hot spray easing the aches in his tired muscles.

When he got out, still no Kristine.

What did she mean about him being a summer romance? Was he supposed to romance her? Should he go over there?

What were the rules in this so-called relationship?

He opted to call her.

"Hi," she said on the second ring.

"Hi." He closed his eyes, her voice like a soothing summer breeze. "How are you?"

"Good, great," she said her tone optimistic. "I made a lot of important decisions today."

"I want to see you," he said.

"I want to see you, too," she returned. "Meet me on the deck?"

"I'm there."

He left the guest house, reaching her as she stepped outside.

"I don't know the rules," he said. "Can I kiss you in public?"

She smiled. "Only if no one is watching. I don't want to confuse Carly."

"So this is a secret summer romance," he teased. He could smell her, light, floral, so feminine. His body tightened.

"Yes, if that's okay." She settled into a lounge chair.

He took the chair next to her. "I'll take what I can get."

She smiled, her hand reaching for his.

Rand squeezed her fingers.

"Mom," Carly called from the kitchen.

Kristine let go of his hand. "Out here, with Rand."

Carly came out, plopping on the end of Kristine's chair. "Nan's mom just bought the ticket. She'll be here tomorrow on the six o'clock train. I told her we'd be there waiting."

"Okay," Kristine said, smiling. "I'm so glad she's coming."

"Me, too," Carly said. "It's going to be so fun." She hopped up. "I'm going to go and make us a playlist for tomorrow." She looked at Rand. "Can we do a beach fire tomorrow night?"

"Sure," Rand said, glad to be included. "I'm game."

"We could roast stuff," Carly said. "Make s'mores with candy bars."

Kristine laughed. "Sounds good, honey."

Carly ran inside, leaving them alone.

171

"Where's Mom?" Rand asked.

"Watching television in her room," Kristine said. "Something on PBS she watches every week."

"Lucky?" Rand asked.

"Out, I have no idea where."

"My place?" he suggested.

"I don't know."

"Carly's busy," he said, smiling. "I want you, Kris."

He could read the indecision on her face. "Okay, go. I'll pop inside, make sure everything is fine, then head over."

Rand stood. "Don't be long."

Kristine shook her head.

Rand laughed as he headed to the guest house, a giant smile on his face.

Chapter Fifteen

An hour later, Kristine left the house via the back door. When she'd gone to check on Carly, the pre-teen had wanted Kristine to help her pick out music for the upcoming visit with Nan.

Unable to say no, Kristine had sent Rand a quick text telling him she'd been delayed. She'd spent the next hour helping Carly get ready for her visit from Nan.

She was about to head over to Rand's when Lucky came in.

"Hey," she said.

"Hi." He went to the fridge and snagged a beer. "Want one?"

"No thanks. Everything okay?" He seemed off, upset.

"Your boyfriend wanted to meet," he said, taking a long swig of beer.

"My boyfriend?" she asked, unsure of whom he was referring to.

"Kyle."

"Oh," she said. "He's not my boyfriend, Lucky. I went out with him once—as friends."

"Said you told him to clear things up with me." Lucky frowned. "That true?"

"Yes, but not for my sake," she said. "For yours. I don't know what happened between the two of you, but I don't want to be in the middle."

He studied her. "I never should have come back here."

His words made her sad. "We need each other."

"Do we?" He frowned. "I'm not so sure."

"Promise me you won't disappear," she said, panic rising inside her. "I need you in my life. We can start over together."

"Not here." Lucky glanced away from her. "People here will never forget."

"That's not true," she said, even when she felt he might be right.

"It is true," he said. "I can't make it here, Kris. Even if I wanted to open a restaurant, who would come?"

"I will," she said. "Rand, Ro, Carly."

"Not enough to keep me in business." He took another long pull of beer.

"Don't run away," she said. "We are stronger together."

He didn't reply.

"Stay for the summer," she said. "Please."

"I don't know."

"Promise me," she said. "I just got you back. I need help going through Dad's stuff. I'll need you when we find Cameron. I can't do it all alone."

He set his beer on the counter. "Okay. You win. I'll stay through the summer. I'll help you, but after, I'm not making any promises."

"Fair enough," she said, relief filling her. "Thank you."

"You deserve better than Kyle King," Lucky said on his way out of the kitchen. "The guy's a dick."

"Will you tell me what he did?" she asked.

"Nothing I can prove." Lucky shook his head. "It doesn't matter to anyone but me anymore." He left the kitchen.

Whatever Kyle had done, it was obvious Lucky still didn't like him or believe his story.

Kristine sat at the table, her lust for Rand gone for the time being. She hated how Lucky kept everything inside. Whether

Kyle was guilty of something or not, she wanted her brother to find peace. Tired, sick at heart, she headed upstairs and got ready for bed.

If you're still up, she texted to Rand, *I'm sorry. Too much going on here. I'm going to bed.*

He didn't reply. Great. Now Rand was mad at her too. Kristine turned out the light. She'd only been in bed a few minutes when the outside door to her room edged open.

"You awake?" Rand asked.

She sat up. "Yes."

He came inside, closing the door. "Need some company?"

Her sad heart picked up a beat. "What did you have in mind?"

"Scoot over," he said.

She did. He got under the covers, drawing her into his arms.

"Let me hold you," he said. "That's what summer boyfriends do."

She smiled. "Really?"

"Really."

She snuggled against his chest, her arm going around him. His strength seeped into her, eased the ache in her heart.

"Sleep," he said. "Just sleep."

Kristine did. When she woke up a little after two a.m., Rand was gone.

* * *

The following day, Nan arrived on the six o'clock train.

Kristine and Carly were waiting for her on the platform when she disembarked.

Squealing, the two girls embraced.

Kristine smiled. The girls both started talking at once. They sat together in the backseat on the drive home from the station. Once at the house they ran upstairs to Carly's room.

Seeing the girls together lightened Kristine's spirit.

Rowena had gone out with her knitting club tonight. Lucky was nowhere to be found.

The girls were occupied. Kristine didn't think. She headed down the path to Rand's. His truck was parked out front so she knew he was home.

Hussy met her halfway.

"Hey, girl," she said, petting the dog behind the ears before continuing on.

She could hear the shower the second she stepped inside. She closed the door to the guest house, locking it behind her.

On her way to the bathroom, she removed her tank top and her bra, stepping out of her shorts and panties.

Never had she done anything so bold in her life. Inside the bathroom she had a clear view of Rand, all of him. His back was to her. His soapy hands were in his hair.

She slid the shower door open. "Room for one more?"

He turned, smiling. "Hell, yes."

She slid the door closed.

Rand stepped under the spray washing the soap from his hair, then he reached for her.

Kristine laughed as he pulled her close.

"Where are the girls?" he asked.

"Getting ready for the fire. Painting their nails, and changing their outfits in case boys should walk by."

"So how long do we have?" His eyes took on a feral, predatory glow.

"How quick can you be?" she asked as he gathered her to him, kissing her mouth, her chin.

"Quick and dirty, darlin'," he replied before opening the shower door and returning with a condom.

Rand gave her a devil's smile, then turned her, coming up behind her. Kristine's hands found the tile. Rand nudged her legs wide, his hands on her hips and he pulled her butt against him, his sex bumping at her opening.

Kristine moaned as he slid into her. His hands covered her breasts, his fingers teasing her nipples as he thrust against her.

She couldn't think, only feel, all of him, solid and firm around her. He kissed her ear, her neck.

Rand groaned. "Kristine."

She climaxed, and would have lost her balance if he hadn't been holding on so tight. She pushed against him, and he moaned again, tensing, finding his own release.

"Quick enough for you?" he whispered into her ear.

"Yes, sir."

She moved in his arms, facing him now. He soaped them both up, using the removable showerhead to rinse them clean.

"What are you going to do about your wet hair?" he asked as they dried off.

"Use your hair dryer." She laughed. "I needed this time with you. Thank you."

"No," he said, "the pleasure was all mine. Use the hair dryer and I'll go and get the fire going."

"Okay." She finished up, putting her hair in order. She mopped up the water on the floor and hung their towels up. One last check in the mirror, and she went to the window. The girls ran down the path to Rand.

Kristine waited until they'd gone by before letting herself out of the guest house. She went back to Wilding House and packed up the food, setting the bag and cooler on the deck.

Rand came toward her. "Thought you might need some help."

"Thanks." She smiled.

They walked to the fire together. As soon as they got there, the girls headed down the beach to explore.

Kristine settled into a sand chair. Rand did the same.

"This is nice," she said.

"This is nice," Rand agreed. "The shower, however, was spectacular." He reached for her hand, his fingers playing against hers.

Her insides curled. They'd just had sex and she wanted him again. Never had she experienced lust like this, the pull heavy and low in her center. Her fingers traced his tattoo, the tall trees, the line of the lake. "Tell me about this. There has to be a story here."

His mouth tightened. "It's a place I used to go. Tall Pines."

"And it's significant because?"

"It just is."

She studied him. Clearly he didn't want to talk about the tattoo, and for now, that was okay. His silence didn't upset her. Their relationship was new. Best guess told her the tattoo had something to do with his lifestyle change.

The girls ran toward them. Rand let go of her hand. They spent the next minutes eating the fried chicken and fresh-cut watermelon she'd packed. Summer food.

Eaten with a summer boyfriend.

Kristine smiled.

Two kids came from the beach toward them.

Carly hopped up. "Okay if Patty and her brother Kevin come over?"

"Sure." Kristine smiled at the brother and sister who joined them. "You two live a few houses down, right?"

"Yes," Patty said.

Introductions were made. Kristine kept the kids supplied with drinks, then helped them all make s'mores.

Around ten, Patty and Kevin's parents walked down to get them.

"Hi, I'm Candy and this is my husband, Bill," the woman said. "We're the parents of these two."

"I'm Kristine," she said. "And this is Rand. Carly is my daughter."

"I hope it was okay for Patty and Kevin to crash your beach fire," Candy said.

"Of course." Kristine smiled.

"You're all welcome," Rand said.

"You live in Wilding House?" Candy asked.

"Lucas Wilding was my father," Kristine told her.

"Was?" Bill prompted.

"He passed away a little over a week ago."

Candy exchanged a stricken look with her husband. "We are so sorry, Kristine."

"Thank you," she said. "He was very ill. He's at peace now."

"Are you home to stay?" Candy asked.

"Carly and I are trying the place out this summer," Kristine explained. "We are keeping our options open." She smiled at Carly, but Carly only had eyes for Kevin.

"Well," Candy said, "we should get these two home. It was so nice to meet all of you. I'm sure we'll see a lot of you this summer."

"Yes, nice to meet you, too," Kristine said.

Rand stood, shaking Bill's hand.

As the family walked away, Rand said, "Nice people."

"They are," Kristine said, her eyes on Carly, whose eyes were on Kevin. She gave a nod toward her daughter. "Not sure if this is good or not."

Rand grinned. "Ah, summer romance."

"Shut up," she said, kicking some sand on him.

His smile widened, causing Kristine to smile back.

Summer romance indeed.

* * *

Rand let himself into the cottage.

In the bathroom, he noted the towels draped over the shower door. The hairdryer neatly put away. A woman's touch.

Not just any woman.

Kristine Wilding.

She was something all right. Sexy as hell and possibly up for anything.

He liked her—a lot.

He liked being her summer boyfriend, even if the role was on the down low.

Rand got into bed, picking up his phone.

"Hello," Kristine said on the first ring.

"Just wanted to say good night."

"Thanks for a wonderful evening," she said.

"Are we allowed to go on a real date?" Rand asked.

"Hmm," she said. "Let me think for a minute."

"Just dinner, wine, summer romance," Rand coaxed. "No one has to know. We could go into the city."

"I'd love to," she said. "I'd have to get Rowena on board as a sitter."

"Easy," he said. "She lives for that stuff."

"We'll have to wait until Nan goes home," Kristine said. "I'm in charge of her."

"You're worth the wait."

She laughed softly.

"You sure you can't sneak over?"

"Positive," she said. "And don't come over here. I'm a responsible mother tonight."

"Pity," he said with regret. "I smell like campfire. I could use another shower."

"Go to sleep, Rand," she said in a playful tone.

"You, too," he said. "See you tomorrow."

"Okay. Good night."

The line went dead. Rand rolled over, closing his eyes, reliving every moment of his shower with Kristine. Perfect. Then she'd asked about his tattoo. For some reason, he'd been unable to tell her about Grif, about the tattoo. She hadn't pressed him for details.

The familiar sadness ran through him, but the emotion wasn't quite as strong. His sorrow had faded some and he knew that had to do with Kristine. She was slowly pulling him back to the land of the living.

He had to make a decision soon. His six-month sabbatical was nearly over. The clock was ticking. If he didn't go back to New York, return to work, he'd lose his job. His boss, the firm, had both been so patient with him. They'd gone above and beyond giving him the time off.

Was he ready to go back? No. Yes. Maybe. He didn't know. Just the fact that his answer wasn't a solid no told him he was moving forward again.

Maybe he wasn't as broken as he'd thought.

Chapter Sixteen

Nan stayed until Friday.

Early Friday afternoon, Kristine put Nan and Carly on the train. Carly was spending the weekend with Nan, heading out to the family's beach place in Lincoln City.

That left Kristine free for the entire weekend.

She needed a break. She'd spent the week going through her father's office. She'd found several years' worth of canceled checks made out to Cameron's mother, confirming everything the attorney had told them.

She'd recycled tons of paper, packed up books and knickknacks neither she nor Lucky wanted. She hadn't tackled her father's bedroom yet. She wasn't ready for the task and probably wouldn't be for a long time. In fact, she wondered if Rowena would rather tackle his room on her own.

Lucky had helped during the week. He'd been her muscle, schlepping paper and boxes out to the recycle bin. Hauling garbage bags to the can. She could sense how unhappy Lucky was, yet she wasn't willing to release him from his commitment to spending the summer with them.

There'd only been one unpleasant note to the week. Kyle had come by, wanting to see her. She'd told him no, but he'd persisted, drawing Lucky outside.

The two men had faced off. Kristine had stepped between them, asking Kyle to leave. He'd done as she'd asked. Lucky had stormed away.

The whole scene had been unpleasant. What had really gone on between Lucky and Kyle? She had no intention of getting between the two men. Dating Kyle had been nice, but not firework fantastic like she had with Rand. And although Rand wasn't permanent, she wasn't willing to settle for a man who didn't ring all her bells.

Rand came in through the back door. "I have an idea."

"Oh?" She put the glass she held in the dishwasher and closed the door.

"We could stay here for the weekend," he said, "but my mother and Lucky are here. Not very private."

She smiled. "I'm listening."

"What about a weekend away?" he suggested. "Snoqualmie Falls, or Sapphire Lake Lodge?"

"Do you really think we could get a reservation at either of those places? It's summer."

"Don't know, but I'll check if you're game." Rand closed the space between them, kissing her. "I want you all to myself."

"Are you kidding?" Lucky asked as he walked into the kitchen. He shook his head. "And I was worried about Kyle."

"Busted," Kristine said, smiling. She didn't care if Lucky knew. He barely said a word to anyone. He was no tattletale.

"Shall I make some calls?" Rand asked, his eyebrows raised in encouragement.

"Sure." She leaned against the kitchen counter.

Rand left, whistling as he walked.

"I knew he'd get to you," Lucky said, snagging an ice tea from the fridge.

"We're friends," she said.

"With benefits," Lucky shot back with a smirk. "Don't bother to deny it."

"So what if we are? I like him. He gets me. I'm not stupid. I know he doesn't belong in this town. What we have is a summer romance. You should get one yourself. Might make you easier to be around."

Lucky shook his head. "Not much chance of finding a willing woman in this town."

"You'd be surprised if you put yourself out there," Kristine said. "You are a handsome guy. Some women like the brooding, dangerous type."

"With a nice, long police record," he reminded her.

She shrugged. "Your record's not long. You made one mistake. It just takes the right girl. Don't close yourself off to love, big brother." She patted his shoulder as she passed.

Upstairs, she took a look at her wardrobe. Did she even have anything nice enough to take to one of the places Rand had suggested?

She was cruising through her closet when Rand called.

"Sapphire had a cancellation. We got a room for the weekend."

"I've never been there. What do I need?" she asked, excitement in her belly.

"Shoes for hiking. Something nice to wear to dinner, they have a top-notch restaurant. We might kayak. There's lots to do."

"Okay, got it. When do you want to leave?" she asked.

"We can check in tonight if you're game," he said.

"I can be ready in half an hour," she returned. "What are you going to tell your mom?"

"I got you to agree to go hiking," he said. "She'll buy it, and it's the truth."

Kristine laughed. "Meet you downstairs in thirty minutes."

Kristine quickly assessed her wardrobe. Hiking clothes were easy. She even had a pair of sturdy hiking shoes with her. She'd thrown in her black dress from the memorial service, and could use it for dinner. Into the suitcase went the black dress, and two sun dresses. She packed two pairs of dressy sandals, flip-flops, shorts and tops. Too many clothes for one weekend, but she didn't care. She added toiletries, and a light jacket before zipping the bag.

"Big bag," Rand said when she came downstairs, "for hiking."

Rowena smiled. "I'm so happy you two are doing something fun. Lucky didn't want to go with you?"

"No," Kristine said. "He's not much of a hiker."

"Have a good time," Rowena said. "See you Sunday."

They made the four-hour drive to Sapphire Lake Lodge, much of the drive along the coast. They chased the sun the entire way, arriving as the sun went down. While Rand checked them in, Kristine wandered outside. The lake was breathtaking, deep blue, gorgeous. A fire blazed near the shore. Several people sat in the Adirondack chairs placed around the property, drinking wine or cocktails. There was a gazebo, a young couple necking inside.

The place reminded Kristine of an old-time beach club. So civilized, yet brimming with summertime fun.

"Nice," Rand said as he joined her.

"Gorgeous." She kissed him. "I can kiss you here."

"Freedom." Rand kissed her back. "We can't get in the restaurant tonight, so I ordered us some room service and a bottle of wine."

"Sounds perfect."

Their room looked out at the lake. It was an older room, but quaint and cozy. They quickly unpacked. Their dinner arrived and the waiter set the food up on the small table in front of the window.

They ate giant scallops with a hot bacon salsa, garlic mashed potatoes and fresh green beans. Rand had ordered a pinot that complemented the shellfish perfectly.

When they finished the meal, they set the tray in the hall and set out on a moonlight walk along the water. They found the path easily, taking their time, enjoying the beautiful scenery.

They came upon a bench and sat.

"It's beautiful here," Kristine said. "This was a great idea."

"The best is yet to come." Rand kissed her cheek.

Kristine met his mouth, kissing him, her hands in his hair.

They kissed until the sound of distant laughter caused them to come up for air.

"Let's go back," Rand whispered against her mouth.

She stood. "Let's go."

They made the short walk back to their room. With frantic hands they tore off each other's clothes, and then they were on the bed, naked.

Rand took her quick and hard, leaving her gasping.

Slowly, Kristine floated back to earth, her eyes closed, his body covering hers, his rough breath caressing her neck.

Had anything ever felt so right?

"Perfect," Rand said, as if he could read her thoughts.

"Perfect," she agreed, a contented smile on her face.

*   *   *

After a fabulous breakfast of salmon benedict, Kristine and Rand spent the morning doing a five-mile hike. In the afternoon, they lazed around on deck chairs, soaking up the sun. Before dinner they kayaked around the lake. They made it back to the lodge in time for happy hour, wine and cheese in front of the big fireplace in the lobby.

Their dinner reservation wasn't until seven-thirty, giving them time to enjoy their wine, then take a nap before dinner.

"What a great day." Kristine sipped her merlot.

"I'd forgotten what it's like to live like this," Rand said.

"What do you mean?" she asked.

"Fine dinner, good wine, being pampered."

"The life you had before you came back to Wilding Point." She gave him her full attention. "You were on the fast track, right?"

He frowned. "For what it was worth."

"I know you loved your life," she said. "Don't bother to deny it. It's okay."

"I did," he admitted. "But that life comes with a dark side. A price."

"How so?"

"It just does," he said. "I don't want to talk about my past now. Let's just enjoy the moment."

Kristine leaned back in the chair. "All right."

Rand frowned. Was he remembering his old life, his real life? Would she lose him now to those memories?

You're going to lose him eventually, she reminded herself. He's your summer boyfriend. *Summer*. Not forever.

Rand's fingers laced with hers. "I'm here now. This is the life I want."

She bent and pressed a kiss to his tattoo. She didn't believe him. He was capable of so much more than he was doing, just as she was. She understood the need for something greater.

Kristine sipped her wine. "I could stay here forever."

"I know." Rand gave her a tender smile. "Believe me, I know."

* * *

Sunday morning, after another fabulous breakfast, this one country potatoes with poached quail eggs and the best homemade blueberry coffee cake ever, Kristine and Rand headed out for another hike.

Checkout time was eleven. They got an early start, completing the hike, leaving them plenty of time to make love slowly before packing up to head home.

Kristine glanced at Rand as she zipped her suitcase. Something had shifted in him. He seemed more thoughtful, quiet. Had she stirred up memories with all her talk about his tattoo and the life he'd left behind? Was he, even now, thinking of what he'd given up?

A life that would never include her. She didn't want fast-paced or exciting. She wanted to raise her daughter, study, get a job she could be proud of—all of it in Wilding Point.

Kristine paused. She wanted to stay in Wilding Point. She wanted it so much. She'd all but quit her life in Oregon, even without Carly fully on board.

"You okay?" Rand asked as he passed, rubbing his hand on her back.

"Just thinking," she said.

"About?"

"Starting over in Wilding Point." She smiled. "Until this moment, I didn't realize how much I wanted to stay here, raise Carly here."

He nodded. "It's a great area, for sure."

"Are you okay?" she asked. "You seem distracted."

"Are you kidding?" he replied, grinning. "I had the time of my life this weekend."

She smiled. "Really?"

"Absolutely."

"Me, too."

He kissed her, and Kristine forgot all about Rand's funky mood. This was the Rand she loved, her summer boyfriend, sexy and passionate.

"Stop," she said, breaking the kiss, "we have to check out."

"I'm going to miss this when we get home," he said. "Back to sneaking around."

He grabbed their suitcases and started for the door.

"You have to admit, it's kind of fun." She laughed. "There's a certain sexy danger to all the sneaking around."

He shook his head. "All this weekend did was whet my appetite for you. Prepare to get creative on the sneaking around. I want you more than ever."

His words sent her pulse racing and instant lust filled her.

"I look forward to the pursuit," she said, giving him a push toward the lodge lobby. "Let's go before we get creative here in the hallway."

Rand's smile widened.

She'd miss him when he left her. For now, she'd enjoy Rand as long as she could.

She hoped it was going to be a long, hot, summer.

Chapter Seventeen

"Mom, can I go over to Patty's?" Carly called from upstairs.

In the kitchen, Kristine walked to the base of the staircase. Carly stood at the top, her phone pressed to her ear. "I suppose, but I want you home for dinner."

Carly smiled. "I can come," she said into her phone. "Be there in five."

Since Carly's return on Monday, she and Patty had been inseparable. While this was what Kristine wished for, that Carly would make friends, as a mom she worried a little about Patty's brother, Kevin. Carly was only twelve. Way too young to be boy crazy, but boy crazy she was, and Kevin was just old enough, by two years. She had a bad case of puppy love for him.

A few minutes later Carly bounded down the stairs. "Bye," she called on her way out.

"Bye." Kristine finished wiping down the counter. It was too soon for Rand to be home. Too bad. The perfect time to sneak around was while Carly was out.

Tired of sorting through her father's papers, Kristine sat in front of the computer. She booted it up and searched for the University of Washington, typing in "Nursing."

She spent an hour reading through the information provided, including how to apply. She had her Associate of Arts degree, and she prayed those credits would transfer to the UW, or whatever school accepted her.

Restless, she decided to go for a walk. She hit the beach, the sun warm on her head. She had to go back to Oregon and tie up their lives there. She needed to move out of her apartment, go by the hospital and pick up her things.

First, she had to talk to Carly, get a clearer idea of how her daughter felt about staying on in Wilding Point, now that she had had a chance to think about it some more.

Her phone vibrated. Kyle's name flashed on the screen.

"Hi, Kyle," she said. Kyle was nothing else if not persistent.

"Kristine," he replied, his tone warm. "How are you?"

"Busy," she said. "There's a lot to do when settling someone's estate."

"Of course there is," he said. "Look, I'm sorry my relationship with Lucky has come between us, but does it have to? I like you, Kristine. I'd love to take you out again."

In her heart she was done with Kyle. He'd never been exactly the right fit for her, no matter how much she'd wanted him to be.

"I'm sorry, Kyle," she said. "It's not you, or even Lucky, it's me. I need some time."

"Of course," he said. "You're grieving. I'm being insensitive."

"No," she said. "You're not. I want to take the summer to reassess my life. Everything has changed for me."

"You have my number," he said, the words heavy with disappointment. "When you're ready, call me."

"Thanks for being so understanding," she said.

"I think we could be great together, Kristine."

"Good-bye, Kyle."

"Good-bye."

She slid her phone into her pocket, her attention on the water. She finished her walk and was approaching the path to the house when she spied Rand pulling in. Kristine quickened her step. He was home early.

Rand was already inside when she reached the guest house. The front door was open.

"Hello?" she called.

"Come in," Rand said.

He stood in the kitchen, unloading groceries.

Kristine pulled the screen open, stepping inside. "You finished early today."

He shut the fridge, then took her in his arms.

"I've missed you," he said, kissing her. "It's torture to have you so close, yet so far away."

Kristine kissed him back. "I've missed you, too."

"Where's Carly?" he asked.

"At Patty's."

He grinned.

Kristine smiled back.

And then his hands were tugging her T-shirt up over her head. She tore at his shirt, his fly, as she shimmied out of her shorts.

Rand picked her up, and she wound her legs around his hips. He carried her to the bedroom.

He was so hard for her, so ready, and Kristine was frantic to have him.

"No foreplay," she rasped. "Take me."

His eyes darkened as he quickly rolled on protection. He entered her in one thrust. Kristine arched off the bed. This is what she wanted. Wild sex. Rand drove into her again and again, taking her to a full-out orgasm quicker than he ever had before. She shattered into a million glittering pieces.

"Rand," she said, his name sounding like a dirty word.

He thrust, finding his own release, tensing.

She stroked his back, her hands running over his butt. Slowly, he relaxed until his body grew heavy against hers.

"That was so good," Rand said, his breath coming fast. "Man."

Kristine smiled. "Well, it's been a few days."

He laughed. "I guess it has."

The sound of young voices caused them both to freeze.

"Carly," Kristine whispered. "We left the front door open."

Rand rolled from her, pulling on his pants.

"My clothes are out there," Kristine said, panicked now.

"Shhh." He held a finger to his lips before slipping out of the bedroom. He returned a few seconds later with her clothes. "They're up on the deck."

Kristine shot off the bed and into the bathroom, dressing quickly.

Rand was in the kitchen when she emerged.

"They're just hanging out." Rand pointed to the house.

Kristine saw the kids—Patty, Kevin, and Carly—sprawled on the deck chairs.

"I heard her call for you," Rand said.

Kristine peeked out the window. "She'll see me if I leave."

"Would that be so bad?" He shrugged. "We're dressed. You could be visiting. She knows we're friends."

"I think it looks bad," she said, unsure of what to do.

"You could go out my bedroom window and come back via the beach path."

"Seriously?" She shook her head.

"You wanted the thrill of sneaking around," he reminded her with a chuckle. "What's the matter? Don't think you can do it?"

"Oh, I can do it," she said, her competitive streak rearing up. "Watch me."

Rand followed her into the bedroom, an amused smile on his face. Kristine opened the window and climbed out, landing in the soft dirt.

"I'll see you later," Rand said, blowing her a kiss.

Kristine ran for the beach, then back to the path.

Rand was sitting on his porch when she passed. He waved.

She waved back, giving him a wide smile.

"There she is," Carly said when she spotted her mother.

"Hi." Kristine came up the steps. "What are you kids up to?"

"Can I spend the night at Patty's?" Carly asked. "Her mom said it was okay. Her dad is going to barbecue tonight."

"I don't know," Kristine hedged, her eyes on Kevin. He looked innocent enough, but he was still an adolescent boy.

"Please, Kristine," Patty said. "I really want Carly to spend the night. Mom said we could sleep on the sun porch."

"I suppose it's okay," Kristine said, "but I'd like to talk to Candy just to confirm."

"Sure," Patty said, dialing up her mom.

Kristine had a quick conversation with Candy, who told her all the same things the girls did. Kristine agreed to the overnight. The girls shrieked with joy, running inside to pack Carly's bag.

Kevin stayed put.

Rand joined them. "Hey, Kevin."

"Hey," Kevin said with a nod.

"What's happening over here?" Rand asked. "Lots of girls screaming."

"Carly is going to spend the night at Patty's," Kristine told him, her mind spinning with all the possibilities for them tonight.

"Great," Rand said making eye contact with her.

Kristine knew his thoughts echoed her own.

Kevin stood, probably bored with them. "I think I'll go home."

"Bye, Kevin." Kristine watched him go.

"She'll be okay," Rand said, reading her mind. "He's a guy, but I doubt he knows what to do with a girl."

"Don't be so sure," Kristine said. "I think all guys are born with one goal in mind: getting a girl to sleep with them."

Rand laughed. "I suppose you're right."

Rowena came outside, bringing them each an ice tea.

"Thank you." Kristine accepted the glass from the older woman.

"Thanks, Mom," Rand said.

"I hear the girls are out for the evening." Rowena sat in Kevin's vacant chair. "Anyone up for playing a board game tonight?"

Rowena loved to play games, but playing board games was the last thing Kristine wanted to do while Carly was gone.

"I was just about to invite Kristine out to dinner," Rand said.

"Oh, that's nice." Rowena smiled.

"But we could stay here," Kristine said, her heart going out to Rowena. The woman had just lost her lover. She had to be lonely, and Kristine knew she was sad.

Rand was no dummy. He caught on quickly. "Sure, Mom. We'll play."

Rowena beamed. "Fantastic. I have beef stew on the stove. We can eat first, then play." She stood. "I'll go finish getting dinner ready."

"Thanks, Ro," Kristine said.

"You didn't have to say okay to the game," Rand said, "but thank you."

"She needs us," Kristine told him. "She's probably grieving more than anyone."

"Yeah." Rand ran his fingers through his hair. "But once she's in bed, you're all mine, Kristine Wilding."

"Yes, sir, I am." She grinned.

The girls ran out of the house, Carly with her backpack on.

"See you tomorrow, Mom," she said.

"Wait a second." Kristine stood, hugging Carly. "Have fun, girls."

They giggled before running down the steps, arms linked as they ran down the beach.

* * *

Kristine came awake to the feel of Rand's lips against her neck.

"Hmm," she said, her mind clicking on. They'd made love twice during the night, and Rand was at it again.

The man had stamina.

"What time is it?" she asked.

They were at his place, and she didn't want to get caught there.

"Seven-thirty."

Carly wouldn't be home yet, but Kristine knew Patty had a nine-thirty orthodontist appointment.

Kristine rolled into Rand's waiting arms. He kissed her like a starved man. Never had she been kissed like this. Each time felt like the first time. Sex with Rand never felt routine, but instead was charged with sexual energy.

She never got enough of him.

Maybe it was her, not him. He did something to her no other man had ever done before. She wanted him—all the time. She'd never been as attracted to anyone else, and if she wasn't careful, she'd get her heart broken.

He ran his hand down her hip, lower, his fingers finding her most sensitive spot.

Kristine forgot to think. She opened for him, and he quickly brought her to orgasm.

He rolled her on her back, and she stretched her arms above her head, giving him total access to her body. He kissed her everywhere and just when she couldn't take it anymore, he entered her, taking his time, using his most male part to tease her until he drove her wild.

She wanted to reciprocate, do all the things to him he'd just done to her, but he found his release, crying out, the sound so arousing, she climaxed again.

When they parted, he said, "I've never been with anyone as responsive as you, Kristine."

She made a purring sound. "I've never been so responsive. You bring it out in me."

"Do I?" he asked, sounding insanely pleased.

"Yes, you do."

He gathered her to him, and again she wondered if he would break her heart. For now she decided he was worth the risk. Yes, Rand was definitely worth the risk.

* * *

Rand breathed in the scent of Kristine's hair. Flowers, sunshine, salt air. She felt so good in his arms. It was so easy to pretend this was real life, but he knew it wasn't, knew it deep in his gut.

Since his conversation with Kristine about his "real" life, pieces of his past kept resurfacing.

He'd left his life in New York behind so easily, and he knew why. He'd been a coward, unable to face his guilt, his demons.

His life dream had never been to live in Wilding Point. He'd never wanted to do manual labor. He'd studied his butt off to get his master's in business, and he'd been damn good at his job. Too good. So good he'd gotten caught up in the hype, in the risk. So much so he'd lost his best friend.

He'd been a terrible friend.

Rand touched his tattoo. Every time he looked at it, the trees, the lake, his guilt returned one hundred fold. It's why he'd gotten the tattoo. He never wanted to forget his part in Grif's death.

He never wanted to forget Grif.

How did he get past his guilt? He'd left his life behind and thanks to Kristine, he now recognized what he'd done. He'd punished himself, taking himself away from the job and lifestyle he loved. In a sense, he'd put himself in hell, if one could call Wilding Point hell.

Did he want to leave Wilding Point and go back to New York?

Rand inhaled again, Kristine's scent winding though him, clear to his gut.

He liked her, a lot, but deep down was she enough to keep him here? He wasn't fool enough to believe she'd go with him to New York. She didn't belong in the city. No, he couldn't picture her there. She belonged here, the princess of Wilding Point.

Rand closed his eyes. He didn't want to think anymore. For now, he just wanted to be in the moment. Always in the moment.

Chapter Eighteen

Lucky was waiting for Kristine when she entered the kitchen, via the deck door. "Have fun?" He gave her a cocky smile.

She slid the screen closed. "What do you mean?"

"You know what I mean." Lucky poured himself a cup of coffee. "I know Rand's a good guy, but he's a player, Kris."

"I know who he is," she said defensively.

"And you're okay with getting played?"

"How do you know I'm not the one playing him?" she asked.

"Are you?"

"Maybe." She poured her own cup of coffee. "I know what I'm doing, Lucky. Rand and I know what we have. A summer romance."

Lucky shrugged. "Well, okay." He drained the last of his coffee before putting his mug in the dishwasher.

"You haven't been around much lately," she said. "What have you been up to?"

"A little of this and that," he said, totally non-committal.

She eyed him. "What does that mean?"

He shrugged again, smiling.

Smiles were rare from Lucky. This smile led her to believe he had something up his sleeve. She prayed it was something good.

"I'll see you later," he said on his way out of the kitchen.

She let him go, his words heavy on her mind. Rand had been a player, but was he still? Kristine frowned.

"Mom," Carly called as she burst into the kitchen via the deck doors.

"Hi," Kristine said, Rand forgotten. "How was the sleepover?"

"So fun," Carly said with enthusiasm. "Patty and I are going to hang out at the beach today after she gets back from her orthodontist appointment."

"That sounds fun," Kristine said. "Did you get breakfast?"

"I had a bowl of cereal," Carly told her.

"Can I talk to you for a minute?" Kristine asked.

"Sure." Carly sat at the table.

Kristine took the seat opposite her daughter. "Let's talk about staying in Wilding Point again."

"Okay," Carly said.

"I vote to stay," Kristine told her, deciding to just be blunt. "I'd love for you to finish growing up here."

Carly pursed her lips together. "Can I think about it a little longer?"

"Of course you can," Kristine said. "Your happiness is the most important thing. Like I said, we both need to want to make this move, to change our lives."

Carly stood. "Message received, Mom. I'm going to go and get ready for the beach."

Kristine watched her daughter leave. Would Carly vote to stay? She hoped so. This decision was right. She knew it in her heart.

Kristine went upstairs to her childhood bedroom. She looked at the pink walls, the white bedspread with the pink rosebuds and green leaves. It was time to make changes, update this room, make it hers. Carly had been staying in the guest room. The girl also needed her things from the apartment as well as new, updated decorations fitting her upcoming teen years.

It was time to go to Oregon and close up the apartment.

Their things would make Wilding House feel more like home.

Decision made, Kristine knew it was also time for her to check in with the attorney. Time to get her affairs in order.

Their new life was calling. Kristine had never been more sure about anything.

* * *

Kristine, Rowena, and Carly were having dinner on the deck that evening when Rand pulled in next to the guest house.

Kristine's heart sped up and she wondered if Rowena or Carly could see the excitement on her face.

She'd missed Rand today.

He exited the truck and went inside.

Kristine assumed he was showering before joining them. When he didn't appear after thirty minutes, she began to worry. Why wasn't he joining them?

Patty and Kevin came up the path. Carly jumped up, running to meet them halfway.

"New friends," Rowena said. "I'm glad."

"Me, too," Kristine agreed.

Patty and Kevin followed Carly up the steps.

"We're going to watch a movie," Carly announced on her way by.

"Okay," Kristine said. "Have fun."

Rowena stood and began clearing the table.

Kristine helped her. When the dishes were done, Rowena produced a plate of food.

"Would you mind taking this over to Rand?" Rowena asked, a spark of mischief in her eyes.

"Sure," Kristine said, with a knowing shake of her head.

She carried the food to Rand's, knocking on the door. "Rand?"

"Come in," he said.

She found him sitting on the couch, a bottle of tequila in front of him. Not good.

"I brought you some dinner." She set the food on the coffee table. "Drinking alone?"

"More like having a toast with an old friend," he said.

"May I sit?" she asked, wondering if he would finally tell her everything.

"Thanks for bringing the food over," Rand said, "but I want to be alone, okay?"

His words stung. "Okay."

Kristine left him, her heart heavy. Back home, she went to Rowena.

"Will you tell me what happened to Rand?" she asked.

Rowena gave her a long look before asking, "What's wrong?"

She didn't know how much to tell Rowena.

"Is Rand okay?" Rowena asked.

"I'm not sure," Kristine admitted. "He's sitting there alone with a bottle of tequila."

"I'll go over," Rowena said, starting for the door.

Kristine caught her arm. "No. Don't. He wants to be alone."

Rowena's eyes took on a worried look. "He holds too much inside."

"I agree," Kristine said. "I think it's my fault. I said some things to him about running away from his life. I think I made him think about things he's buried."

"Some things can't stay buried forever," Rowena said sadly.

"What happened, Ro?" Kristine pressed.

"His friend, Grif, took his own life. Grif was Rand's friend from college. They did everything together, even got jobs with the same brokerage house. Rand didn't see it coming, and I think he blames himself for what happened."

"Oh, boy," Kristine said, blowing out a breath.

"After the funeral, Rand took a leave of absence from his job and came here. You know the rest."

"So he is running away from his life," Kristine said with resignation.

"He's in pain." Rowena pressed her hands together. "My boy's in pain."

Carly burst into the kitchen. "Mom, will you make us popcorn?"

"Sure, honey," Kristine said.

"I'll do it," Rowena said. "You go and see if you can get my boy to let go of his grip on the liquor bottle. Tequila never solved anything."

"He doesn't want me there," Kristine reminded her.

"He doesn't know what he wants," Rowena said. "It's you or me. You choose, but I think we both know it's you he wants near."

Rowena set the pan on the stove to make popcorn, ending their conversation.

Unsure of what to do, Kristine stepped outside, her eyes on the guest house.

Did Rand want her close? His words told her no. Her heart told her yes. Taking a deep breath, Kristine set out for Rand's.

*   *   *

Rand shot the tequila, welcoming the burn. "To you, old friend." He set the shot glass on the coffee table. "I'm sorry. So sorry."

He couldn't shut off his memories of Grif. Today would have been Grif's thirty-fourth birthday. His friend would never grow older.

All day long Grif had been on his mind. Images of his time with Grif hammered at him, to the point he'd needed the tequila to dull the memories.

The scent of food filled the guest house, but he didn't touch the dinner Kristine had brought. It seemed wrong, considering how he'd sent her away. And she'd gone without an argument, making him feel like ten times the jerk he was.

He poured himself another tequila.

"I'm back," Kristine said from the other side of the screen door.

Suddenly, he knew why he'd sent her away. He didn't want her to see him like this, weak, beaten down, pathetic.

"Go away, please," he said, regretting the tequila.

"It's me or your mother," she said. "She ordered me over here. Said if I didn't go, she was coming."

He frowned. The last thing he needed was his mother crying all over him, begging him to stop drinking. "Come in."

She let herself in. "Your mother told me about Grif, about what she knows, but I'd like to hear about him from you. Does he have something to do with your sudden need for tequila?"

His hand closed around the shot of tequila he'd been about to take.

"Is this a pity party?" Kristine asked. "Help me understand."

"Not pity," Rand said. "More like a pain dulling party, or a guilt drowning party."

"Why?" she asked. "You weren't responsible for what happened to Grif. He made his own choice."

"You don't know anything about me," Rand said, the words sounding harsh to his own ears. "Not really. What we have isn't real. You said it yourself, it's a summer romance, a fling, a way to help us both forget."

She took the shot of tequila from him, downing it herself. "You're right. Absolutely right."

He didn't see any hurt in her eyes, or condemnation, he saw acceptance. Did she really get him?

Her fingers closed over his, and she gave his hand a squeeze. "Right now, you're being a crappy summer boyfriend. Let's agree to let our problems simmer."

"Simmer?"

"We both know our past lives were crap, let's acknowledge the crap, and move on," she said. "We can't change the past, only the future. I didn't know your friend, but my guess is he wouldn't approve of this." She pointed to the tequila. "I doubt he'd want you to feel guilty."

"Today is his birthday," Rand said sadly.

"I see." She gave him a soft smile. "Of course you'd want to remember him today, honor him."

Was he drunk, or was she making sense?

She poured another shot. Hefting the glass, she said, "To Grif. Happy birthday." She downed half the shot, then passed the glass to him.

"To Grif," Rand said before finishing the shot.

Kristine uncovered his food. "Beef stroganoff." She retrieved a fork from his kitchen, tasting the meal. "Delicious." She passed him a forkful, bringing the beef and noodles to his mouth.

Rand took the bite, the flavors exploding on his tongue. Suddenly, he'd never felt hungrier.

She smiled, passing him the fork. He dug in. While he ate, she removed the tequila and brought him a glass of water.

He realized she'd tricked him, but he didn't care. She'd been right, he'd been having his own private pity party—a party Grif would have hated.

"Let's go for a walk," she said when he finished eating, offering him her hand. "Get some fresh air."

His fingers closed around hers and she pulled him up.

They walked to the water's edge.

Rand inhaled, not caring that anyone could see they were hold hands. Right now, he needed this, needed this woman.

Kristine Wilding was getting under his skin, but in a good way, a healing way. He let go of her hand, and put his arm around her. Her arm snaked around his back.

They stood together a long time, just breathing.

And maybe it was what they both needed at that moment.

Air. Each other. The water.

Rand closed his eyes as the pain left his mind, and the fresh healing air filled the space.

Chapter Nineteen

Kristine, Rand, Lucky, and Carly hit the road for Oregon early Saturday morning to pack up the apartment.

Carly still hadn't made a decision about the move, but for now, they were bringing their things to Wilding House, storing most of it in the garage until a decision was made about where they would live.

Kristine had applied to both the University of Oregon and to University of Washington for winter quarter. By then, she'd know where Carly wanted to be. She'd have money from the estate. She'd be ready to go back to school. The idea of completing her nursing degree excited beyond her wildest dreams. She'd had time to think about it, and she truly felt hospice nursing was for her.

Kristine pulled into the parking lot at their apartment complex, noting the only emotion she felt for their former home was relief they were leaving here. The unappealing brown building looked even sadder to her after living on the beach for a few weeks. A glance at Carly revealed nothing about the girl's state of mind. Maybe Carly didn't see the poverty around them. After all, she'd grown up here.

Lucky exited the backseat, Rand the front.

The drive had been mostly silent, with Carly and Lucky both wearing earbuds, listening to music. Rand had kept the conversation to a minimum and she wondered if he was still thinking about the friend he had lost. She'd definitely noticed a restlessness in him since the night of tequila and confessions, and that worried her.

Inside the apartment, a musty smell greeted them and Kristine instantly longed for the salt air at Wilding Point.

"Home, sweet home," she said to no one in particular, her tone dry.

Lucky brought in a load of boxes and began building them. Rand helped.

Carly made a beeline for her room. A second later, music came on.

Kristine went to her own room, boxes in hand. She worked to pack up her bedroom and bathroom, while Rand and Lucky concentrated on the kitchen and living area, throwing questions at her when they couldn't decide if something should stay or go. They packed all day, going to bed early, intending on getting an early start in the morning.

Carly gave her bed up to Rand. Carly and Kristine shared her bed, with Lucky sleeping on the sofa. They were up early, and the two men left around eight to pick up the U-Haul truck they would use to transport their bigger items to Wilding Point. Once the truck was there, it only took them a couple of hours to load it. They didn't have much.

Around one Lucky took her car, heading home with Carly in the passenger seat.

It took Kristine and Rand another hour to finish up the cleaning of the apartment, then they too were on the road in the rental truck.

As Rand pulled onto I-5 Kristine said, "I'm beat."

"Me, too."

"Thank goodness it's not raining," Kristine said, her eyes on the dry pavement. "Thank you for all your help today."

"You're welcome." He smiled. "You fed me Chinese takeout. I'm a happy man."

She laughed. "Then you're easy to please."

He glanced at her, grinning. "You know I am."

Yes, she did. Happiness filled her chest, making her glow from the inside out. Rand always made her feel better, even when she was dead tired.

The drive home took longer than usual because Rand took it slow and easy. When they pulled into the driveway at Wilding House it was close to ten p.m., with the house already dark.

"Is there anything here you have to have tonight?" Rand asked.

"Just this." She picked up her tote bag. "The rest can wait."

"Any chance you can slip over to my place?" he asked.

"I'd love to, but I don't know." She exited the truck. "Let me check on things inside. I'll text you."

"Okay."

He walked her inside, exiting through the kitchen.

Kristine trudged up the stairs. Every bone in her body screamed for sleep, yet the lure of sleeping part of the time with Rand called to her like some kind of mythic siren.

Carly's soft snores met her ears when she poked her head into her daughter's room. Canned television laughter came from Lucky's room. She rapped on the door.

"Come in," he said.

"Hey." She stepped into the room. "The drive go all right?"

"Fine," he said. "She fell asleep just as we hit Des Moines. I roused her enough she got herself to bed."

"Thanks." She blew out a breath. "Ro asleep?"

"Yeah." He gave her a measuring look. "Just head over to his place. I'll keep an ear out for Carly."

"Really?" she asked.

He nodded. "Go. And let Rand know Hussy is sleeping in Carly's room. That dog loves her."

"She does," Kristine agreed. "Thanks, Lucky. I won't stay all night, just long enough to—"

He put his hand up. "Stop talking. I don't want to know what you're doing over there."

Kristine shook her head. "Sleeping, just doing it together. I need to decompress and Rand is good at making me smile."

"TMI." Lucky tossed a pillow at her. "Get out."

Kristine left him, stopping by her room long enough to snag some clean clothes before slipping out the back door and running down the stairs to the guest house. The porchlight was on. Kristine let herself in. Rand walked out of the bedroom naked, a towel wrapped around his hips, his hair wet.

"Thought I heard you," he said. "Shower?"

"You read my mind." Kristine went into the bathroom and shucked her clothes, stepping under the hot spray. She washed the dirt, grime, and sweat from her body. Clean, she wrapped herself in a fluffy towel before joining Rand in the kitchen.

"I take it Carly was asleep?" he asked.

"Yes, Lucky's listening for her." She walked to him. "Hussy's with her."

"Do you want a drink or something?" he asked.

"All I want is you." She stood in front of him now, tugging at the towel at his hips. The towel fell to the floor.

Rand released the towel she wore and they came together naked.

"I told Lucky we were just going to sleep," she said as he drew her into the circle of his arms.

"You lied."

Kristine laughed as he swept her off her feet and bore her to the bedroom.

* * *

The sound of a ringing phone pulled Kristine from a deep sleep. Groggy, it took her a second to remember she was at Rand's. She located her phone.

"Lucky," she said, "what's wrong?"

"Carly's awake. She had a bad dream."

"Be right there."

"What's going on?" Rand asked.

"Carly had a bad dream." Kristine went into the bathroom, dressing quickly.

Rand sat up. "Do you want me to come with you?"

"No," she said. "I've got this." She blew him a kiss. "See you later."

"Count on it."

Kristine ran up the steps and into the kitchen. She met Carly in the foyer.

"Where were you?" Carly asked, her tone heavy with accusation.

"I fell asleep on the deck," Kristine lied, noting the wild look in her daughter's eyes. "What's wrong?"

"I had a bad dream."

"I'm sorry, honey." Kristine hugged Carly. "Do you want some warm milk?"

"Will you put honey in it?" Carly asked in a small voice.

"Sure."

Kristine put some milk on to heat. "What was your dream about?"

"Grandpa," Carly said. "He was covered with dirt, trying to get in the house."

"Yikes, what a bad dream," Kristine agreed. "We've had a couple of long, emotional days. We ate wild food. Makes sense you'd have a wild dream."

"I guess." Carly sat at the table.

Kristine added honey to the warm milk. "Here you go."

"Thanks." Carly took a sip and yawned. "Can I sleep with you?"

"Sure." Kristine glanced at the clock. Three twenty three a.m. "Let's take the milk upstairs."

Carly crawled under the covers in Kristine's room. Kristine changed into cozy pajamas. By the time she crawled in bed, Carly was asleep.

She stroked her daughter's hair as her own body became heavy. When Kristine woke again, the bedroom was hot, stuffy.

Carly was gone.

Kristine stretched. If she'd learned anything last night, she'd learned she wouldn't be sneaking over to Rand's when Carly was home. She'd had a close call. She needed to quit acting like a teenager and start acting like the seasoned mother she was.

When she finally made it downstairs, she found Carly and Patty sitting on the deck playing cards.

"What time is it?" Kristine asked.

"Noon," Carly said. "You slept a long time."

"Moving is hard work," Kristine said. "What time did you roll out of bed?"

"After ten," Carly said. "Go fish, Patty."

Patty groaned, drawing a card.

"I'm getting some coffee," Kristine told the girls.

It was Monday, but she knew Rand was home—she could see his truck. Her heart sped up. She really did have it bad for him. Shaking her head, Kristine snagged the coffee pot, no doubt made for her by Rowena.

She was cruising the fridge for something to eat, when Rowena and Rand walked into the kitchen, their arms filled with groceries.

"You're up," Rowena said.

"I see you've been shopping," Kristine observed.

"Yes," Rowena said. "Rand was nice enough to go with me."

"Any more coffee?" Rand took a mug from the cupboard.

They all had coffee. Rowena produced a plate of croissants and a jar of Nutella. Heaven in the form of food as far as Kristine was concerned.

"Mom, Patty and I are going to her house for a while," Carly called.

"Okay," Kristine said. "Don't wear out your welcome there."

The girls burst into laughter.

"What?" Kristine asked.

"Patty's mom says the same thing." Carly tugged Patty's arm. "Let's go."

"I need to start a load of wash," Rowena said, setting her mug in the sink on her way out.

Rand smiled at Kristine. "You slept late."

"You wore me out." She grinned back.

Rand's phone buzzed. He pulled it from his pocket and frowned. "I have to take this. Excuse me."

"Hello?" he said on his way outside.

Kristine tidied up the kitchen, heading out to the deck. She planned on taking it easy today. Her muscles were still sore from all the lifting during the weekend.

A book in hand, she reclined in the padded deck chair, the sun warm on her face.

Rand paced his small porch, the phone pressed to his ear. He ended the call, going inside. A few minutes later, he jumped in his truck and drove off.

Well! She guessed he wasn't worried about cluing her in on anything in his life. He was taking her words to heart—summer lovers, no real strings attached. Kristine's heart ached a little at the thought.

Around five, Keith pulled into the parking area in front of the guest house. Rowena saw him, and went to talk to him. When she returned she told Kristine he'd come by to see if Rand wanted to have dinner. Rowena had sent Keith on his way, having no idea where Rand was.

When Rand still wasn't back by dinner time, Kristine resisted the urge to text him. She wasn't that kind of summer girlfriend, clingy, needy.

Rand drove in as the sun was setting.

She prayed he didn't have another bottle of tequila with him. Where on earth had he been all day?

"Hey," she called from the deck, waving.

He turned, raising his hand in greeting. "Be right there."

Maybe she was imagining things. He sounded fine. Rand went inside the guest house briefly before joining her.

"Hi," he said, the word a caress.

"Hi." She searched his face for a clue as to what he'd been up to. "Where have you been all day?" She kept her tone light, casual.

"A pipe burst at Keith's place. I went over to give him a hand."

"That was the call you had earlier?" she asked, praying he wouldn't lie to her.

"Yeah."

Kristine's stomach rolled. This was how it had started with Carly's dad. Evasive answers, lies. She didn't need this. He had no reason to lie to her. She'd placed zero demands on him. Why couldn't he trust her with the truth? He's just a summer fling, she reminded herself. They weren't committed to each other. She'd gone in with her eyes wide open.

So why did she feel like she'd taken a direct punch to her heart?

Rand followed her into the kitchen.

"Have you eaten?" she asked, not knowing what else to say.

"We grabbed burgers," he replied, patting his stomach.

"Carly's watching a movie," Kristine said, needing some space from Rand and all he made her feel. "I'm staying put tonight."

Rand's forehead wrinkled. "Can I sneak a kiss?"

"You better."

He kissed her and Kristine wound her arms around his neck, giving everything to the kiss. A desperate kiss. Fear settled in her belly.

They parted.

He stroked her back. "I'll miss you tonight, Kristine."

She forced a smile. "I'll miss you, too."

"I should go," he said. "I need a shower and a change of clothes."

"I'll see you tomorrow," she said.

He nodded. She watched him go, his body a dark silhouette against the purple twilight.

Did she want to know what Rand was up to?

Her stomach twisted, reminding her she was more invested in Rand Bell than she should be. Was it happening? Was he pulling away from her, fighting to regain the life he'd once had? A life far away from her and Wilding Point.

Her heart heavy, Kristine turned out the kitchen light. She wasn't going to get any answers tonight. For now, she just wanted to be with her little girl and remember all the reasons she wanted to stay put right where she was.

Chapter Twenty

Rand took a seat on the guest house porch, his eyes on Wilding House.

Why had he lied to Kristine tonight? It would have been so easy to admit he'd been thinking a lot about Grif and what had happened in New York, what had gone wrong. She'd understand. He knew she would. Yet he'd kept silent and he wasn't sure why. Maybe he was afraid she'd think less of him if she knew the entire truth about Grif's death.

For now, his past was his problem. And today the past had rolled right in to Wilding Point in the form of Cory Phillips. Cory, Grif's girlfriend.

After his conversation with Kristine at the Lodge, he'd done nothing but think about Grif and what had led him to take his own life. While deep into that bottle of tequila, unable to help himself, he'd called Cory, hoping she could help him understand. When she hadn't called him back, he'd thought he'd received her message, loud and clear. She wanted nothing to do with him, blamed him for Grif's death. Then Cory had turned the tables, showing up here, wanting to see him in person.

They'd spent the day together, struggling to understand what had gone on in Grif's mind prior to the suicide. Cory's grief, like his, still colored her life in every way. She'd lost weight, her already model-thin body becoming a mere shell of the woman she'd been.

She'd told him he looked like hell; he needed a shave and a haircut. She reminded him that he needed to call his boss, make a decision about his job. They'd spent the day talking about their lost friend, crying together, the day ending when he'd taken her back to her hotel near the airport. Cory had given him a type of closure no one else could. Together they'd shared a horrific tragedy, something he was still unable to fully share with anyone else. Even Kristine, and for one important reason.

Cory had helped him remember the life he'd once had, painting a vivid picture of the rush he'd gotten from the job he'd loved. She'd reminded him of his love for New York. They'd talked about everything from his great loft apartment, to their favorite place to get a slice, to the job they both loved, investment banking.

Cory had begged him to come back, to give New York a second chance.

And a part of him wanted to.

That was why he couldn't tell Kristine about Cory. Not yet. What he had with Kristine was special, different, but she'd said from the start it was just a summer romance.

Was it?

"Hey."

Lucky came up the path from the beach, looking more relaxed than he had in a long time.

"Walking?" Rand asked.

"Yep," Lucky said, "had some thinking to do. Mind if I sit?"

"Be my guest." Rand settled back in his chair. "What's on your mind?"

Lucky blew out a breath. "What isn't?"

Rand chuckled. "Everything has changed for you, too."

"Understatement of the year."

"Will you stay in Wilding Point?" Rand asked.

"I don't know," Lucky said, his eyes on Wilding House. "I don't think this town is going to welcome me back."

"You were a kid, Lucky," Rand said. "Kids do stupid things."

"Yeah."

"Kristine needs you," Rand pointed out, knowing Kristine would need her brother even more if he decided to return to New York.

"I know." Lucky pushed his hands through his hair.

"You could try it here, see how you like it," Rand suggested. It was what he had done. "Nothing ventured, nothing gained."

Lucky studied him. "Why are you here, Rand?"

"I'm asking myself that exact question. I suppose I'm running away." Saying the words out loud filled him with a deep sense of relief.

Lucky shook his head. "Aren't we all?"

"Beer?" Rand asked.

"Love one."

Rand brought them each a beer.

"You've got it bad for my sister, don't you," Lucky said, eyeing Rand.

Rand took a sip of beer. "I like her. A lot."

"Don't break her heart," Lucky warned. "She already got tangled up with a jerk. If you're thinking of leaving, cut her loose, man. Be honest with her. Don't make her fall in love with you."

Rand's hand tightened on his beer. "Message received."

The light came on in Kristine's room.

Lucky stood. He held up his beer. "Thanks for the beer."

"Any time."

Lucky headed to Wilding House.

Rand finished his beer, his eyes on Kristine's window. He didn't move until she turned out the light. Only then did he go inside, his heart heavy in his chest.

* * *

Unable to help herself, the first thing Kristine did when she woke up was go to the window and look for Rand. His truck was gone.

Maybe he had an early job.

Or was something more going on?

His lie about where he'd been yesterday festered in her stomach like a stab wound. She turned away from the window. She wasn't ready to give him up yet, but it was happening, he was pulling away from her.

She had a decision to make. Did she back away from him now before he broke her heart completely? Or did she stick to her original proposal and make the most of this summer romance?

Summer romance! Right now, she couldn't imagine her life without Rand in it. He made her feel alive, wanted.

Who was she kidding? She'd take Rand as long as she could get him. She needed him right now. Rand Bell was better than any other artificial mood enhancer. Being with him was right on so many levels.

Decision made, Kristine hit the shower. After breakfast, she finished packing up her father's office. She'd sorted and boxed up most everything, keeping only a few of the books from his shelves. If she was going to live here, this would be her office now. It felt weird to think she and Lucky owned Wilding House.

"There you are." Rowena glanced around the room. "My, you're almost done in here."

"I know." Kristine looked around. "It's like a blank slate now."

Rowena inhaled. "I miss him."

Kristine smiled. "I know you do."

"I know it's not the same for you and Lucky," Rowena said.

"I don't miss him exactly," Kristine admitted. "I'm sad he's gone, but he hasn't been a part of my life for a very long time."

Rowena smiled. "Carly's looking for you. She's wondering if you could run her and Patty into town. They want to go to the five o'clock movie."

"Sure," Kristine said. She glanced at the clock on the wall. "We should get going, then."

She found Carly and Patty in the kitchen. A few minutes later, they were on their way. She dropped the girls off, then stopped at the store before returning to Wilding House.

When she got back, Rand's truck was at the guest house.

She quickly unpacked her groceries, then started for Rand's place.

At the door she called, "Knock, knock."

"Hi," he said, from the kitchen. "Come in."

She let herself in.

He smiled. Her heart melted. His hair was wet, as if he'd just come from the shower. He opened his arms and she walked into his embrace.

Rand kissed her hair, her mouth.

"I've missed you," he said, and she knew he meant it.

"Me, too," she returned, her arms around him.

"About yesterday…"

Suddenly she didn't want to know. "I don't need to know anything. Summer romance. No strings attached."

He stared into her eyes. "I'm just trying to figure things out. It's not you. You are the best thing that's happened to me in years."

"I know," she said softly. "Like I said, no strings. Do what you have to do. I want you to be happy."

He gave her a slow nod. "I know what I want to do right now."

"What?" She kissed his neck, inhaling his clean scent. Her heart began to beat wildly.

His hands found the hem of her T-shirt and he pulled it up and over her head. "How much time do we have?"

"An hour. The girls are at the movies."

Rand's mouth claimed hers in a searing kiss. They kissed their way to the bedroom, shucking the rest of their clothes on the way. They fell onto the bed together, naked, their hands on each other's bodies.

Rand took her from zero to ten in seconds. Kristine ached for him. Lust beat in her gut. When he entered her, she climaxed, her world spinning out of control.

"Kristine," he called as he found his own release.

His fingers slipped into her hair. His lips brushed against her forehead before kissing the tip of her nose, her mouth, her chin.

"Wow," she said, her eyes closed, the afterglow of sex charging every cell in her body. "What is it about you?"

He laughed. "I was thinking the same thing about you."

"Really?" she asked, pleased.

"Really." He kissed her again. "We've only used up about ten minutes of our hour."

"We did." She smiled against his mouth. "What do you want to do with the other fifty minutes?"

"Are you kidding?" He gave her a sexy grin. "Let me show you."

He rolled over, taking her with him, so now she was on top.

Kristine laughed. "Hmm, I think this time I'm in charge."

"Bring it on, baby," Rand said. "Bring it on."

Kristine did.

* * *

When Kristine returned with the girls, Rowena had dinner waiting, barbecued chicken, green salad, and corn on the cob.

She had the outdoor table set, and Lucky and Rand were on the deck talking.

Kristine's body still hummed from her interlude with Rand earlier. She refused to think about the end to their romance, instead concentrating on the here and now.

They were just finishing dinner when Rand's phone rang. He excused himself to take the call.

Immediately, Kristine's antenna came up. Another call from his past? *Stop it*, she told herself.

Rand paced back and forth in front of the guest house, his phone pressed to his ear. She kept tabs on him via her peripheral vision, telling herself she wasn't really interested in his conversation.

When Rand rejoined the group, he said, "Just Keith with instructions for the job tomorrow."

She wanted to believe him, she really did, but there was something in the way he said the words that bothered her.

"We could use an extra set of hands, Lucky," Rand said, "if you're interested."

"Sure," Lucky said. "Be good to have something to do. I'm not cut out for a life of leisure."

Kristine smiled, happy Rand had included her brother.

The table broke up. The girls went inside to hang out in Carly's room.

Rowena insisted the young people sit while she cleaned up tonight.

Rand met her gaze, and smiled. Lucky must have gotten the romantic vibe because he said, "I'm going for a walk. Mind if I take Hussy?"

"Go for it," Rand said.

"Come on, girl," Lucky said to the dog who lounged nearby. "Want to go for a walk?"

Hussy jumped to her feet, readily going with Lucky.

"Let's move to the comfy chairs," Kristine suggested.

They settled into the padded lounge chairs, watching the sun go down. The air held the most intoxicating scent, sun-warmed roses and salty beach.

"It's so beautiful here," Kristine said. "I never get tired of the view."

"It's gorgeous," Rand agreed, but he sounded distracted.

"But it's not for you, is it?" she asked, turning her head to look at him. Something was different between them, but she wasn't sure what.

"I wouldn't say it's not for me," he replied. "I grew up here, same as you. Right now I'm not sure what I want."

"Will you tell me about your tattoo now?" She touched the trees etched on his skin. She needed to understand him, wanted him to trust her with his secret. "It's unusual."

He didn't reply and she wondered if she'd pushed him too far. Then he said, "It's a place I used to go with Grif. It's where he went to die. It's where I found him. I don't ever want to forget him. Every day, I see these trees inked on my skin, and I remember."

She started to pull her hand away, but he captured her fingers. Their eyes met and she saw pain there, raw and definitely still fresh. "I'm so sorry, Rand."

"Me too," Rand said simply. He let go of her hand. "All that is in the past now. I'm ready to let Grif go."

She didn't believe him. Grief marred his features in the tightness of his mouth, the wrinkles on his forehead. Rand was aching inside and she had no idea how to make things better for him. She never should have asked about the tattoo.

He touched her cheek. "You make me happy, Kristine."

She smiled, but her heart was sad for him and all he'd been through. "Ditto."

Melancholy now, they watched the sun slip into the Sound, casting a scarlet hue on the water. Lucky returned, bypassing them to go inside. Hussy resumed her place on the deck. Carly came out.

"Patty has to go home now," she said.

"We can walk her." Kristine rose.

The four of them walked the short distance down the beach to Patty's. They waited until the girl was inside before starting back.

"How are you liking it here?" Kristine asked Carly. "Any thoughts?"

"I love it, Mom," Carly said, her words elbowing the sadness from Kristine's heart.

Rand trudged alongside, silent, thoughtful—reliving his past?

"Enough to stay permanently?" Kristine asked, unable to keep the hopeful note out of her voice.

"I want to, Mom," Carly said. "I'll miss Nan, but I really like Patty. She's told me all kinds of stuff about the kids at her school. And I love living in a house."

Not for the first time, Kristine wished she'd been able to give her daughter a house sooner. They reached the steps leading to Wilding House. She stared at the house, a jewel of a house, lit with golden light from inside.

"Well, kiddo, you're home." She gave Carly a one-armed hug. Her daughter smiled up at her.

"So are you, Mom."

"Let me be the first to welcome you both back to Wilding Point," Rand said, his eyes less haunted now.

A mix of sadness and joy filled Kristine. She'd lost her father, a man with whom she'd had a contentious relationship, but from that loss had come security, a great place to live, and when the estate settled, enough money to set her own dreams in motion.

She felt Rand's hand on the small of her back. His touch connected with her soul. She didn't want to lose him, not yet.

"Can we celebrate with root beer floats?" Carly asked, grinning.

"Absolutely," Kristine said, focusing on her daughter. "Join us, Rand?"

"You know I will."

Carly ran ahead. Rand's hand slid up Kristine's back as they walked up the stairs.

"You belong here, Kristine Wilding," Rand said, the words low.

He was right. She did belong here. Nothing had ever felt so right.

Chapter Twenty-One

The following day, Kristine's phone rang. The attorney's name flashed on the screen.

"Hi, John," she said into the phone as she let herself out the glass doors onto the deck.

"Hello, Kristine," John said in a pleasant, upbeat tone. "I hope you're settling in."

"I am. How are things going with the estate?" she asked.

"Fine. You and Lucky will have some decisions to make soon with regard to Wilding House and the other properties, but that's not the reason for my call."

"Oh?"

"Cameron Butler has been found," John said. "He's been living in Italy, doing freelance work in Cortona."

"Wow," she said, unsure how she felt about her new half-brother. "Has he been told about Dad, about us?"

"He has," John confirmed. "I've asked him to come to Wilding Point, but he's refused."

Her heart sank. "Really?"

"He has a life there. As you can imagine, this has all come as a shock to him. I'm not even sure he believes Lucas was his father."

"It was a shock for us, too, but surely he wants his share of the money?"

"He declined at first," the attorney told her, "but I think he'll come around."

"I think the money should be placed in an account for him," Kristine said.

"All of that is being handled," the attorney assured her. "His signature is required on documents and I've explained this to him. However, most of the paperwork can be handled via long distance."

"Okay," she said. "I guess that's all we can do. Maybe he will change his mind someday."

"You sound sorry he's not coming," the attorney said. "I'm surprised. I thought you would be relieved."

"I'm not sure what I feel," Kristine admitted. "Nothing Dad did or said could really shock me, I suppose. He had a secret life we knew nothing about. Maybe I expected that, I don't know."

"At any rate," the attorney said. "We've done our part with the notification, and thankfully, your father's set up Cameron's share to function alone, for him."

"I guess that's something," Kristine said.

"I'll be in touch if I learn anything more," the attorney told her.

After she disconnected, Kristine stared out at the water. Cameron Butler wasn't interested in them. But he'd grown up here. He had to know who they were, how they lived. Was he still that same free spirit she remembered from high school? Time would tell.

Her gaze cut across the deck, to the guest house. Rand's truck was gone. He'd taken Lucky with him that morning on the new job.

Kristine brushed the hair from her eyes. Things were going her way. Carly wanted to stay in Wilding Point. Lucky was working, and seemed in no rush to leave. Her relationship with

Rand was hot. She frowned. Life never swung in her favor. Was it time for the other shoe to drop, the one that sent her spiraling backward?

She hoped not. She really needed to read a self-help book on being more optimistic.

Smiling now, she set out for a walk, her thoughts focused on the good things in her life.

*   *   *

The following morning, Rand poured himself a cup of coffee, his eyes on Wilding House, his thoughts on the woman inside…Kristine.

Yesterday, he'd placed a call to his boss in New York. Now, he waited for a call back, his stomach a pit of nerves.

In his gut, he knew what he wanted, but was he strong enough to reclaim his former life?

A part of him wanted to, wanted a do-over. He'd barely made the move into private client services when Grif had died. There was big money to be made there, and the thought excited him, made him remember his love of the job.

A smaller part of him filled with regret when he thought of leaving Kristine behind. His summer romance. She'd said no strings. He had no reason to feel guilty, yet he did.

In a perfect world, he'd take more time, spend it with Kristine, but his sabbatical was up. A decision had to be made.

He knew for certain his life in New York was not over. There had been no closure. He'd run away with his tail between his legs, his heart and spirit broken. His mistakes were all so clear now.

And while some of his guilt still lingered, Rand now saw the bigger picture of the mental illness Grif had suffered from. And that bigger picture was helping Rand heal, helping him deal with the guilt he felt.

His phone rang. The name Greg Rogers flashed on the screen.

"Boss," he said. "Good morning."

"Good morning, hot shot," Greg Rogers said, using the nickname he'd pinned on Rand when he'd first hired him. "Tell me you're coming back."

"I am," Rand said, the nerves in his belly changing to raw excitement.

"Excellent," Greg said.

He had to go back, for himself. He didn't have to stay, but he had to finish what he'd started in New York. "Thank you for giving me the time off. I appreciate it. My head's on straight now."

"Good to hear," Greg said. "I'll let you work out the details of your return with HR."

"Thanks again," Rand said. "See you soon."

Rand ended the call. Suddenly, he had a million things to do. He had to pack. He needed to find a place to live, although Cory had offered to put him up until he found something.

He had to tell Kristine.

Would she be okay with his decision? He had no idea, but he was about to find out.

No matter the outcome, he'd never regret his time with her.

He'd miss her, no doubt about it, but the time had come to go back to New York.

New York was in his blood, his soul. He needed the city like he needed a drug.

"Hey," Lucky called through the screened door. "Ready?"

"You bet," Rand said, starting for the door. Lucky could take over for him with Keith. He'd done a great job for them yesterday. He'd have a job with Keith until he figured things out.

"It's going to be another hot one," Lucky said as they climbed into the pickup.

"Yeah," Rand agreed. He'd miss it here. He'd especially miss Kristine, but he had to do this for himself.

He was going home.

* * *

Kristine hadn't been alone with Rand in a few days, and she was beginning to ache for him in a way that scared her. She was too attached, she knew it, yet she couldn't give him up. When Carly had told her earlier that Patty's family had invited her camping this weekend, Kristine had somehow managed to hold her happiness in check until Carly had left the room.

Kristine was free of all parenting for three whole days.

She couldn't wait to tell Rand.

Better still, Rowena had her book club tonight. They wouldn't have to sneak around.

She was waiting on the deck when Rand's truck pulled in. Lucky hopped out, calling, "See you later, man."

Kristine passed her brother on her way down the stairs.

"Booty call?" Lucky asked, smirking.

"Shut up." She grinned. She couldn't help it.

"Hey," Rand said, waiting for her to come to him. "Long time, no see, pretty lady."

"I know, it seems like forever." She reached him, pulling his head to hers for a kiss.

He kissed her back, every bit as hungry for her as she was for him. Her heart sang. She needed this, needed him.

"I take it Carly's not home," he said against her mouth.

"Gone for the weekend." She kissed him again. "Your mom has book club."

He gave her a wicked smile. "I need a shower. I'm sweaty and filthy."

She grinned. "You look good to me."

Rand tugged her into the bathroom. They undressed quickly, then stepped under the hot spray.

Kristine took her time soaping him up, running her slippery hands down his arms, his back, his butt. She wanted to memorize every sexy inch of him. Rand turned and she spooned him, her arms going around him to his chest, her hands sliding down his corded abs, and lower still to his sex. She soaped him up, and he slid between her hands, so ready for her.

Rand moaned, thrusting against her hands. "Oh, baby."

Kristine stroked him, faster, encouraged by his need.

"Kristine."

Her name burst from him as Rand found his release. She held him until he stilled, then he turned, coming face to face with her. The hot water poured over them. Kristine wound her arms around his neck and he kissed her, the kiss hungry, seeking, his tongue mating with hers.

"My turn," he said, his voice hoarse with need. He picked up the soap, working up a bubbling lather before putting his big hands on her. His hands slid over her breasts, lingering just long enough to make her crazy. Those hands slid lower, over her belly, cupping her woman's place before finally slipping inside her.

Kristine moaned as his fingers stroked her. She struggled to keep herself from slipping into orgasm too fast, but his lips found her neck and she was lost.

Not thinking he'd be ready for her, she was surprised when he lifted her, her back to the shower wall. She wrapped her legs around his waist and he entered her, bringing her to orgasm again so quickly, she had to hold on for dear life.

Rand called out, holding her tight.

For a full minute they didn't move. Water washed over them, around them. Kristine closed her eyes, holding tight to the delicious sensations rocking her body.

Rand let her down. Her feet touched the floor. The water was lukewarm now. Removing the hand-held showerhead, Rand rinsed her off before cleaning himself, then shut off the water. He exited first, wrapping her in a towel.

"I'm feeling a little more dirty now than when I went in," Rand joked.

Kristine smiled. "Me, too."

They dried off, then got in his bed. She snuggled against him.

"Can we stay in here all weekend?" she asked.

"I can't all weekend," Rand said with regret. "But I can tonight."

"No, don't tell me you have to work," she moaned.

"Something like that." He kissed her forehead. "I don't want to talk about it now. Let's just be together, enjoy each other for as long as we can."

"I like the sound of that," she said, right before she kissed him.

* * *

Around midnight, Rand got out of bed, his mind alive with all his coming life changes. Restless, he located his phone, checking his messages, finding a text from Cory.

Call me when you land.

I'll take a cab in, he texted. *Call you once I'm en route.* He set his phone on the kitchen counter.

What was he going to do? He never should have taken Kristine to bed tonight without telling her of his plan to go back to New York. He'd been unfair, but something happened to him whenever she offered herself to him. He couldn't resist her. The sex was too damn good.

Rand ran his fingers through his hair. He'd tell her in the morning, come clean with everything. It wasn't like he was saying good-bye forever. He just needed to get his head on straight, figure out what he wanted.

Rand slipped back into bed.

"Everything okay?" Kristine asked.

"Yes, go back to sleep."

She burrowed against him, making a sexy sound of contentment.

Rand's heart grew sad. He'd miss her. Maybe they'd met at the wrong time, or maybe the timing had been exactly right for both of them.

Only time would tell.

Chapter Twenty-Two

The cry of a seagull woke Kristine.

She rolled over, stretching, as incredible warmth filled her.

What a night, a beautiful, wonderful night. Magical.

Rand. She reached for him, finding air. He was already up, greeting the day.

Kristine left the bed, finding Rand's robe on the back of the bathroom door. She shimmied into it, belting the robe closed on her way out of the bedroom.

"Rand?"

She didn't see him inside, so she went to the window.

He stood at water's edge, Hussy a few feet away from him. What was Rand thinking about? Was he just enjoying the moment, the beauty before him?

The ping of a text message sounded.

Thinking it was her phone, she went to the kitchen, finding Rand's phone lit. Not meaning to be a snoop she saw the name Cory, followed by *Okay, waiting for your call.*

Cory? Who was Cory? Was Cory a guy or a girl, and why was Cory waiting for Rand's call?

A lump formed in Kristine's stomach. She'd been right. Something was going on with him. Something he wasn't telling her. Was Rand leaving Wilding Point? Was Cory the distraction he'd been dealing with?

"Good morning," Rand said, the screen door snapping shut behind him. "How are you today?" He smiled, stealing a kiss.

"Good," she said, fighting to ignore the dread growing in her gut. "Slept like a baby."

"Wish I could say the same," he said.

She looked into his eyes, searching for a clue as to what was going on. "Something on your mind?"

"Yeah." He pulled away from her.

Her stomach dropped. "You just got a text from Cory. I'm sorry, I didn't mean to look. I thought it was my phone. Does your lack of sleep have something to do with Cory?"

He frowned. "Indirectly."

"Indirectly?" she repeated. "What does that mean? Who is Cory?"

"Cory was Grif's girlfriend. My friend."

"And why is she waiting for your call?" Kristine asked, knowing she wasn't going to like his answer.

"Cory was here a few days ago. We talked about Grif, about his death, about what it did to us."

"And you didn't think that was important enough to share with me?" she asked, hurt filling her. Cory was the lie he'd told her. It all made sense now.

"Summer lovers," he said, throwing her own words back at her. "I didn't want to lay anything heavy on you. You've been through enough this summer."

"Don't make this about me." She pressed her lips together to keep from crying. "You're going back, aren't you?"

He took a step toward her. "I have to."

She held up her hand. "Just stop. Don't touch me, not now."

"Kristine," he pleaded.

"No, I'm fine," she said, sucking up all her hurt. "You're right, we were summer lovers, no strings. I know you don't belong here. I get it. I just wish you'd told me you were thinking of leaving. I feel blindsided."

"I'm sorry." He hung his head. "I didn't know how to tell you. I was going to tell you last night, but then you showed up and we—"

"I know what we did," she said. "It's okay. Really."

He shook his head and she could see the sorrow in his eyes. "I want you to understand. I have unfinished business in New York. Cory made me see that. She helped me to understand that what happened to Grif wasn't my fault. He was messed up. I blamed myself for not seeing the signs, but Grif hid so much from me. Cory set my guilt free. I have to go back. If nothing else, I need closure. The firm I work for, they've been holding my job for me. I have to go back now or lose my job. I want to go back. I have to."

She could see the regret in his eyes.

He came toward her again. Kristine stepped back.

"I can't move forward here until I go back," he said. "Cory, she's stuck, too. We need to help each other move forward, make sense of what happened to Grif."

"Is she pretty?" Kristine asked, knowing the question was petty.

He shook his head. "It's not like that with us. She will always be Grif's girl. We are friends."

His answer didn't make her feel any better. "When are you leaving?" She had to go, or she'd be crying soon.

"Tonight, the red-eye."

She nodded, already feeling his loss. "Okay."

"Don't be sad," Rand said. "Because of you, I'm trying to put my life back together again. You made me feel alive. You made me feel hope for my future."

Tears filled her eyes. "You did the exact same thing for me." She had to get away from him before she became a blubbering idiot. "I need to go."

"Kristine, wait," Rand said.

Kristine ran from the guest house. In her room, she locked the door. Hot tears filled her eyes and she pressed her face to her pillow to stifle her sobs. She'd fallen in love with Rand. The one thing she'd vowed not to do.

She'd been so stupid to think she could have a casual fling. She was not that kind of girl, had never been.

No, she led with her heart. She'd wanted him all to herself from the beginning. She could see that now.

Kristine dried her eyes on the sleeve of Rand's robe. Time to pull on her big-girl panties and kiss Rand good-bye. He deserved his shot at happiness and she wasn't going to stand in his way, or make him feel bad.

She was a Wilding. She was made out of stronger stuff and had been through much worse in her life than a broken summer romance.

Like Rand, it was time for her to make her own way in the world, realize her own dreams.

She didn't need a man. Rand was doing her a favor, cutting her loose.

And someday, she just might believe that.

* * *

"Are you going to let me say good-bye?" Rand asked.

They stood in the kitchen at Wilding House, Kristine with her back to him, her hands on the counter.

"I don't want to say good-bye," she said, her voice strong. "Good-byes are ugly. You'll make me have an ugly cry."

They'd spent a wonderful, yet bittersweet day together, walking, making love, the act frantic and desperate.

Rand wound his arms around her, her back to his chest. She leaned against him and he felt her surrender, felt the fight leave her body.

"I'm going to miss you," she said. "And I'm mad at myself for making what this was into something more in my mind."

He kissed her head. "No regrets, that's what you told me."

"No regrets." She turned in the circle of his arms and he kissed her, one last, sweet time.

She peeled away from him. "Go before you see my ugly cry."

"I'll call." He hated hurting her, but he knew she understood his need to go back.

"No." She shook her head, her hands pressed tightly together. "Calling will make it harder."

Rowena came into the kitchen, her own eyes filled with tears. "Kiss your mother good-bye."

Rand kissed his mother, hugging her tight. "I'll miss you, Mom."

"I'll miss you more," Rowena said. "Let me know when you land."

"I will. Take care of Hussy." Rand separated from his mother, turning back to Kristine. He gave her a slow nod before letting himself out. He climbed into the waiting taxi, his bag already in the car. As he drove away from Wilding House, a lump formed in his chest, or was it his heart?

Leaving Kristine was hard, but going back would be harder still, something he had to do for himself.

Yet the regret he'd told Kristine not to feel filled his body, his soul. Rand closed his eyes, focusing on the life he was going back to, the life that made him happy, the life that would make him whole again.

* * *

With Rand gone, Kristine threw herself into reorganizing Wilding House and submitting college applications. Personal money was already beginning to land in their bank accounts. Wilding House ran itself with the trust account her father had set up. She had free rein with the checkbook, her name on the account. For the first time, she and Carly were financially secure. Next week she'd register Carly for school. Everything was falling into place.

If only her heart didn't ache for Rand.

"Mom," Carly called, cutting into her pity party. "Can we go to town? I need a couple of things."

"Sure." Kristine straightened, putting a lid on the box of books she'd just packed. "Now?"

"Yes," Carly said. "Please, Mom. Fred Meyer has the cutest flip-flops on sale. Patty got a pair. I have to have them."

Kristine laughed. "Okay, but while we are there I'm going to do some grocery shopping."

Carly clapped her hands. "Okay with me."

"Let me freshen up and get my purse," Kristine said.

"I'll meet you at the car." Carly took off for the garage.

Kristine did a quick check on her hair and makeup; snagged her purse from the foyer table, and five minutes later they were on their way to town.

When they reached the store, Kristine followed Carly to the shoe section where they both picked out the cute flip-flops. Fred Meyer was a one-stop shopping store in the neighborhood, so they also picked up a small rug for Carly's room.

For the first time in her adult life, Kristine didn't have to worry about money. Shopping was actually fun. An alien feeling came over her and she knew this new life would take some getting used to.

In the grocery area of the store, she and Carly separated. Carly went in search of the cereal she liked while Kristine cruised the produce section. She was adding peaches to a bag when a voice said, "Well, hello."

Kristine turned. "Kyle."

"It's my lucky day running into you here," he said, smiling. "I've been wanting to call, but wasn't sure I'd be welcome."

"You're welcome with me," she said. "Lucky, I'm not so sure about. Did the two of you make up?"

He shook his head. "No. He won't listen to reason, won't admit he's bitter about Beth."

"Sounds like Lucky," she said with a shrug as she placed the bag of peaches in her cart.

"Have dinner with me, Kristine," Kyle said. "I don't want to get between you and Lucky, but I like you. Beth is history. She shouldn't come between Lucky and me, or between me and you."

"I like you, too," Kristine said, although in her heart she knew Kyle could never take the place of Rand. "But I'm not sure I'd be good company right now."

"I understand," he said, sounding a bit lost.

"No," she told him, not wanting to hurt him, "you don't. It's not my father. I was seeing Rand until a few days ago."

"I see." His mouth tightened and some of the sparkle left his eyes.

"It didn't work out," she said, surprised to find telling him didn't hurt as much as she thought it would. "He's left town."

Kyle's face relaxed with hope. "It's just dinner, Kristine, between friends. I won't press you for more, not yet."

"You're sweet, Kyle, but I don't know. I'm not sure I'd be the best company."

"Hi, Kyle," Carly said, joining them.

"Hello, Carly." Kyle smiled. "Nice to see you. I was just trying to convince your mother to have dinner with me."

"You should, Mom," Carly said. "You never do anything fun."

If Carly only knew the fun Kristine had had with Rand that summer.

"Say yes, Kristine," Kyle said.

"I could use a night out," Kristine admitted, suddenly tempted by the prospect of a no-strings good time. Kyle knew where she stood. Rand was gone. She was here. She needed something good in her life. Maybe Kyle King was her something good, a new friend.

Kyle grinned. "Then it's settled. I'll pick you up at six-thirty?"

"Six-thirty is fine." Kristine smiled, her eyes locking with Kyle's for a second. She didn't feel the spark, the instant chemistry she'd felt with Rand, and for now, that was okay with her. She wasn't ready for another all-consuming summer romance. Kyle was a friend, a distraction, and she needed both right now.

* * *

They stood at the base of the Ferris wheel on Elliott Bay. Seattle's Great Wheel, in an electric neon green tonight, slowly spun, as locals and tourists alike took a turn in the gondolas, getting a bird's-eye view of the pier.

"Are you game?" Kyle asked, a mischievous glint in his eyes.

Kristine took a breath. She'd always been a little afraid of heights, but she felt the need to challenge herself, experience life more fully. "Yes."

Kyle grinned. "I'll be right back."

Kyle purchased the tickets and they got in line.

When their turn came, they climbed in. The gondola rocked and Kristine grabbed Kyle's hand.

"Don't worry," he said with confidence. "You're safe with me."

And she did feel safe. Kyle had been the perfect gentleman all night. They'd had dinner at The Pink Door, then taken a stroll along the waterfront, watching as the sun went down, ending up here, at the Wheel.

An enchanted summer evening, the air just the right temperature you didn't need a sweater. All around them the city came alive as lights came on, twinkling.

The Ferris wheel began to climb. Butterflies took flight in Kristine's stomach, but nerves didn't stop her from admiring the breathtaking view from the top of the Wheel.

"Beautiful," she said, embracing her fear of heights.

"Yes," Kyle agreed, but she found him staring at her.

Kristine smiled, returning her focus to the pier below.

When the Wheel finally slowed, and their ride was coming to an end, her stomach began to return to normal. She'd done it, taken on a new challenge, and she felt great.

They disembarked, heading back the way they'd come.

"It's been a wonderful evening," Kyle said.

"It has," she agreed.

"But your mind is somewhere else," Kyle observed. "It's Rand, isn't it?"

Kristine blew out a breath. "You're right. I guess I'm sad. It's been a sad summer on so many levels, but in other ways it's been great. I have no regrets."

Kyle took her hand, squeezing it. "I can help you forget him, help you move forward."

"I'm not ready for romance," she said, wanting to be clear.

"I'm a good friend." He stopped, looking into her eyes. "I'm a patient man. We can take things slowly."

"Friends for now?" Kristine asked, wondering if any guy could really just be friends with a woman. Her mind jumped to Rand and Cory. Were they really just friends?

Kyle nodded. "Friends for now."

They walked, hand in hand to the car. On the drive home they were mostly silent. Words weren't needed and Kristine liked that.

At Wilding House, Kyle walked her to the door.

"The awkward moment," she said with a laugh. "Good thing we are just friends."

He pressed his lips together. "I won't deny it. I want to kiss you, but I won't." Taking both of her hands in his, he gave them a squeeze. "Good night, Kristine."

"Good night, Kyle. Thank you for a wonderful evening."

Kyle let go of her hands. She smiled at him before letting herself inside.

The house was quiet, and she expected Carly to be in bed. Wanting to snag a bottle of water, Kristine went to the kitchen. Lucky sat at the table, a crossword puzzle in front of him. He glanced up and she could see the disappointment in his eyes. Ro must have told him where she'd gone.

"Don't look at me like that," Kristine said.

"Like what?" Lucky asked.

"Like I stabbed you in the back because I had dinner with Kyle."

Lucky stood. "What you do is your business, but when the SOB shows you his true colors, you'll understand why I don't like him."

"Maybe because you never tell me anything." Kristine grabbed a bottle of water from the fridge.

"I told you, there's nothing to tell, no facts, nothing to support the way I feel about Kyle," Lucky said. "What I feel for him is in my gut."

"Okay," she said. "I still don't get it, but I can tell you this, Kyle and I are just friends."

"Like you were friends with Rand?"

His words stung, hurt. "No, not like that."

Lucky sighed. "Not my business." He tried to pass her.

"I need a friend," Kristine said, not willing to let him go yet. "You barely talk to me. I have no idea what you're thinking."

"Believe me," Lucky said, "you don't want to know. I was going to tell you this later, but you might as well know. The tenants in the beach cabin have given notice. Once they're out, I'm moving in."

"Because of Kyle?" she asked.

"Not exactly," Lucky said with a frown, "although I can't stand the thought of you and him together. Kyle doesn't have any influence over the way I run my life."

"If not, Kyle, then why? Wilding House is huge," Kristine said. "We can live here together."

"I need my space, Kris," he said simply. "This house is great for you and Carly. I'll be a silent owner."

"If you have to move, I'm happy you'll be close by, that you're staying in Wilding Point." She couldn't lose Lucky, too. She needed him.

"For now," Lucky said. "Testing the waters, trying to figure things out."

"You know I'll help you any way I can," she offered.

"I know." He touched her arm as he passed.

"I love you, Lucky," she said.

Their eyes met, and she saw his love for her, their bond, was still there, as solid as it had ever been.

"I love you, too, sis," Lucky said. "It's me and you against the world. I won't forget our pact."

"Me either." She gave him a small smile.

Lucky was staying in Wilding Point for now. This was a victory for her, for their family.

She went to the window, looking out at the dark guest house. Her heart ached, the pain sudden and sharp, so much worse than she'd ever imagined. Where was Rand? What was he doing right now?

A veil of sadness engulfed her.

She needed to focus on the blessings in her life—Carly, Rowena, Lucky, and maybe even Kyle.

Move forward, Kristine, she told herself. *Don't backslide. Be happy.*

She turned away from the window, her stride purposeful. She shut off the kitchen light and headed upstairs to check on her beautiful daughter.

Chapter Twenty-Three

Rand hailed a cab. "Rumors Bar," he said to the driver. He gave the address.

"Sure thing." The cab driver pulled away from the curb.

Rand tugged at his collar, the air sticky and hot. Not the crisp, fresh beach air he'd become accustomed to in Wilding Point. No, this heat was different, crushing, the late summer heat of New York City.

He pulled his focus to the view from the window. The Brooklyn Bridge, alive with people walking, enjoying the last bit of evening as night began to fall. Cars. Horns honking. Always.

Rand willed himself to unwind, unplug.

The crush of the workday was over, but the streets were far from empty. He spotted tourists in their tennis shoes and shorts. Local couples strolled arm in arm, maybe heading to or from dinner. A group of teenagers hung out on the corner.

He thought of Carly, so far removed from the city life, safe, in Wilding Point.

His heart took a hit.

Stop it. This is what you wanted. You need this.

Rand inhaled, not letting his mind go to Kristine. He was home, in the city he loved. Since arriving he'd been swamped, pulled back into his job with a vengeance. He ate Chinese takeout at his desk. He went home to sleep. He'd missed so much. The world had gone on without Rand Bell. Try as he might, he couldn't shake the feeling of being behind. Each day was a struggle to catch up.

This was the rat race in its purest form.

"Rumors," the cab driver barked.

"Great." Rand passed him cash. "Thanks." He exited the cab.

The bar was crowded but he spied Cory almost immediately, her red hair a beacon in the room.

She sat at a small two-person table in front of the window facing the street.

"Hi," he said, taking the seat beside her.

"Hi, you." Cory smiled. She really was pretty. Green-eyed. The red hair. The slim, almost boyish figure.

So not his type. No, he preferred curvy blondes.

"I just got here," she said. "I'm lucky to have snagged a table."

The waitress joined them. "What'll you have?"

"White wine, please," Cory said.

"Draft beer," Rand said.

"Menus?"

"Yes," Cory said. "I'm starving."

The waitress dropped two menus on the table. "Be right back with your drinks."

Cory turned to him. "How was your day?"

"Busy," he said.

"But you love it, right?" she asked.

He heard the worry in her voice. She was afraid he'd leave her again. He got it, but he couldn't be her everything, her substitute Grif.

"I do," he admitted. "I love the rush."

Their drinks arrived and Rand took a long pull of his beer, his mind bouncing to Kristine, to beers on the beach, the fire roaring before them, the sun going down.

"Rand," Cory said, her tone snapping him back to present.

"Sorry," he offered.

"Where were you just now?" she asked. "You didn't even hear me the first two times I called your name."

"Just thinking," he said, not wanting to share even a small part of Kristine with her.

"Um hum," she said, sounding totally unconvinced. "As I was saying, an apartment has opened up in my building."

"Really?" He sat forward, interested now. He'd been bunking at Cory's since hitting town. He was more than ready for his own place. "Think I'd have a chance?"

"I do." She beamed. "I've spoken with the manager. You can do the application online, but I have a feeling you'll get it. Sam, the manager, likes me."

Rand smiled. "I'll fill out the application tonight."

"Any food here?" the waitress asked, a tray on her hip.

"Burger for me, medium," Cory said.

"Same for me," Rand said, "only medium rare."

"You got it." The waitress headed back to the bar.

"Rand," Cory said, "you know I love having you here, but before you take an apartment, make sure this is where you want to be."

"I'm here," he said with resolution, almost sure he meant it. "In every sense of the word."

"I know being here is difficult," Cory told him. "It's difficult for me, too. But this is where we belong."

"I see Grif everywhere," Rand admitted. "At work, in your apartment—hell, here in this bar."

She nodded, her eyes filling with tears. "I'm glad you're back."

"Me, too." Rand squeezed her hand, the gesture meant to comfort.

They finished their drinks and ordered another round before their food arrived. When they were through eating, they shared a cab home.

Alone in Cory's guest room, Rand brought up the application for the soon to be vacant apartment.

He typed in his information. When the application was complete, he stared at the blue submit button. This was it, a real commitment to staying in New York.

Rand hit the submit button.

The application disappeared.

His stomach knotted. He was doing the right thing, wasn't he?

Kristine. What was she doing now? Would she take his call?

Rand palmed his phone. No. If he heard Kristine's voice, his second thoughts would charge him full force. Not yet. He needed time to forget her and time to remember the life he had before he met her.

If he returned to Wilding Point, he'd lose a big part of himself, a part he wasn't willing to give up.

Exhausted, Rand crawled into bed, but sleep eluded him. Instead, Kristine Wilding filled his thoughts until he ached for her.

He couldn't even begin to process what that meant.

*   *   *

Kristine dipped her paddle into the gray waters of Puget Sound.

In front of her, in their two-person kayak, Carly did the same. Kyle followed alongside in a one-person kayak.

Today had been idyllic, a perfect Sunday. They'd started with brunch at The Salt Shack, feasting on crab legs, delicious cheeses, and delicate crepes filled with ricotta and sour cherries, then from there, they had gone back to Wilding House in search of the kayaks. After a thorough scrub, Kristine had pronounced the boats ready.

They'd put the kayaks in the water at the beach in front of Wilding House. It had only taken Kristine a few seconds to remember what to do. She'd chosen the two-person kayak, wanting Carly with her the girl's first time out. They paddled close to the shoreline. Kristine had loved to kayak as a child and had often done so with Lucky, or with friends. She couldn't believe it had taken her most of the summer to get out on the water.

Summer was slipping away at an alarming rate. Rand had been gone almost four weeks. Next week Carly would be starting school at the middle school. Lucky was moving out the first of September. Cameron Butler was still absent, but Kristine didn't worry about him, didn't know him. If he showed up, fine. His share of the money was waiting for him. In her mind, he'd be a fool to let the money go, no matter what he thought of them, or their father. She hoped he'd take what Lucas Wilding had offered him.

Kristine's paddle sliced through the water. She lifted her face to the sun and inhaled deeply.

Life was changing. Money was pouring into Kristine's bank account now as accounts were closed, money dispersed. There was a freedom that came when one didn't have to worry about money. She could take care of Carly properly, no more scrimping and eating macaroni and cheese three nights a week. She even had an investment broker now.

"You're really good at this," Kyle said, his kayak even with hers.

"Loved kayaking as a kid," she said, smiling. "Being on the water was a great escape."

"How are you liking it?" Kyle asked Carly.

"It's fun," Carly said, as her paddle cut through the water. "I can't wait to try this with Patty. I think she's pretty good at it."

Kyle always made sure to include Carly in their conversations, and most times, in their plans. He'd mentioned once he hadn't wanted children, yet he seemed fine with Carly. He was slowly worming his way into Kristine's heart. He was so giving. She still didn't understand what he'd done to Lucky, or why her brother disliked him so much, but figured if Kyle had done something really bad, Lucky would tell her, really warn her off Kyle. Instead, Lucky kept his opinion about their relationship to himself now, and that suited her fine.

"Should we turn back?" Kyle asked, when they'd been kayaking for about an hour.

"Okay," Kristine said, "wouldn't want to wear you two out your first time."

"Mom," Carly said. "I'm way younger than you."

"Ouch." Kristine exchanged a smile with Kyle.

They turned their kayaks, heading back to Wilding Point. Again Kristine took the time to just breathe and savor the air. When the house came into view, they beached the kayaks. Kyle climbed out first, then gave the girls a hand up.

"That was fun," Kristine said. "I love it so much I might make it part of my day every day."

"Can I go and get Patty?" Carly asked. "I want to show her the boats."

"Sure." Kristine smiled as Carly ran down the beach.

"I'm glad she enjoyed it," Kyle said, bringing her attention back to him.

"Me, too." Kristine faced Kyle now. "What's on your agenda for the rest of the day?"

"Not a thing," he said, spreading his arms wide. "I'm all yours, Kristine. Whatever you want to do. Name it."

She eyed the deck. "How about relaxing with the Sunday paper, maybe mixing up a Bloody Mary this afternoon?"

Kyle smiled. "I'd say you read my mind." He offered her his hand.

Kristine intertwined her fingers with his.

Did her heart beat faster when she touched him? A little, but not like with Rand.

She knew from Rowena that Rand had found an apartment. He was scheduled to move in September first. An apartment made his departure so final. A one-year lease would be involved. She had to let him go.

Kristine smiled at Kyle as they settled into the deck chairs. Kyle was nice, safe, solid. In so many ways he was exactly what she needed.

"I like you, Kristine," Kyle said, his tone warm. "I like you a lot."

"I like you, too, Kyle," she said.

He leaned over, kissing her cheek. When he pulled back, she could see the longing in his eyes, the questions.

"I'm not ready for more," she said sadly, not wanting to lead him on.

His fingers grazed her cheek. "You are worth waiting for."

She gave him a soft smile. "This is nice. Right here, right now. I know this won't be enough for you forever."

"Let's just see how things go," Kyle said, settling back in his chair.

Kristine did the same, her eyes on the water.

Carly and Patty ran down the beach to the kayaks. Their giggles reached Kristine's ears. There was nothing better than a happy child.

"Mom," Carly called. "Can you take us out?"

"Sure." Kristine smiled at Kyle. "Want to come down and help me get the girls loaded?"

"Of course," Kyle said, rising.

"Okay." Kristine followed Kyle down the path, wishing again he was the one who made her heart beat faster.

Chapter Twenty-Four

Rand let himself into his apartment.

He'd spent yesterday moving in. Cory had helped him.

He paused in the doorway, taking in the room. Loft style, the apartment was open and airy, filled with natural light. The place came furnished with mid-century modern pieces. Not really his taste, but the quality of furniture made up for it. The black leather sofa was supple and soft to the touch. The coffee and end tables were solid pine.

The small modern kitchen was sleek, the black granite counter tops gleaming. A large island completed the kitchen. Six tall bar chairs held court, waiting for a meal he would never cook.

Rand smirked. The loft was too nice for him. He would have been happy in a crappy studio apartment that was a quarter of the price. Why had he let Cory talk him into this place?

He set his computer case on the counter before taking a seat on the sofa.

What now? He had an apartment for a life he didn't really have. He had a year lease. A year.

Sadness filled him.

What was he doing here? Sure, he loved his job, but he wasn't finding the work as fulfilling as he'd hoped and he didn't want to ask himself why.

He palmed his phone. It was almost six p.m. in Wilding Point. Dinner time. What was Kristine doing? Was Carly in school now? How was his mother?

He could call his mom and get all the details, but it wasn't his mother he wanted to speak to. It was Kristine.

Rand hit the call button, then held the phone to his ear. The call went to voicemail. Kristine's voice asked him to leave a message. He didn't.

This wasn't the first time she hadn't taken his call, and it stung. How badly had he hurt her?

But it was more than that. Kristine had become a friend during their time together, and he missed the friendship part of their relationship more than he missed the sex.

Rand looked around the sterile loft. This was his life now, the life he'd chosen.

With a sigh, he hefted himself off the sofa and retrieved his laptop, taking the computer to the built-in desk in the corner of the room.

Might as well get some work done.

He turned on the computer, his mind not on his work, but on the life and the woman he'd left behind.

* * *

September seventh, Kristine sat in the parking lot of the middle school, waiting for the bell to ring, the stuffy air in the car making her sweat.

They were having an Indian summer, with temperatures still in the eighties. She loved the sun, but not while she was sitting in a parked car.

Kristine prayed Carly had had a great first day. More than anything she wanted her daughter to be happy here. The coming of September had brought more changes for them. Lucky was gone now, all moved into his cabin on the beach.

Kristine missed having him around. Rowena was doing her best to fill the gap, but the older woman had her own life to lead. Rowena had thrown herself into her women's groups, knitting, book club, and she volunteered at the food bank and at the community center, all while running Wilding House. Kristine realized Rowena stayed busy to keep her grief at bay, and that made her love Ro even more.

But with both Rand and Lucky gone, Kristine had a big hole in her life and in her heart.

It would be so easy to return Rand's calls, but she knew better. She'd be sucked right back into all her feelings for him. The one-year lease he'd signed said it all to Kristine. He was gone for good. What was the point of torturing herself with phone calls? They wanted different things. She understood. Heck, she'd been the one to set the rules for their relationship. Rand hadn't done anything wrong. He'd merely taken what she'd offered him.

The bell rang. Kristine got out of the car, her eyes on the school. Kids began pouring out. It took a few minutes before she spotted Carly and Patty. Kristine raised her hand.

Carly waved before tugging on Patty's arm.

The girls made their way to the car. Carly was smiling, and Kristine hoped that was a good sign.

"Hi," Kristine said. "How was it?"

"Good," Carly said, her eyes bright.

"Fine," Patty told her.

"Good, fine?" Kristine asked as they got in the car. "I need more details. Are we waiting for Kevin?" Patty's brother had found his own romance during the summer with a girl named Sandy, much to Kristine's relief.

"No," Patty said. "He's riding home with Sandy."

"Okay." Kristine started the car, joining the line of cars trying to exit the busy parking lot. "Details, girls. How were your classes?"

"Pretty good," Carly said. "I really liked my history teacher."

"Mr. Jacks," Patty confirmed. "He's super cute."

"I see." Kristine smiled. "Anything else?"

"I have homework in English already," Carly moaned. "On the first day."

"I know," Patty chimed in. "Me, too."

The girls continued to chatter about their day. Kristine's heart soared. This was what she'd hoped for. Carly liked it here, she had friends, felt included, like she belonged.

When they pulled into the driveway at Wilding House, Carly said, "Okay if Patty and I work on our English?"

"Sure." Kristine got out of the car. "Rowena has snacks in the kitchen."

The girls grabbed their backpacks.

Kyle's BMW came up the driveway as the girls headed inside.

Kristine walked out of the garage to meet him. He rolled his window down. "Hi. What brings you around?" she asked.

He smiled. "Thought I might take you girls to dinner tonight to celebrate the first day of school."

"That's nice of you," Kristine said, leaning down to better see him. "Carly and Patty are working on homework now. Maybe around six?"

"I'll be here," he said cheerfully. "I have a couple of things to do, then I'll swing back around."

Kristine nodded. "See you then." She watched him drive off. How long would Kyle be content to be her friend and not her lover? Eventually Kyle would make a move on her. She could see the longing on his face, feel the tension in his body. Would she ever be ready?

Her phone buzzed. Kristine fished the phone out of her purse. Rand.

Her knees went weak. Suddenly, she wanted to hear his voice. She pressed the talk button.

"Hi," she said, her heart racing.

"Kristine," Rand said, sounding surprised. "You answered."

"I did," she said.

"I'm glad."

"I hear you are all moved in to your new place," she said on her way to the front porch. She sat on the bottom step, praying she wouldn't cry.

"Yes," he said, "not sure I'm loving it, but it's a nice place."

"How's your job?" she asked, not knowing what else to say.

"Great. How are you?"

The rich timbre of his voice made her weak. She closed her eyes. "Fine. I'm all set to start school winter quarter."

"That's wonderful," he said, the words warm.

Silence stretched between. There was so much she wanted to say, but the words wouldn't come.

"Are you still there?" he asked.

"Yes." Her throat tightened. She bit her lip to keep from crying.

"Is Carly in school?"

"Today was her first day," Kristine told him. "She had a great day, it sounds like. She's with Patty now."

"I miss you," Rand said the words soft and filled with longing.

"Don't," she said, her heart breaking. "I can't, Rand. I need to let you go."

"Do you?" he asked. "I'm not so sure. I think about you all the time."

"I can't do long distance," she said. "Our lives are too different."

He sighed. "I guess they are."

"I've moved on," she lied, the words heavy on her tongue. "You should, too."

"What if I don't want to?"

Her heart beat faster. "You made your choice."

He didn't reply right away and she imagined him pacing in his trendy apartment. "I guess I did."

"I'm glad you called," she said, "but I have to go. We are getting ready to go to dinner."

"I see," he said. "Take care, Kristine."

Tears stung her eyes. "You, too." She pressed the end button.

There. She'd done it. She'd spoken to Rand and survived.

He wasn't coming back. It really was over between them. The time had come to move forward, start living again.

Kristine stood and wiped the tears from her eyes with the back of her hand. She was going to go inside, let Carly know about their dinner plans, then get ready for dinner with Kyle. She was going to open her heart to the possibility of a relationship with him.

She was going to leave Rand Bell behind. He would become a beautiful memory of a wild summer romance. A memory that would keep her warm when she was old and gray.

* * *

Dinner with Kyle and Carly and Patty went off without a hitch. They went to Wally's in Des Moines and feasted on fish and chips. Their bellies full, they finished the evening with a walk in the marina, strolling out to the end of the fishing pier before circling back to Kyle's car.

They'd dropped Patty at her place on the way home. Back at Wilding House, Carly had gone up to shower and get ready for bed, leaving Kristine alone with Kyle.

"Thank you so much for dinner," she said to him as they entered the kitchen. "Good food. Great company."

"Do you mean that, Kristine?" Kyle asked, his eyes on her.

"You know I do."

He reached for her hand. "I care about you a lot."

His fingers closed over hers, and the panic she always felt when he got romantic jumped to life in her stomach. "I know."

"Do you care about me?"

"You know I do," she said, meaning it. "You've been a wonderful friend, and you've been more than patient with me."

"I want to kiss you," he said, the words low. "Let me, Kristine. Let's see if the magic is there."

Her lips parted. She couldn't deny him. A part of her did want to know what his kiss would be like.

Kyle's fingers brushed against her cheek, before finding the back of her neck. Gently, he coaxed her to him.

His mouth brushed against hers.

Kristine's lips parted and Kyle deepened the kiss, his arms going around her. Her eyes slid shut and she gave herself to the kiss. He pressed more tightly against her, and she felt his arousal.

Kyle moaned. "Magic," he said against her mouth. "I want more of you."

His words stirred something inside her. He felt good against her, but her heart wasn't in it.

"Come home with me," Kyle said before kissing her again.

"Oh!" Rowena exclaimed.

They broke apart.

"Excuse me," Rowena said, backing out of the kitchen.

"Well, I guess the cat's out of the bag now," Kyle said, smiling, obviously pleased with himself.

Kristine stepped out of Kyle's embrace. "I suppose so."

"Come home with me," he said again. "Rowena can watch Carly."

Kristine shook her head. "I can't. It's a school night."

"Then this weekend?" Kyle asked hopefully.

"I don't know."

He stepped toward her. "Did you enjoy the kiss?"

She looked at him. "You know I did."

"Then I think we owe it to ourselves to explore this—us." Kyle smiled, pulling her into his arms again. "For now, I'll take another kiss good night."

Kristine returned his smile, kissing him, putting everything she had into the kiss.

But in her heart she knew it wasn't ever going to be enough. She just didn't love Kyle the way she loved Rand, and she was scared to death she would never love anyone like that again.

* * *

Rand's phone rang, his mother's name on the screen. "Hi, Mom."

"Rand," his mother said, happiness filling the word. "How are you?"

"Pretty good," he said, his emotions still raw after his earlier conversation with Kristine. "How are things there?"

"Moving along," his mother said. "Carly's in school now. She's doing well."

"That's great." He moved his phone to the other ear.

"Kristine is also moving along," his mother said.

"What do you mean?" he asked, his gut tightening.

"She's been seeing Dr. King," his mother told him. "She has a big date Saturday night."

Rand's fingers tightened on the phone. He stood, pacing to the window. "Really."

264

"Really," his mother said matter-of-factly. "Let me ask you something."

"What?"

"Are you really happy in New York?"

He rubbed his temple. "Of course."

"Well, if that's the truth, then I'm happy for you, but if you have some feelings for Kristine, you better come back here and deal with them. Dr. King wants her. Oh, she's resisting, but I can see he's wearing her down. Ask yourself what really makes you happy. Is it your job, your apartment, or is it the people in your life?"

Rand swallowed, his gut beginning to burn.

"Rand?"

"I know the answer," he said. "Thanks, Mom."

He ended the call.

He'd known the answer all along.

Kristine made him happy. He'd been a fool. Rand took a seat at his desk and popped a couple of antacids. It was after ten and he was still at work. Seriously?

When had he changed? Had Grif's death changed him? When had his dreams shifted? He didn't know, but he knew one thing for certain: He didn't belong in New York when everything he wanted was in Wilding Point.

Rand smiled as happiness filled him for the first time in weeks.

He was going home to Wilding Point and once he got there, he was going to beg Kristine to forgive him for being a fool.

Chapter Twenty-Five

Kristine sat on Kyle's patio, her eyes on his pool.

They'd just finished a lovely dinner, cooked by Kyle himself, steaks on the grill, baked potatoes, and a wonderful arugula salad. Kristine toyed with the stem of her wine glass.

"Have I told you how beautiful you look tonight?" Kyle asked.

"Thank you." He wanted to have sex with her and she was receiving the message loud and clear. Was she ready to sleep with him? She couldn't answer that question.

"What are you thinking about?" he asked, his gaze on her. "You seem far away."

"Us," she admitted. "You deserve so much more than me."

The lines on his forehead deepened. "What do you mean? You are everything to me, Kristine."

"That's what I mean," she said, wanting him to understand. "You deserve someone who loves you with her heart and soul."

"And that's not you?" he asked, the words sad.

She shook her head. "No."

"I can help you forget him." Kyle left his chair, coming to her. "Give me a chance."

He pulled Kristine up and into his arms, his desperation making her feel even worse. "I can't, Kyle."

He kissed her, but seemed to realize immediately that she wasn't kissing him back.

"So we're done?" he asked, still holding her in his arms.

"We never really started," she said sadly. "I'm so sorry. I didn't know. I thought maybe…"

"I see." He let her go. "I'm nothing if not a gentleman. I'll take you home."

She nodded.

The ride home was silent, strained. When they reached Wilding House, Kristine exited the car on her own. Kyle met her at the front of the vehicle.

"I'm going to miss you," he said.

"I'll miss you, too. Thank you for everything," she said. "You've been wonderful."

He kissed her softly, then, when she moved to leave him, he yanked her to him, but this kiss was rough, punishing.

She shoved at his chest, breaking the kiss. "Kyle!" She wiped her mouth with the back of her hand.

"I'm sorry," he offered, glancing away from her, then back. "I lost control. I hope you find what you are looking for."

He got in his car, driving away. Kristine watched him go, her heart heavy. She'd never meant to hurt him.

She trudged up the steps and went inside, leaving her purse on the foyer table.

The house was quiet. Rowena was out tonight and Carly was spending the night at Patty's.

"Hussy?" she called. "Where are you, girl?"

The dog was never far from Carly when she was home, but Carly wasn't here.

Puzzled, Kristine called, "Hussy," on her way to the kitchen. Once there, she poured herself a glass of wine before heading outside to see if Hussy was out back.

The guest house was ablaze with light.

Her heart leapt, paused, then started beating again.

Who was in the guest house? An intruder? Lucky? Rand?

She set her wine down and headed over, not caring about her personal safety at all. She had to know who'd turned on the lights.

At the door, she called, "Who's here?"

Rand stepped into view, Hussy on his heels.

She clutched the handle on the screen door for support.

"Finish your date with Dr. Love?" he asked, the words bitter.

Had he seen Kyle kiss her? What right did he have to be upset about Kyle? Rand had left her behind. Left her.

Angry, she yanked the door open. "What are you doing here?"

He looked so good—thinner maybe, clean-shaven, hair cut short. His eyes held a hunger, a hunger for her. Kristine's heart sped up. Had he come for her?

He set the beer he held down on the counter with a *thunk*, then came toward her, like a predator, heat rolling off of him.

Kristine froze, her feet rooted to the spot.

When he reached her, Rand kissed her, hot, erotic, tongues mating. She couldn't resist him, didn't want to. She'd missed him with every fiber of her being. She didn't care why he was there, only that he was.

They tore each other's clothes off, and Rand took her against the wall, the sex wild, desperate and blazing hot.

Kristine clung to him, taking everything he gave her, until she spiraled out of control, his name bursting from her lips.

For several seconds they didn't move, their frantic breathing the only sound in the room.

Kristine's wits returned. What had she just done? She unwrapped her legs from his waist, her feet finding the floor. Rand stepped away from her.

"I'm sorry," he said gruffly. "I didn't mean for that to happen."

He was sorry? The words crushed her. Kristine gathered her clothes, getting dressed.

Rand did the same.

"Why are you here?" she asked, feeling more broken inside than ever.

"I came home for you," he said softly.

Her head snapped up. "What?"

"I came back for you, Kristine." His eyes held all the pain of a man who'd made hard choices.

Was he for real?

She didn't move, couldn't breathe. "Why? Don't you get it? Being with you is torture. We don't want the same things. And if I've learned anything, I've learned I don't want you part time. I can't. I've discovered I'm an all or nothing kind of girl."

He shook his head. "You don't understand. I'm not going back to New York. My life is here, with you, Carly, and Mom."

Kristine wasn't sure she'd heard him right. "But your job, your apartment?"

"I quit, and they let me sublet the lease."

He took a step toward her. Kristine backed up.

"Don't run from me," Rand said, advancing on her. "I saw Kyle kiss you. Tell me I still have a chance with you."

"I—" she began, "No, I mean yes. Kyle's not the man for me. I told him so tonight."

"I love you, Kristine," he said with passion. "I fell in love with you this summer. You are the part of me that's missing. Not Grif. You."

Her eyes filled with tears.

"Tell me you feel the same way," Rand said.

"But what about your dreams?" she asked, wanting more than anything to say yes to all he was offering.

"I'll get a job here, doing what I love," he said. "It's people who make a home, a life—not a job, not a city, and not things."

Kristine smiled. "Really?"

Rand smiled back. "Absolutely." He took her hands. "I love you. I want to spend the rest of my life with you. Marry me, Kristine Wilding."

Kristine looked into his chocolate eyes. Never had she wanted anything more. Her heart, her body, flooded with happiness. "Yes, I'll marry you. I love you so much. I've been lost without you."

"Well, why didn't you say so?" Rand asked, grinning madly. "I would have come back sooner. You didn't take my calls, and when you did, you cut me loose."

"My heart was broken," Kristine said, winding her arms around him. "Now it's whole."

"I'm going to spend the rest of my life, making you happy," Rand said. "You and Carly."

"I like the sound of that," Kristine said.

Rand kissed her, slowly this time, tenderly, before he swept her off her feet.

Kristine laughed as he hoisted her in his arms. "What are you doing?"

"I'm taking you to bed," Rand said. "I'm going to make love to you all night long."

Kristine smiled. "You better."

Rand kissed her quick, then bore her to the bedroom, kicking the door shut behind them.

Epilogue

Ten Months Later—July

"You may kiss your bride," the minister said.

Kristine stepped into Rand's arms, and he kissed her, a long, passionate kiss, a kiss born out of love and pure joy. When they broke apart, applause filled the room.

Kristine turned to her maid of honor, Carly.

"Congratulations, Mom."

Kristine hugged her daughter, kissing the top of her head.

"My turn," Rand said, hugging Carly.

"I guess I can call you 'Dad' now," Carly said, smiling.

"I'd be honored," Rand said, and Kristine could see how touched he was.

She took one of Carly's hands, Rand the other, and they walked down the aisle as a family.

They passed her mother and Lucky, who sat in the front row with Rowena. Patty and her family were there. Keith. Lauren, the hospice nurse. Kate and Nan from Oregon, as well as some of Kristine's former co-workers. Cory was there. Everyone happy for them.

Kristine's heart sang.

In the vestibule, they formed a reception line.

"I love you, Mrs. Bell." Rand kissed her again.

"I love you, Mr. Bell." In his eyes she saw their future.

She finally had it all, everything she'd always wanted. Her family all near, with her. Someone to love, someone who had her back and would walk with her through life.

She had her fresh start in Wilding Point.

Lucky came through the line first. He'd cut his hair, trimmed his beard for the wedding, and to Kristine, he'd never looked more handsome.

Lucky hugged her. "Love you, sis."

"Love you, too."

Lucky shook Rand's hand. "Brothers now."

"Brothers," Rand echoed, grinning.

Carly ran up. Lucky took her hand. "Come on, kid, you can help me get this party started."

Kristine exchanged a smile with Rand, and she knew he understood her happiness in a way no one else could.

They joined hands.

Her wild summer romance had turned into a forever love affair.

She had it all now, love, family, a home.

All here in Wilding Point.

ABOUT THE AUTHOR

Small town settings, ranch living, and quirky characters are all
things that have long intrigued award-winning author Joleen
James. For as long as she can remember, Joleen's been spinning
stories centering around home, family, and of course, true love.
When she's not busy writing, Joleen can be found with her family
on their party barge, traveling, or indulging in her hobbies of
home decorating and recipe collecting. Visit Joleen James at
www.joleenjames.com and on
Facebook and Twitter.

Cozy up with A Wilding Point Romance!

After vowing to never set foot in Wilding Point again, single mother Kristine Wilding comes home to take care of her dying father. But watching someone die isn't easy, and Kristine soon finds herself in need of a shoulder to cry on. From the start, Kristine underestimates the power of the caring, mysterious Rand. Does she dare let passion carry her into Rand's embrace and into the wildest adventure of her life? ~ **WILD ABOUT RAND on sale now**

She's everything he's ever wanted…He's everything she can never have.
~ **WILD ABOUT LUCKY coming April 2019**

What happens when an uptight, single mom is reunited with the one man who has the ability to turn her life upside down and drive her wild?
~ **WILD ABOUT CAM coming June 2019**

Watch for book 4 in the series to release Fall 2019!

Visit me at www.joleenjames.com!

Thanks for reading!

Joleen James

www.ingramcontent.com/pod-product-compliance
Lightning Source LLC
Chambersburg PA
CBHW071120170626
46809CB00002B/443